MW01007963

Also by Jennifer L. Schiff

A Shell of a Problem

Something Fishy

In the Market for Murder

Bye Bye Birdy

Shell Shocked

Trouble in Paradise

Tinder Fella

A novel

Jennifer Lonoff Schiff

Shovel
& Pail
Press

Tinder Fella: A Novel
by Jennifer Lonoff Schiff

© 2020 by Jennifer Lonoff Schiff

Cover design by Molly Burton with Cozy Cover Designs

Formatting by Polgarus Studio

ISBN: 978-0-578-67894-8

Library of Congress Control Number: 2020913321

No matter how your heart is grieving
If you keep on believing
The dream that you wish will come true
—Cinderella

CHAPTER 1

Once upon a time, in a magical city called New York, there lived a young man named Allen who dreamed of becoming a famous author, finding his true love, and living happily ever after.

Allen Bartholomew Whitford III had been a happy baby and toddler. So easy going, always with a smile on his cute little round face. Or so his mother would tell people. Then came 9/11, when Allen's world, quite literally, came crashing down. Allen's father was a firefighter and, along with his engine company and the rest of the FDNY, had rushed to Lower Manhattan as the first World Trade Center tower came tumbling down. He never made it back home.

Allen had been six at the time and had just started first grade. He had been nervous that morning, which was unusual for Allen, and he hadn't wanted to go to school. It was as if he sensed something was wrong. But his mother, Rose, who taught high school English at the private school Allen attended, had chalked it up to first-grade jitters and had dropped Allen off in the before-school classroom, as she had every other morning, and had gone to get ready for her first class of the day. Then all hell broke loose.

Allen adored his father and wanted to be just like him

when he grew up. He loved going to the engine company and climbing on the fire trucks and sliding down the pole. But after those two airplanes crashed into the World Trade Center towers, bursting into flames and taking so many lives, including his father's, Allen withdrew. He no longer wanted to play outside or with his friends, preferring to stay inside and read a book or watch *Thomas the Tank Engine* or some other show that took place in a make-believe place that didn't resemble New York. And he would start to cry at the sound of a fire engine.

His mother did her best to keep it together, though Allen would hear her crying in her room at night. She had been given a leave of absence by the school; Allen, too. But after a week of staying at home, the apartment a constant reminder of who and what she had lost, she returned to teaching, taking Allen with her to school.

Allen had not wanted to go back. He was suddenly afraid of everything and lashed out when anyone came near him. His teachers understood and were patient with him. But his behavior caused most of his classmates to keep their distance.

Only Eric, Allen's best friend, stuck by him. The two had known each other since kindergarten and were both in the before-school program. After school, they would hang out at one or the other's house, playing games and watching TV. Allen loved going to Eric's apartment, which was near Central Park. Eric always had the best toys, and the best sister, at least in Allen's opinion. Emily was two years older than Eric and had the same blonde hair and blue eyes. And while she wasn't always nice to Eric, she was kind to Allen and would give him great big hugs, her parents having told her and Eric that Allen had lost his daddy, so she should be extra nice to him.

As they grew older, Allen and Eric continued to be friends. They called themselves brothers from other mothers. Though they looked nothing alike. Allen was tall and thin with dark, wavy hair and hazel eyes, while Eric was average height and fair and wore glasses.

They would still hang out at each other's apartments, often having sleepovers, and would play pranks on Emily and her friends whenever they were at Eric's.

By the time Allen entered middle school, he had lost some of his shyness and fear of new situations and had made several other friends. Though he and Eric would remain best friends, and he would never lose his love of books and reading.

Then, in seventh grade, his world was rocked once more.

His mother, who had remained resolutely single since Allen's father died, was being courted by the father of one of her students, a man by the name of Jonathan Larson, a successful New York attorney.

Jonathan had met Rose at a school Open House, the first he had ever attended, his schedule typically making it impossible to attend such things. He had been sitting a few rows back, checking his phone, when Rose began her presentation on the high school English curriculum. Something about her voice made him look up. And he was instantly smitten, not just by her looks but by the way she talked so passionately about *Romeo and Juliet* and *Pride and Prejudice*.

He had gone up to her afterward and invited her out for a coffee. But she had politely refused, citing school policy. So he had signed up for a parent-teacher conference. And then another one. And another. Until Rose finally agreed to have dinner with him.

Many more dinners and longer outings followed, until finally one day, just over a year after they had begun dating, Jonathan asked Rose to marry him, and she had said yes.

When Rose told him the news, Allen didn't know how he felt. He liked Jonathan okay. Jonathan was always nice to him. He bought Allen books and took him to movies and baseball and basketball games. And while Allen hadn't been keen on sports, he enjoyed his outings with Jonathan and had even begun to watch baseball and basketball games on TV. Though he refused to try out for any of the sports teams at school.

He also saw how happy Jonathan made his mother. But he was nervous about leaving the only home he had ever known and living with Jonathan's sons, Leighton and Liam.

Unlike Allen, who attended school on a faculty scholarship and didn't have the latest video games or the coolest clothes, and didn't care, Leighton and Liam Larson were spoiled rotten and flaunted their affluence, always coming to school dressed in the latest fashion with the latest phone and talking about the latest video game or concert they had gone to.

The Larson boys, who were older than Allen, were also jocks, who preferred football and lacrosse to studying, whereas Allen was the opposite. They would tease and bully the less-sporty kids, including Allen, making fun of them and shoving them against lockers and giving them wedgies. So Allen did his best to avoid them.

Fortunately, it turned out that both boys would continue to live with their mother, at least most of the time. And Allen's new bedroom, in the prewar Upper East Side building Jonathan and Rose had moved into, was almost twice the size of his old one and had a wall of bookshelves.

By the time he started high school, Allen had settled into his new life. Mostly. Then came a new blow.

Over the years, Allen's puppy love for Emily had turned into something more. And he would often daydream of the two of them dating and eventually getting married. Even though Emily still treated him like a little brother and dated other people.

Still, it came as a huge shock to Allen when Emily began dating his stepbrother Leighton. Leighton was now a senior, the captain of the football team, and a bully. Emily was a junior, the captain of the volleyball team, and had spearheaded the school's new anti-bullying program.

Granted, both Leighton and Emily were in the popular group, but Allen just couldn't understand it. How could Emily date a bully like Leighton (especially when Allen was pining away for her)? Eric couldn't understand it either. And he would lock himself in his room or make sure he was out whenever Leighton came over.

Worse, it seemed everyone at school was talking about the new power couple, referring to them as "Lemily." It made Allen sick.

Allen had begun to wonder, once again, if the universe had it in for him when a miracle occurred, actually two miracles. The first was Leighton breaking up with Emily right after the senior dance. He was headed to the University of Florida to play football in the fall and had told Emily he didn't want to be tied down. Emily was furious and swore she'd never speak to Leighton again. Which had delighted Eric and Allen.

Then Eric's family invited Allen to spend the summer with them in the Hamptons, where they had a place.

Allen had visited Eric in the Hamptons before, but he had never gone for more than a week. Now he would be spending the entire summer there, working at the day camp where Eric and Emily were counselors. Allen was thrilled. Not only would he get to spend the summer with his best friend, he'd be spending the summer with the woman he loved. Even though she had no idea Allen had an enormous crush on her.

Allen liked being a counselor. He enjoyed working with kids and hanging out with the other teens and twenty-somethings who worked at the camp. And he got to see Emily every day. But when Emily began dating one of the other counselors, Allen went into a funk. Seeing them grinning at each other and holding hands made him sick. Though he wouldn't reveal the cause of his bad mood when Eric would ask him what was up.

Finally, summer was over, and it was the start of sophomore year.

Allen joined the literary magazine and penned several articles. And the more he wrote, the more he envisioned a career as a writer.

He had been keeping a journal for years, at the advice of a therapist his mother had taken him to, and he had begun to think about writing a novel based on his own life as a child left fatherless by 9/11.

He would still see Emily, now a senior, at school, but she was too busy with AP classes and applying to colleges to pay him much mind. Allen had asked Eric where Emily was applying, but Eric didn't know as she was keeping it a secret.

That summer, Allen stayed in the city. His stepfather had gotten him an internship at his law firm, even though Allen was younger than the other interns. One of the perks of being the son of a partner. And even though Allen had no interest in becoming a lawyer, he did his best to pay attention and be helpful.

Eric had enrolled in a college prep program up in Massachusetts. And although he and Allen texted regularly, it wasn't the same.

Eric returned the city late August, in time for Emily's college going away party. She had been accepted at the University of Southern California, her first choice, and would be leaving for the West Coast the following week.

Allen had been invited to the party and mostly hung out with Eric. However, near the end, Emily had gone over and given him a big hug and a kiss (on the cheek) and laughed about how she now had to stand on her tiptoes to kiss him.

As Emily had kissed and held him, pressing her body against his, Allen had felt lightheaded and something stirred in his stomach (or farther south). Then she was gone, saying goodbye to another guest, and he felt bereft, as though she had taken a piece of him with her.

That would be the last time he would see Emily for many years.

Before he knew it, Allen was a senior and applying to colleges. His mother had told him she would happily take him to visit anyplace he might want to check out. But Allen knew where he wanted to go: New York University. Not only was the school located in one of his favorite neighborhoods, Greenwich Village, which was filled with cool shops and restaurants and old ivy-covered brownstones. It also had one of the best Creative Writing programs in the country. And more than anything, Allen wanted to be a great writer.

However, to humor his mother, he looked at a few other schools outside the city, in New England and Pennsylvania. But he ultimately applied to NYU early decision and was accepted.

Eric hadn't been sure where he wanted to go or what he wanted to study, though he was leaning toward History and wanted to stay close to New York. After visiting a dozen schools, he applied to six of them, including NYU and Columbia, and wound up enrolling at the former as Allen would be there.

It was during freshman orientation week that Allen and Eric met Molly Malloy.

Molly Margaret Malloy, whose personality was as fiery as her red hair, came from a rowdy but loving Irish family in New Jersey. She was the youngest of three girls and her father's favorite, at least that's what he had told her. (She suspected he told her two older siblings the same thing.)

Molly and her family lived just over an hour from Manhattan. Her father was a detective with the local police department, and her mother was a school nurse. While the Malloys were not wealthy, Molly had never felt deprived growing up. All three girls were given an allowance, provided they did their chores. And they babysat or helped out their neighbors to earn extra spending money.

When she was a junior in high school and kids were looking at colleges, Molly knew exactly where she wanted to go: NYU. She had dreams of becoming a writer one day, and NYU had an excellent Creative Writing program, though undergrads could only minor. Still, just the thought of living in the city and meeting lots of famous authors and poets excited her.

Molly had always loved stories, listening to them and reading them. Her father, whose parents had emigrated from Ireland, would recite the story of "Fair, Brown and Trembling," an Irish Cinderella tale, or tell her of Cuchulain the warrior or the mythical giant Fin McCool, and she would always beg him to tell her just one more. He would still occasionally sit on the edge of her bed as she was going to sleep and tell her tales of life back in the old country and of the wee folk or fairies.

Now Molly wanted to make up her own tales.

When she had told her father she wanted to be writer and go to NYU, he didn't question her choice. He just told her she had better be prepared to work hard and earn a living doing something else as writers were notoriously poor. She had given him a hug and told him she wouldn't let him down. Then she had sent off her application.

CHAPTER 2

Molly had spied Allen right away. He was over six feet tall, with a mop of curly brown hair that made him appear even taller. And he had that sensitive, brooding look, like Heathcliff in *Wuthering Heights*, that she found irresistible.

Being naturally gregarious, she had gone over to him and introduced herself and then stood next to him and Eric as the dean gave his welcome speech. Afterward, she suggested they grab a slice of pizza. Although she was unfamiliar with the Village, she had looked up popular NYU student hangouts before orientation, so she wouldn't seem like a clueless Jersey girl, and led them to a local pizza place students had raved about.

As they ate, Molly asked them about themselves and what they planned on majoring in at NYU. Eric told her he was undecided, but he was leaning towards History. Allen had said he planned on being an English major, with a minor in Creative Writing. That was her plan, too, Molly told him, and then she quizzed him on who his favorite writers were.

Although they had not discussed schedules, Allen was not surprised to see Molly in his Introduction to Fiction and Poetry class the next week. She was seated in the first row and signaled for him to sit next to her, but Allen demurred. He was not a front-row kind of guy, preferring to sit towards the back and observe.

After class, Molly waited for him and suggested they go grab a coffee. It soon became a ritual. Molly would sit in the front row, raising her hand every time the teacher would ask a question, while Allen sat several rows back, taking notes. When class was over, Molly would wait for him, and they would go for a coffee or a walk around Washington Square Park, discussing class or what they were reading.

Even though Allen had gone to an elite prep school, he had never met anyone quite like Molly. She was so sure of herself and smart, not afraid to speak her mind. She reminded him of Hermione in Harry Potter.

Eric, who, like Allen, considered himself an introvert, had felt intimidated by Molly at first. Even though he considered himself a reader, Molly had seemingly read so much more than he had. And she was politically outspoken, too, with opinions on seemingly everything.

When the three of them would get together, Eric would just listen as Allen and Molly would discuss whatever. But eventually he began to join in their conversations. And by the end of freshman year, it was as if the three of them had known each other forever.

Eric just had one little problem: he had developed a crush on Molly. But he suspected she didn't feel the same way and was too nervous to say anything. It wasn't until nearly the end of spring semester, as he and Allen were sharing a six-pack of beer (fake IDs being easy to get in New York) in Allen's room that Eric confessed his feelings.

"You have a crush on Molly?" Allen had said, taken off-guard by the news.

Eric took another sip of his beer and nodded.

"Did you tell her?"

Eric shook his head.

"Are you planning on telling her?"

Again, Eric shook his head.

"Why not?" asked Allen.

"Why do you think? Molly would never go out with me."

"You don't know unless you ask."

"Trust me," said Eric. "I know. Remember Monica Metzger?"

Monica was a girl Eric had had a crush on in high school, who had laughed in his face when Eric had asked her out.

"That was what, tenth grade? This is totally different. And Molly's no Monica."

"Maybe."

The two of them sipped their beers, not saying anything for several minutes.

"You should ask her out," said Allen.

"Really?" said Eric, looking at him.

"Sure. Why not? I don't think she's seeing anyone."

"What about you?"

"What about me?"

"You sure you don't want to ask her out?"

Allen stared at his friend.

"Me?"

"Don't act so surprised," said Eric. "I see the way you two look at each other."

Allen didn't know what to say.

"At least admit you find her attractive."

"Sure, Molly's cute and all. But we're just friends."

"You sure about that?" said Eric, looking at him.

"Of course I am!" said Allen. But as he said it, he didn't feel so sure. "So are you going to ask Molly out or what?"

"I'll think about it," said Eric.

Sophomore year flew by, and Allen, Eric, and Molly remained best friends. Then it was junior year, and they decided they would all study abroad spring semester. They had thought about going to the same place. But in the end, Molly went to Ireland, Eric to London, and Allen to Paris. Though they vowed they would meet up at least once a month.

That didn't happen. Though they finally managed to arrange a long weekend in Nice, in the South of France, towards the end of the semester. Molly said she would find a place for the three of them to stay on Airbnb, and they messaged back and forth about things they wanted to do once they got there.

The day before they all were to arrive, however, Eric sent Allen and Molly a message saying he had been violently ill the night before with some kind of stomach bug and would not be joining them.

Allen had called to see if he was okay and if they should cancel, but Eric had insisted he go to Nice without him. Allen had then called Molly. And while she said she felt bad for Eric, she told Allen she still planned on going to Nice, having already paid for the apartment.

Allen then spent a restless night, wondering if he should still go to Nice or not. The next morning he boarded the train to Nice as planned, telling himself it wasn't safe for Molly to be there alone.

On the train ride down, he had felt guilty. But as soon as he saw Molly, he knew he had made the right decision. He dropped off his bag at the little two-bedroom flat Molly had rented them in Old Nice, not far from the water, and the two immediately headed out.

They wended their way through Old Nice, checking out the local farmers market and eyeing the displays in the little shops they passed. Then they stopped and had pizza for lunch. Afterward, they walked up to the old chateau and admired the view of the Mediterranean below. Then they strolled along the Promenade des Anglais, gazing at the sunbathers on the stony beach, many of them topless.

The next day they hiked up to the Matisse Museum in Cimiez and listened as a group of local musicians played in a nearby park. Then they took a day trip to Saint-Paul-de-Vence, a charming Medieval town known for its art and artisans.

On their last night, they dined at a little café near their apartment that their host had recommended.

"You were smart to study in France," Molly told Allen, as she dipped a piece of bread in the broth from her fish stew.

"I'm sure Ireland is nice, too," Allen said, finishing his wine.

"It is. But the food in France is better, especially the bread and the ice cream."

The waiter came by to clear away their plates.

"Would you care for some dessert or coffee?" he asked them.

"Sure, why not?" said Molly.

He returned a minute later with two dessert menus.

"See something you like?" asked Allen.

"It all sounds delicious," said Molly, staring at the menu. "But how about we just go get some ice cream?"

"I thought you'd never ask," said Allen, grinning.

They got the check, then made their way to Fenocchio, the go-to place for ice cream in Nice, where they had stopped their first day. They each ordered two scoops, or *boules*. Then they slowly made their way back to their rental.

"I don't want to go back to the States," Molly said as she flopped down on the couch.

"Neither do I," said Allen, who was standing in the little kitchen. "You thirsty?" he called.

"Totally," said Molly.

He opened the refrigerator.

"Hey, we still have that bottle of Champagne."

"Take it back to Paris with you."

"Nah, we were supposed to drink it together. Let's just open it."

"If you insist," said Molly.

She watched as Allen held a cloth over the bottle and then gently turned it, holding the cork steady until it came out with just a slight hiss.

"Bravo!" said Molly. "Or whatever they say in France. Where'd you learn to do that?"

"From my stepfather. He made sure us boys knew how to open a bottle of Champagne before we went off to college. Said it was an important life skill."

Molly laughed.

"Here you go!" Allen said, handing her a glass. "*Salut!*"

"*Salut!*" said Molly.

They clinked glasses and drank.

Molly closed her eyes. The tiny bubbles tickled her throat. She opened her eyes and took another sip.

"Not bad," said Allen.

"Shall we take our glasses out onto the balcony? It's a beautiful night."

They headed to the balcony, which was located off the living area. There was a little metal table with two metal chairs, and you could see all the twinkling lights of Nice.

Molly leaned on the railing and took another sip of her Champagne.

"It's so beautiful here. I wish we could stay longer."

"Me too," said Allen, looking out onto the city.

He put his glass on the table and turned to look at Molly. In the moonlight, her coppery hair seemed to glow. As if sensing he was looking at her, she turned her head. A part of her wanted to reach up and touch him. He was so beautiful standing there, the moon illuminating his face, the wind rustling his wavy hair. She wished that he would kiss her.

As if obeying her unspoken command, he took the glass from her hand and placed it on the table. Then he took a step toward her, closing the distance between them, and leaned down, brushing his lips against hers.

Molly was so surprised she knocked over her glass, but she barely noticed. Allen was kissing her! And she was kissing him back.

"Let's go inside," Allen whispered into her ear.

Molly nodded.

But as they went to go back in, she heard a crunch.

"What was that?" she said. She looked down and realized it was her wine glass. "Oh no! I broke the glass!"

Allen followed her gaze. It was difficult to see in the dark, but he could see light reflecting off pieces of broken glass.

Molly grabbed Allen's arm.

"What if the owner gets mad that we broke one of his glasses and doesn't return my security deposit? Or he leaves me a bad review, says I'm bad guest?"

Allen placed a hand on Molly's shoulder.

"It's going to be fine. I'm sure this kind of thing happens all the time. It's only a glass. We can go look for another one in the morning before we leave."

Molly looked up at him, tears ready to spill from her moss-green eyes.

"Let me see if I can find a broom and a dustpan."

Molly nodded and let Allen go.

"Ta-da!" he said, holding up a broom and a dustpan a minute later.

He did his best to sweep up the pieces of broken glass, picking up the larger shards with his hands.

"Be careful!" Molly called.

He headed into the kitchen and emptied the pan into the garbage bin.

"I'll check again in the morning, when it's light out," he said. "But I think I got most of it."

"Thank you," said Molly.

Allen yawned.

"It's been a long day. I'm going to head to bed. You going to be okay?"

"Yeah," said Molly.

They stood there awkwardly for several seconds, the mood of a few minutes before broken.

"Well, goodnight," said Allen.

"Goodnight," said Molly.

Then she watched him walk away.

As hard as she tried, Molly couldn't fall asleep that night. She kept replaying the kiss in her head. She had wanted it to go on, and had thought Allen did, too. And she had been a bit miffed when Allen hadn't picked up where they had left off. Had he changed his mind? When she finally got out of bed the next morning, she was tired and out of sorts.

"*Bonjour!*" said Allen, cheerfully, as soon as he saw her.

He was in his pajama pants and a t-shirt, making coffee in the giant French press.

Molly yawned and tried not to stare at him.

"Is the coffee ready?"

"Almost. How'd you sleep?"

"Okay," she said, yawning again. "And you?"

"Like a baby," said Allen.

At that moment she hated him. Clearly, he hadn't tossed and turned all night, thinking about her.

"Here you go," he said, pouring some coffee into what looked like a giant teacup.

"Thanks," said Molly, taking the cup.

She added milk and sugar and drank. Allen did the same. Several minutes went by, with neither of them speaking.

"Okay if I take first shower?" he asked her.

"Be my guest," she replied.

He took a final sip of his coffee, then headed to the bathroom.

As she nursed her coffee and nibbled on a leftover croissant, Molly could hear the shower running. For some reason, her brain began imagining Allen, naked, water streaming down his back and chest.

"Stop it," she hissed. But that part of her brain ignored her.

"All yours!" called Allen, a few minutes later, emerging from the bathroom with a towel wrapped around his waist.

Molly tried not to stare, but she could feel herself blushing. What had gotten into her?

"Thanks," she said.

She waited until Allen had gone into his bedroom, then she scurried into the bathroom and locked the door.

CHAPTER 3

Allen had texted Eric over the weekend, to see how he was doing. As it turned out, it had been one of those 48-hour bugs, and Eric was now feeling fine.

"So, how was Nice?" Eric asked. Allen had called him as soon as he had gotten back to Paris. "Did you guys miss me?"

"Of course we did," said Allen. Though in truth, he had barely thought about Eric.

"Anything I should know?"

"What do you mean?"

"Come on. You, Molly, a romantic city…"

Allen could feel his face growing warm.

"Nothing happened."

"If you say so."

"So did Penelope take good care of you?"

"She brought me some chicken soup."

Eric had met Penelope, a Brit attending the University of London, his first week abroad, when he had gone to a local pub with some other American students. He was bringing a set of pints back to his table when he had literally bumped into her, spilling beer on her shirt. He had apologized profusely, and she had smiled at him and said it was no big deal, but that if he was truly sorry, he'd buy her a pint. And he had.

The two had wound up talking late into the night and had

been seeing each other regularly since.

"So, come on, tell me about Nice," said Eric. "You didn't say much in your messages. Though the ice cream looked great."

"It was."

"So, spill."

"You know," said Allen. "We did a ton of walking and eating. It's a cool place. Lots of old buildings and history. We went to this little Medieval village, supposedly one of the oldest in the South of France, and visited the Matisse Museum."

"Sounds like fun."

"It was. You should go if you get the chance. Maybe invite Penelope to go with you."

"I'll think about it. Hey, speaking of Penelope, I have to go meet her. But thanks for calling. You still coming to London?"

"I wouldn't miss it. So will I finally get to meet her?"

"Only if you promise not to steal her away."

"I promise," said Allen, who found the very idea ridiculous. Women rarely gave him a second glance.

Back in Ireland, Molly brooded.

"What's wrong with you?" asked her roommate, Diana.

"Nothing," replied Molly.

"Oh, please," said Diana. "You've been in a mood ever since you got back from Nice. You not have a good time?"

"I had a great time," said Molly.

"So what's the problem?"

"That's just it. I had a great time."

Diana looked confused.

Molly sighed.

"It was perfect. And now I'm worried he'll never speak to me again."

"Who'll never speak to you again, Allen?"

Molly nodded.

"And why is that?"

"We kind of fooled around while we were there."

"Oho, the plot thickens! I thought you said you guys were just friends."

"We are just friends," said Molly.

"But you said you fooled around," said Diana.

"We did."

"So did you *fool around* fool around or…"

"We just kissed."

"Oh. So what's the big deal?"

Molly sighed again.

"I've had a crush on Allen Whitford since freshman year."

"So?" said Diana. "If he kissed you, he must have a crush on you, too."

"He doesn't have a crush on me. It was the Champagne. We'd had a lot to drink, and he probably just got carried away."

Though just thinking about the kiss made Molly wistful.

"Please," said Diana. "A guy doesn't kiss you unless he wants to."

Molly didn't look convinced.

"So, how was it?"

"Amazing," said Molly. "Probably the best kiss I've ever had."

Diana leaned forward.

"So what happened? How come you two didn't, you know?"

"I broke a glass and shattered the mood."

"Bummer," said Diana.

"Yeah, tell me about it."

They sat in silence for several seconds.

"So, have you talked to him since you've been back?"

"No," said Molly.

"Why not?"

"What am I supposed to say? Thanks for the kiss, let's do it again sometime?"

"You could."

Molly shook her head.

"I can't. Like I said, Allen and I are friends. I don't want things to be weird between us."

"But what if he wants to kiss you again?"

Molly hadn't thought about that. She shrugged.

"Well, I'm heading out. You want to join us? Danny and I are grabbing a drink at the pub."

"I'm good," said Molly. "Besides, I should probably study for my final."

"Suit yourself," said Diana. "You're more than welcome. I'm sure some of his mates will be there. And a few of them are pretty cute."

She grinned at Molly, then shrugged and headed out.

Molly opened her laptop. She stared at it for several seconds, then closed it again. She wasn't really in the mood to study. She got up and grabbed her bag, then raced out the door and down the stairs.

"Hey, wait up!" she called.

Allen was suffering from writer's block. The assignment had been to write a love story. But he was struggling. He had thought he had been in love with Emily, but he realized it was probably a childhood crush. And he hadn't felt in love since then. Though he had felt something when that cute blonde drama student had flirted with him the other night. She was also at the NYU Paris campus for the semester, and he had seen her around. But the two had barely spoken, until the other night.

He stared at his computer, willing the words to form on the screen, but nothing happened.

"I need a break," he announced.

He got up and pounded on the door to the room next door.

"Hey, Mitch, you there?"

Mitch, a fellow NYU student, opened the door. He was dressed in a pair of sweats and a t-shirt.

"What's the emergency?"

"You want to go grab a drink?"

"Is that a trick question?"

"No," said Allen.

"Just give me a sec to change."

He closed the door and reemerged a couple of minutes later dressed in jeans and a leather jacket.

"Shall we?" he said.

"We shall," said Allen.

CHAPTER 4

Senior year seemed to zip by. Allen, Eric, and Molly had been busy, working hard to make sure they would graduate and figuring out what they would do next. But by that April, things had settled down.

Molly had secured a job as an editorial assistant at a prestigious New York publishing house. Eric would be working as an instructor at a college-prep program over the summer, then attending Columbia's prestigious History Ph.D. program. And Allen had landed a job at Hipster, a new digital magazine aimed at twenty-somethings, based in Brooklyn.

Now graduation was just a few days away, and the three friends had decided to celebrate together at one of their favorite restaurants, a little Mexican place in the Village known for its killer tacos and equally lethal drinks.

They ordered a pitcher of margaritas and raised their glasses.

"To us!" said Molly.

"To us!" said Eric.

"May we always be friends," said Allen.

"I'll drink to that!" said Eric.

They clinked glasses and drank.

An hour or so later, after sharing some of their favorite college memories and draining the pitcher of margaritas, they leaned back in their seats with nothing left to say (and a bit drunk).

"Shall we get a check and get out of here?" suggested Eric.

"Probably a good idea," said Allen.

Molly was staring into the distance.

"You okay, Moll?" asked Eric.

"I think I drank too much," she replied.

"You do look a little pale," said Allen.

"I just need some air."

They got the check and were making their way to the door when Molly tripped over the leg of a customer and nearly wound up in his companion's lap. It was only Allen's quick reflexes that saved her.

"Sorry!" she said to the couple.

They then hurried out of the restaurant.

"Let me take you home," Allen said to Molly.

"That's really not necessary," she replied.

"Let me see you walk a straight line."

"I can walk just fine," she primly replied. "It's not like I'm driving. That man's leg was just in the way."

The evening was cool, and Molly closed her eyes as a light breeze caressed her face.

"Well, you don't look fine," said Allen. "Come on, I'll call a car."

"I can see her home," said Eric.

"I got this," said Allen, shooting him a look. He pulled out his phone and opened the ride-sharing app. "A car should be here in less than five minutes."

Molly made a face.

"I'm perfectly capable of taking the subway."

"I'm taking you home," Allen retorted.

The two of them stood there, glaring at each other.

"Guess I'll be heading off then," said Eric, feeling uncomfortable. "See you guys at graduation. Feel better, Molly."

"Thanks," she said, still looking at Allen. "But I'm perfectly fine."

Eric looked at them for a few more seconds, then turned and headed down the block.

A few minutes later, Allen and Molly's ride showed up.

"Shall we?" said Allen.

Molly sighed.

"Fine. But for the record, I would have made it home just fine on my own."

Allen held open the door for her and Molly climbed in.

As they sped north, Molly felt her head spinning.

"You okay?" asked Allen. "You don't look so good."

Molly didn't say anything. She had been feeling fine before they had gotten in the car. But now she felt nauseous.

"Here, lean against me," he said, gently putting an arm around her and pulling her close.

Molly leaned her head against his shoulder and closed her eyes.

"We're here, sleepyhead," said Allen, a few minutes later, as the car stopped in front of Molly's building, a brownstone located in Murray Hill, in the East 30s.

Allen thanked the driver, then helped Molly out of the car.

"Is Becca home?"

Becca was Molly's roommate.

"She's away this weekend."

Allen helped her up the stairs.

"Keys?"

Molly started rummaging in her bag.

"They're in here somewhere," she muttered.

"Here, let me," said Allen.

He gently took her bag and in a few seconds located her keys.

"Which one?"

"That one," said Molly, pointing to one circled with a red ring. "The blue and yellow ones are for the inside locks."

Allen inserted the key with the red ring into the front door of the building and led Molly inside. Then he helped her up the three flights of stairs.

"No wonder you're in such good shape," he said, when they reached her apartment.

"You get used to it after a while."

Allen unlocked the door to Molly's apartment and let them inside.

Molly flicked on the light.

"Yeow, that's bright," she said, shielding her eyes. "Let me go turn on the lamp."

She made her way across the room to a freestanding lamp with a dark red shade and turned it on.

"Turn off the overhead," she commanded.

Allen obeyed.

"Much better," she said, flopping down onto the couch.

Suddenly, she felt woozy again. She closed her eyes and leaned forward, holding her head in her hands.

"You should drink some water," said Allen.

"I don't ever want to drink again."

"You'll feel better after you've had some water."

"Why did I have that second margarita?" Molly moaned. "Those things should come with warning labels. How much tequila do you think they put in there, a whole bottle?"

Allen went to the kitchenette and got Molly a glass of water.

"Here," he said, holding out the glass.

Molly opened her eyes and stared at it.

Allen moved it closer.

"Drink."

Molly took the glass and forced herself to have a sip.

"Happy now?"

Allen smiled.

"You want me to sit with you?"

Molly nodded.

Allen sat next to her, and Molly again placed her head on his shoulder.

They sat there, quietly, for several minutes, Allen's arm wrapped around Molly.

"You feeling a bit better?"

"Mmm…" she said, only barely awake.

"Let's get you to bed," said Allen.

He tried to move her, but she didn't budge.

"Do I need to carry you?" he said, smiling down at her.

Molly's eyes were still closed but she smiled.

"Come on," he said.

"Aren't you going to carry me?" she asked, still smiling.

He picked her up and carried her to her bedroom, Molly's arms encircling his neck.

"Here you go," he said, placing her gently down on the bed.

She frowned.

"I should probably get going," he said, moving toward the door.

"Aren't you going to give me a goodnight kiss?"

She was sitting on the bed, her eyes now open.

Allen paused, then went over to her. He leaned down to kiss her forehead, but as he did so, Molly looked up and their lips met. Before either one knew what was happening, they were kissing, Molly pulling Allen on top of her.

"Take off your shirt," Molly commanded, a bit breathlessly.

Allen started to, then stopped and got up.

"What's wrong?" said Molly, confused.

"This. This is wrong."

Molly looked hurt.

"Wrong?"

"We shouldn't be doing this," said Allen.

"Why not? If you're worried about Becca, she's not here."

"It's not that."

"Then what?"

"We're friends. We just had too much to drink."

"Haven't you ever heard of friends with benefits?"

"I have, but that's not me."

"But I want you, and if your pants are any indication, you want me too."

Allen glanced down and felt himself blushing.

"I should go."

"But I don't understand!" said Molly.

Allen sighed and ran a hand through his hair.

"I just don't want anything to get in the way of our friendship."

"It won't."

Molly knew how she sounded and hated it, but she couldn't help herself. She desperately wanted Allen to stay.

"I'm going," said Allen. "I'll check on you in the morning."

"Don't bother," said Molly, not looking at him.

He stood by the door for several seconds, then left.

As soon as the front door had closed, Molly screamed.

"I hate you, Allen Whitford!"

But she knew in her heart she didn't.

Allen experienced a range of emotions as he made his way home. A part of him had wanted to stay. He had definitely been aroused, but the thought of sleeping with Molly had scared him. He still wasn't completely over Sophie, and he didn't want to risk losing Molly as a friend.

Just thinking about Sophie made him angry and sad. They had started seeing each other in Paris, just before their time there was up. (She was the pretty blonde Drama major he had met at that party.) And they had continued to date when they got back to the States. Allen had thought she could be the one. Then Sophie had announced she was moving to L.A. right after graduation.

Allen had been devastated. He knew that she wanted to be an actress and had an audition for a new pilot, a kind of modern-day version of *Friends* set in L.A. But he said he'd be willing to carry on long distance. Sophie had shaken her head. She didn't think a long-distance relationship would work.

Allen had then offered to move to L.A. with her, even though he had accepted the job at Hipster. But Sophie had again shaken her head and had said she wanted a clean break. This was it.

For days after the breakup, Allen had moped in his room. He skipped classes and wouldn't answer his phone. He thought about moving to L.A. anyway, on the off chance Sophie changed her mind. Though he realized that would be stupid. Why throw away a good job? But every time he thought about her, he got depressed.

Finally, his friends had had enough. Neither Eric nor Molly had particularly liked Sophie. And the thought of their friend wasting away because of the self-absorbed drama queen made them angry. So they dragged him out of his room, taking him out for pizza and a movie. And eventually, with their help, Allen felt better, though some days it still felt as though a piece of his heart was missing.

Yes, it must have been the margaritas and missing Sophie that had caused him to behave as he had. Good thing he hadn't spent the night with Molly. That would have been unfair to both of them.

As he rode the elevator up to the tenth floor and unlocked the door to his parents' apartment, he was already feeling better. He had definitely done the right thing by leaving. And hopefully by tomorrow, Molly would have forgotten all about it.

CHAPTER 5

Allen had been at Hipster for over four months now. And for the most part, he liked working there. Though he still hadn't been assigned a feature, just a bunch of listicles and short pieces talking about the next hot restaurant or bar or boutique. But that was okay, he told himself. He was learning.

He was working on yet another Top Ten list when the publisher, Justin Johnson, known as J.J., a thirty-something recipient of a large trust fund who dressed and acted more like a twenty-something, came over and sat on the corner of Allen's desk.

"Whit-man! Have I got an assignment for you!"

Allen looked up, his eyebrows arching.

"You're going to love it, and the J-Man is never wrong!" said Justin, gleefully. "It's for our 'New Year, New You' edition."

Allen didn't like the look in Justin's eyes.

"Hipster is going to help you find your soulmate in time for the new year!"

"My soulmate?" said Allen. "And how are you going to do that? The new year is just over two months away."

"Okay, maybe not your *soulmate*, but Hipster is going to find you a date for our big New Year's Eve bash!"

Allen looked skeptical.

"You're going to love this!" said Justin, who tended to end

every sentence as though it had an exclamation point. "So, two of our new advertisers are these new dating sites. And as a way to get the word out, we thought it would be fun to have someone from Hipster go on them and bring the winner to the Bash!"

"Winner?" said Allen.

"You know what I mean," said Justin.

"But why me?"

"Because you're perfect! You're young, not bad looking, and you can write."

"Thanks, but I'm not interested."

Justin stared at him.

"What do you mean you're not interested? Do you understand what I'm offering you? It's the chance to meet the woman of your dreams! And did I mention that Hipster will give you a total makeover?"

"Thanks, but no thanks."

Justin shook his head. No one had ever turned down a free makeover or the opportunity to get laid on Hipster's dime.

"Did I mention we'll buy you a whole new wardrobe?"

"I don't need more clothes."

"I don't understand. Are you seeing someone? Or, wait, are you gay? Which is totally fine, if you are. I love gay people. But—"

Allen cut him off.

"I am not gay. And I'm not seeing anyone. I just don't like dating apps."

"But you've never tried *these* dating apps. They're new and different from what's out there, or so their people told me. And did I mention the free makeover and wardrobe?"

Allen knew Justin meant well, but he dearly wished he would just go away.

"Come on, just give them a try."

"If they're so great," said Allen, "why don't you try them?"

Justin scoffed.

"You can't be serious? Me, on some dating app? Besides, Gigi would be furious."

Gigi was Justin's latest model girlfriend.

"Fine. Then ask someone else. What about Dave? He's single."

"Dave? You must be kidding me."

Dave was Hipster's tech reporter, who tended to look like he just rolled out of bed and whose idea of a good time was staying up all night gaming or figuring out how to hack into government websites.

"Okay, maybe not Dave. But there's got to be someone else here."

"Nope, you're it," said Justin. "I already spoke with Natalie and Sara, and they agree with me."

Allen looked distinctly unhappy.

"What's the matter? Don't you want to get laid?"

"Look, J.J., I appreciate the vote of confidence, but I tried dating apps, and they didn't work."

Justin grinned.

"That's because you didn't have Hipster helping you out. Now, are you going to take on this assignment, or do you want to look for another job?"

Allen felt trapped.

"Fine, I'll do it."

"Excellent!" said Justin. "Now, the two sites you'll be checking out are called Spark and Blind Date."

"Never heard of them."

"As I said, they're both new."

"So what makes them different from all the other dating apps or sites out there?"

Justin smiled.

"I'm so glad you asked. The first one, Spark, is similar to some of them. You upload a few photos and create a profile.

But unlike most other apps, it's up to the woman to make the first move. And everyone uses a screen name, kind of like on Instagram, to protect people's privacy."

"Okay," said Allen. "What about the other one?"

"Ah, yes, Blind Date. Have you ever seen that show *The Voice*"?

"Sure, why?"

"It's kind of like that. You don't actually get to see your date unless you like what you hear."

"You mean I have to sing?" said Allen, confused.

Justin laughed.

"No, you don't have to sing. You write letters."

"Letters?"

"Technically emails."

"Emails? You don't just text?"

"No. That's the whole point. You have to woo your prospective dates with words."

"What about photos?"

"No photos. Hence the name."

"But eventually you get to meet these people, right?"

Justin nodded.

"The way I understand it is, they match you with three women they think you'd be compatible with, based on a questionnaire you fill out. Then you correspond with your dates for four weeks. If you make it to the end, you get to meet."

"Did you say four weeks? Who on earth is going to email someone for four weeks, especially not knowing what they look like? That's crazy."

"I'll have you know that Blind Date was just named one of the top dating sites for 2019."

"Huh," said Allen. "So how do you know that the people they match you with aren't ax murderers or whack jobs?"

"Blind Date does a thorough background screening."

Allen still looked skeptical.

"Okay, and what happens if you don't like the people they match you with?"

"You can request new matches."

"So how many dates am I expected to go out on?"

"As many as you like on Spark. And as I said, Blind Date matches you with three people."

"Great," said Allen, sarcastically.

"Oh, and one other thing," said Justin.

Allen raised his eyebrows.

"You can't tell any of the women that this is for an article."

"Won't they get mad, though, when they read about themselves?"

"Not if you change some of the details. People write about stuff like this all the time. And some of them might be thrilled to be in Hipster."

Allen wasn't so sure.

"What if I don't meet anyone I really like?"

"Nonsense. New York is filled with beautiful women. I'm sure you'll find someone. Preferably someone who will impress the advertisers."

"Speaking of the advertisers, won't one of them be upset? Maybe I should bring two dates, one from Spark and one from Blind Date."

Allen was being sarcastic, but Justin looked like he was mulling it over.

"No, probably best to bring just one. I've already explained it to them, and they agreed. I think they rather enjoy the idea of a competition."

Justin was grinning again.

"Oh, and you can't just bring anyone to the Bash. You need to have a real connection with the person. The advertisers insisted."

"How am I supposed to establish a deep connection in just two months?"

"Haven't you ever heard of love at first sight? That's what it was for me and Valaria."

Valaria was Justin's first wife.

"And didn't you divorce her less than a year later?"

"Sad, but true," sighed Justin. "But then I met Mona… and then Courtney… and then Heidi and Gigi."

Allen held up his hand.

"I get the picture. So, when do I have to start?"

"Right away. Natalie and Sara are on standby. Just schedule a time to meet with them."

"Great," said Allen.

"Well, duty calls," said Justin. "Gotta run. Good luck. And keep me posted!"

"So," said Natalie, sitting at her desk and looking over at Allen. "Shall we begin? Let's start with something easy. What are you into?"

Natalie was Hipster's fashion editor and one of the few people who had an actual office.

"You mean, like, hobbies?" asked Allen.

"More like passions," said Natalie. "But whatever. What floats your boat?"

"I like to read."

Natalie fake yawned.

"Bor-ing."

"You know we work for a magazine, right?" said Allen. "If people didn't read, we wouldn't have jobs."

"He's got a point, Nat," said Sara, Hipster's advice columnist.

"Fine. But he needs to say something other than 'I like to read' on his profile. What about sports, or travel, or cooking? Women love a man who can cook."

"I'm not really into cooking, though my mom is. She can make just about anything."

Natalie rolled her eyes.

"What about sports? Did you play anything in college?"

Allen shook his head.

"I'm not that into sports, though I sometimes watch basketball and baseball."

"You work out?"

"I go running in Central Park and belong to a gym."

Natalie got up and walked around her desk. She was eyeing Allen.

"Take off your shirt," she commanded.

"Excuse me?" said Allen.

"You heard me. I said, take off your shirt."

"I will not."

"Don't be such a prude, Allen. Take it off."

"Why?"

"I want to see what the good Lord gave you."

Allen looked at Sara, who was suppressing a grin.

"You embarrassed about your body?" asked Natalie.

"No, it's just… We're at work."

"So? I have models taking their clothes off all the time."

"I'm not a model."

"You are now."

Again, Allen looked to Sara for help.

"Does he really need to take off his shirt?" she asked Natalie.

"If he wants me to dress him properly, he does."

"Fine," said Allen.

He slowly unbuttoned his shirt.

"Now take it off," commanded Natalie.

"I feel like a piece of meat."

"Now you know how women feel."

Allen removed his shirt.

"Now stand up."

"What if people see me?"

"So what?"

"Fine," said Allen, standing up. "But I am not removing any more clothing."

"Now slowly turn around."

Allen scowled but did as he was told.

"Very nice," said Natalie, admiring him. "If I wasn't in a committed relationship, I might ask you out."

Allen felt mortified.

"This is sexual harassment!"

"Chill out, Whitford. I wasn't serious. Now stand still."

She went over to her desk and took out a tape measure.

"What's that for?" asked Allen.

"What do you think?" said Natalie. "Now spread your arms."

Allen reluctantly obeyed and Natalie proceeded to take his measurements, though she allowed him to take the one around his hips and hold the top of the tape measure when she measured his inseam.

"Now can I please put my shirt back on?"

"Go ahead," she said.

Allen quickly put his shirt back on and sat back down. Though what he really wanted to do was get the hell out of there.

"Now, about your hair," said Natalie, eyeing it.

"What's wrong with me hair?" said Allen, defensively.

"It's a bit bushy. I'm thinking it could use some trimming, maybe thin it out a bit, put a little product in it. What do you think, Sara?"

She nodded.

"I'll see if Paolo's available."

"Who's Paolo?" asked Allen.

"Only one of the best men's hairstylists in all of New York."

Allen frowned.

"It feels like cheating. Shouldn't women want me for who I am?"

Natalie laughed.

"And I thought Blind Date didn't allow photos."

"You still need to send them a few," said Sara. "It helps the matchmakers."

"But what if the person in the photos doesn't look like me?"

"Nonsense," said Natalie. "By the time we're through with you, you will look exactly like the person in the photos we'll be taking of you."

"Shall we get back to the profile?" said Sara.

"Fine," said Allen.

"Okay," said Sara. "Tell me something about you that a prospective date might find interesting."

"Well," said Allen, thinking. "I like to travel. I studied in Paris my junior year and traveled all around Europe. And I'm writing a novel."

"A novel, eh?" said Natalie, looking mildly interested. "What's it about?"

"It's about this young man whose parents both die in 9/11, when he's, like six, and he's raised by friends of theirs. And he falls in love with their daughter, even though she's like a sister to him."

"Kinky. I like it!" said Natalie.

"Have you finished it?" asked Sara.

"No, not yet. I'm about halfway through."

"You have an agent?" asked Natalie.

"No, I'm waiting until I've finished the first draft to look for one."

"Well, don't wait too long," said Sara.

"May I go now?" asked Allen. He had another listicle to finish.

"Yes," said Natalie. "But you need to work on your Spark profile and fill out the Blind Date questionnaire this weekend. We can then review both on Monday. And I'll talk to Lucy about arranging a photo shoot."

Lucy was Hipster's art director.

"Great," said Allen, morosely.

CHAPTER 6

Molly stared at her computer. She had opened Blind Date, a new dating site that her friend Felicity, who worked in the Marketing department, had insisted she check out. Unlike other dating sites, Blind Date didn't allow you to post or share photos. And you had to correspond with someone through the site for four weeks before you got to meet them.

Molly thought it sounded gimmicky and wondered if anyone actually met their perfect match through the site, four weeks being an eternity to correspond with someone before actually meeting them. But Felicity assured her it worked. It was, after all, how she had met her boyfriend, Nick.

"This way you really get to know the guy, without all that superficial stuff," Felicity had explained.

"I thought you liked all that superficial stuff," said Molly. "You're the one addicted to *The Bachelor* and *Love Island*."

Felicity sighed.

"I never said I wanted to go on those shows. I just like watching them."

"Whatever," said Molly. "But how do you know the guy they match you with isn't a creep or a rapist?"

"Everyone undergoes a background check," said Felicity. "And when you do finally get to meet your match, it's someplace public, like a restaurant. Totally safe."

"I don't know," said Molly. "What if the guy turns out to

be a midget or looks like the wolfman?"

"Now who's the one being superficial?"

"You know what I mean."

"They're not going to match you with one of the seven dwarfs or some super hairy dude unless you state on your questionnaire that that's what you're into."

"I still don't know."

"Trust me, you'll be so horny after emailing with these guys for four weeks, you won't care what they look like."

"I doubt that," said Molly. She paused. "So really, that's how you met Nick?"

"Yup," said Felicity. "A girlfriend of mine works at Blind Date. She asked me to be a beta tester when the site first launched. At first, I was hesitant, like you. I mean, who knows what kind of guy they're going to match you with, right? But she convinced me to try it out, and I'm glad I did."

"Huh," said Molly.

She had met Nick a few times. He was a total stud. And it seemed like he and Felicity were madly in love.

"So how long have the two of you been together now?"

"It's been four months since our first official date."

"And you had no idea who he was or what he looked like before you met him?"

She couldn't believe Felicity, the original internet stalker, would actually agree to go out with a guy she hadn't met or couldn't find online.

"Nope," said Felicity. "Though it wasn't as though I knew nothing about him. I knew he was a couple of years older than me, worked in finance, and was from Massachusetts. And that he was into football."

"What about where he went to school or where he worked?" asked Molly.

"You're not allowed to reveal your place of employment or where you went to school, but you can say stuff like, 'I work at a publishing house' and 'I graduated from a Big Ten school.'"

Molly tried to imagine what she would say.

"So, you game?" asked Felicity. "You won't be disappointed."

"What the heck? Not like I'm meeting anyone through work. Will you help me?"

"Of course!"

Now here she was, about to take the plunge.

"You're not serious," said Eric.

"I'm totally serious," said Molly.

She and Eric had gone to see a movie and had stopped to get a bite to eat afterward.

"A dating site with no photos? What if they set me up with someone who weighs 300 pounds or is like that crazy chick in *Gone Girl*?" Eric asked.

Molly rolled her eyes.

"They supposedly screen everyone. And they only match you with people they think you'd be compatible with."

"I don't know," said Eric. "It sounds like a scam."

"I thought so, too. But my friend Felicity met her boyfriend Nick through Blind Date, and the two of them seem very happy."

Eric ate another french fry.

"Besides, what have I got to lose? Not like I'm meeting anyone through work. Everyone there is either married, in a relationship, or gay."

"Surely some of them must have single friends?"

"You would think so. But apparently not."

"I'd go out with you," said Eric, trying to look casual while eating another french fry, though his heart was hammering against his chest.

Despite his fling with Penelope, he still harbored a crush on Molly.

Molly reached across the table and put her hand on top of his.

"You're sweet," she said. "But I'm not looking for a pity date."

Eric opened his mouth to tell her it wouldn't be a pity date, then shut it.

"Besides, what have I got to lose, except a little money? And Blind Date guarantees it can help you find that special someone."

"If you want to throw your money away..."

"So are you seeing anyone?" Molly asked.

"You know how it is," said Eric.

"I bet there are lots of cute, smart women in your History program."

"A few, but they want nothing to do with me."

Since Penelope, he hadn't dated anyone, mostly out of shyness and a lack of self-confidence.

"I don't believe that," said Molly.

"Well, it's true. Besides, I'm too busy with work and studying to date right now."

"Nonsense. If you found someone you really liked, you'd make the time."

"Maybe," said Eric.

"Tell you what," said Molly. "Let's both go on Blind Date and see what happens. And if it's a total bust, we can both laugh about it."

"I don't know."

"Come on. Who knows? You may meet your dream girl."

Eric wanted to tell Molly that she was his dream girl. But like so many times before, he didn't have the courage.

"Fine," he said, finishing the last fry. "If it'll make you happy."

"Yay!" said Molly. She paused. "Just don't tell me your screen name, in case they match us up. Wouldn't that be funny?"

"Yeah," said Eric. Though he didn't find it funny at all. In fact, he thought this might be the perfect way to show Molly he really was the guy for her. Assuming Blind Date matched the two of them. "So when are we going to do this?"

"Right away. There's a questionnaire you have to fill it out first. I just started it, so you'll need to get going."

"Have you heard of this new dating site, Blind Date?" Eric asked Allen the next night when they were having a beer.

They had met up after work.

"Blind Date?" said Allen, feigning ignorance.

Justin had told him he was not supposed to discuss the dating article with friends.

"I just heard about it and was thinking of checking it out. You fill out a questionnaire and get assigned three matches. The catch is, no photos. And you have to email with people for four weeks in order to actually meet them."

"Sounds kind of gimmicky," said Allen.

"That's what I thought. But I hear it works."

"What about that woman you told me about, the one you were thinking of asking out?"

"Rob got to her first. I swear that guy is a chick magnet."

"But there must be other women."

"There are," said Eric. "But you know I'm no good at asking women out. This just seems like a better way."

"Mmm," said Allen.

"This way, women get to know me, the real me, without judging me by my looks."

"What's wrong with your looks? If I was a woman, I'd go out with you."

"Thanks, but you know what I mean."

Allen shrugged and took another sip of his beer.

"Well, let me know how it goes."

"You could always try it, too. It's not that expensive."

"Thanks, but I'm pretty busy these days."

"Speaking of being busy, how's the novel coming?"

Allen scowled.

"I've been kind of stuck."

"How come?" asked Eric.

"I don't know. I think spending all day writing listicles has done something to my brain. By the time I get home, I have no energy to write."

"Well, don't give up on that novel. I think it's great. And I want to be able to tell people I knew you when."

Allen smiled and finished his beer.

"I should get going. Got a big day tomorrow."

"I should get going, too," said Eric.

They signaled for the check and left shortly afterward.

CHAPTER 7

Allen groaned as he read through the Blind Date questionnaire. He had thought he could just quickly fill it out at work and be done with it. But there were so many questions, many of them pretty personal, and, he thought, inane. Did it really matter which way he placed the roll of toilet paper on the holder? Like anyone really cared. And did he really want to date someone who did?

He continued to scroll through the questions. Sara had told him to answer honestly. But looking at some of them, he wondered if honesty was really the best policy.

The first section asked for basic information: name, age, height, weight, hair color, eye color. He had dutifully filled in the blanks and moved on to the education and work questions. Those, too, he had filled out.

Next was a section on interests and hobbies. He had typed *Reading* first, then had stopped, remembering his conversation with Natalie and Sara. He stared at the screen and frowned. There were spaces for five answers.

"Screw it," he said, then typed *Reading* again. If Natalie and Sara had any objections, he'd deal with them.

Finally, he came to the personal or intimate questions. Allen's head hurt just thinking about answering them. He was at his core a private person, and he didn't think it was anyone's business how many showers he took a week, if he watched porn, or what his favorite sexual position was. (Did people his age even have a favorite sexual position?)

He felt slightly more comfortable listing his favorite bands, books, movies, and television shows. Though that, too, was difficult. He had many, but he could only put down his top three. He started typing, then deleted what he had written and typed something else, only to delete that and start over.

Over an hour later, he was done, but he had left many of the questions blank. He hit "save," then he fired off a message to Natalie and Sara.

"Took a first pass at the Blind Date questionnaire," he wrote. "Left some blank. Is that okay?"

Seconds later, he received a message from Sara.

"You want some help?"

"Not really," Allen replied.

"Okay. We can go over it Monday."

"You start your Spark profile?" Natalie chimed in.

"Not yet," Allen typed.

"Well, get going!" she wrote back.

"Fine," wrote Allen.

He closed the Hipster messaging app on his computer and opened the Spark app on his phone.

Spark had a wizard that helped you create a profile and didn't ask nearly as many questions as Blind Date had.

Allen had begun setting up his profile when he felt a presence looming over him.

"Whatcha doin'?" asked Dave.

"Nothing," said Allen, quickly turning off the screen on his phone.

"Uh-huh," said Dave, grinning at Allen.

"It's not what you think."

"Sure, sure. Whatever you say. So, is she hot?"

"Is who hot?"

"The chick you were just looking at."

"I wasn't looking at a chick," said Allen.

"So it was a guy? Huh. I hadn't peg you as gay, though…"

"I am not gay, Dave. Not that there's anything wrong with being gay," he quickly added. "And I wasn't looking at anyone. I was working."

"Uh-huh. Then why were you hunched over your phone?"

Allen desperately wanted Dave to go away.

"Is there something you wanted?" he asked.

"Nope, I'm good. Was just passing by and wondering what you were up to. You looked pretty intense."

"That's because I was *working*," said Allen, stressing the last word.

"Okay, dude. No need to get hostile. "But if you're ever looking for a little online action, hit me up. I know all the good sites."

"Thanks, Dave, but I'm good. Now I really need to get back to work."

"So, what are you working on?"

Allen silently counted to three, then turned and faced him.

"I'm working on an article. Don't *you* have an article you need to work on?"

Dave held up his hands.

"Geez, I was just being friendly."

He lingered for another minute, no doubt hoping Allen might say something, but Allen was staring at his monitor, ignoring him.

"Well, good luck with the article."

Allen didn't respond. He was looking at the article on the most fashionable dogs in New York he had been assigned to edit. A few minutes later, he again felt someone standing behind him and wished he had an office—with a door.

"Hey."

It was Natalie.

"Hey," said Allen, turning his head.

"So, which questions were you having trouble answering?"

"I'd rather not say," said Allen, glancing around.

"Gotcha," said Natalie. "Let me guess," she said, leaning over and whispering. "It was the sex ones, right?"

"Can we please not discuss it here?" said Allen.

"No problem. Though, just out of curiosity, what is your favorite sexual position?"

She was grinning at him, and Allen wanted to crawl under his desk.

"Come to my office."

Allen wanted to refuse, but he knew it was pointless.

"There," she said, closing the door, after he had followed her into her lair. "Now no one can hear us."

Allen glanced around, not sure if he should sit or stand.

"So, which questions do you need help answering?"

"I didn't say I needed help," Allen replied. "I said I didn't want to answer some of them."

"So why don't you want to answer some of them?"

"Because they're very personal."

"Don't you want to find that special someone?"

"Not if it means discussing my sex life."

"Don't be such a prude, Allen. I thought all you twenty-somethings were sex-forward."

"Not all of us."

Natalie looked at him sympathetically.

"Look, I get it. You don't want people knowing about your sex life. But it's not like the Blind Date people are going to publish your answers on social media. They're just trying to find you someone they think you'll be compatible with, personally, professionally, and sexually."

Allen stared at a spot on the floor.

Natalie sighed.

"I'm not going to force you to answer all the questions. But the more you answer, the more likely you'll find your perfect match."

"So you say."

"I'm not going to argue with you, Allen. What about Spark? Any problems there?"

"No. It seems pretty straightforward."

"Good. So, did Lucy message you about the photo shoot?"

"I didn't see anything."

"I'll follow up with her. We talked about doing it this coming Tuesday. Can you meet us at eight?"

"At night?"

"No, in the morning."

"Why so early?" asked Allen.

Natalie gave him a patronizing look.

"Right. So before the photographer takes any photos, the model—that would be you—has to go through hair and makeup. Then we need to figure out what clothes you'll be wearing in each shot. And then there's lighting and…"

"Makeup? No one said anything about makeup."

"It's no big deal, Allen. All models wear makeup. Even guys you see on TV, on ESPN."

"But," said Allen.

"I promise, no one will be able to tell."

Allen wasn't so sure about that.

"And I've arranged for Paolo to do your hair."

Allen nervously ran a hand through his mane, dreading the thought of even one lock being cut.

"And, of course, you'll need new clothes."

"What's wrong with my clothes?"

"Nothing, if you plan on spending the day in a library."

Allen scowled.

"I've already arranged appointments at Brooklyn Tailors and Todd Snyder."

"When?"

"Tomorrow."

"Tomorrow?"

"You have a problem?"

"No, it's just Saturday."

"So?"

Allen knew it was pointless to argue.

"What time?"

"I have Soul Cycle at nine. So let's meet at Brooklyn Tailors at eleven. We'll go to Todd Snyder afterward."

"Fine," said Allen. "May I go now?"

"Yes."

Just as Allen was about to leave, Sara popped her head in.

"What have you two been up to? Anything I should know?"

"Allen and I were just discussing his dating profiles."

"How are they coming?"

"Fine," said Allen. "Now if you two will excuse me…"

"Actually," said Sara, "I was just going to suggest you come with us to Milly's after work tonight."

"That's a great idea!" said Natalie.

Sara turned to Allen.

"A group of us get together for a drink a couple of Fridays a month. It's a great way for you to get some feedback."

"I don't need any feedback," said Allen.

"Oh, come on, Whitford, be a sport," said Natalie. "It'll be good for you to know what other women think."

"Just come for one drink," said Sara. "On us."

Natalie nodded.

"Fine, one drink. What time?"

"We'll grab you around six," said Natalie.

"Now can I please get back to work?" Allen pleaded.

"You ready?"

It was a couple of minutes before six and Natalie was

standing next to Allen's desk.

"Give me two minutes to save this article."

He hit "save" and then powered off his computer.

"Where's Sara?" he asked, looking around.

"She's going to meet us at Milly's. She had to run a quick errand."

Allen reached under his desk and grabbed his messenger bag.

"Okay, I'm ready. But remember, I'm only staying for one drink."

"Yeah, yeah, yeah," said Natalie. "Let's go."

CHAPTER 8

"Next question," said Sara, taking another sip of her white wine. "Name three adjectives that describe your dream girl."

Allen took a sip of his beer. The word *pretty* immediately sprang to mind, but he didn't want to sound superficial.

"Let's see..." he said. "*Smart... funny...* and... *well-read.*"

Natalie, Sara, and their two friends, Odette and Mariah, exchanged looks.

"What?" said Allen. "Did I say something wrong?"

"Seriously, the three most important qualities you look for in a woman are that she's smart, funny, and well-read?" said Odette.

"Yeah. Is that so hard to believe?"

"So you don't care at all about looks?"

The four women were staring at him.

"I mean, looks are important, but..."

"Let's say you see a woman on the street or at a bar or a restaurant," said Mariah. "You telling me you don't check out her face or her chest or her ass?"

Allen felt cornered.

"I, uh... I mean..."

"Leave him alone, ladies," said Natalie. "We all know guys are visual. But not all of them judge women solely on looks."

Allen nodded and sent a silent thank-you to Natalie, and Sara suggested they move onto the next question.

"Name three adjectives you would use to describe yourself."

Allen stared at the liquor bottles neatly lined up behind the bar. How would he describe himself? People used to tell his mom all the time how smart and cute he was. But describing himself as smart and cute sounded cocky.

"Need some help?" asked Natalie.

He turned to face her.

"What do *you* think I should say?"

She eyed him, and Allen felt as though she was trying to probe his brain.

"*Intelligent,*" she said, after a few seconds.

"How about *thoughtful?*" said Sara.

"Hmm…" said Natalie, still gazing at Allen. "I'm thinking *athletic.* What do you guys think?"

She looked over at Mariah and Odette.

"We don't really know him that well," said Mariah.

"Though it seems like every dating profile I've ever seen, the guy always describes himself as successful, good-looking, and funny," said Odette.

Mariah nodded.

Natalie was busy typing something on her phone.

"It says here that the top four adjectives that get the best results for men are *honest, intelligent, romantic,* and *funny.*" She looked over at Sara. "What do you think?"

"Sounds about right. What do you think, Allen?"

Everyone turned and looked at Allen.

"What?" he said. (He had been trying to tune out the conversation around him.)

"Would you describe yourself as *honest, intelligent, romantic,* and *funny?*" asked Sara.

Allen drained his beer.

"If saying yes means I can go, then yes."

"Maybe we should put down *grouchy, impatient,* and *rude* instead," said Natalie.

Allen scowled.

"Put down whatever you like."

"You know we're just trying to help," said Sara.

Allen opened his mouth to say something snarky but saw the four women staring at him and closed it.

"I know," he finally said. "It's just... I don't like people picking me apart."

"We're not picking you apart," said Natalie. "We're just trying to show the world what a great catch you are."

Sara nodded.

"Hey, if he doesn't want the help, I'll take it," said Odette.

"I need to go," said Allen.

He took out his wallet to pay but Natalie stopped him.

"Drinks are on Hipster."

Allen raised an eyebrow.

"It's research."

"Well, whatever you want to call it, I'm done. Thanks for the help."

He picked up his bag and threw it over his shoulder.

"See you tomorrow at Brooklyn Tailors!" Natalie called after him.

Allen took the subway to Williamsburg and arrived at Brooklyn Tailors a few minutes after eleven. The place had a clean, modern aesthetic, with clothes hung neatly on metal poles or folded and stacked on wooden tables. Natalie was there waiting for him.

"Everything's waiting for you in the dressing room," she told him. "Just try on each outfit, then let me see."

"I don't get a say?"

"If you really hate something, let me know. But I like to think I have excellent taste."

Allen glanced around the shop.

"Go start trying stuff on," Natalie commanded. "We have a busy day. If something's too big or too small, let Beto know. He can get you the right size."

Allen turned to see a well-dressed man smiling at him.

"I assume you're Beto?"

"The fitting room is this way," Beto said, gesturing.

Allen followed him and examined the outfits Natalie had picked out. There was a suit, a couple of pairs of slacks, a variety of shirts, and a couple of sweaters.

"Let me know if you need anything," said Beto.

"Thanks," said Allen.

He stared at the clothes, which had been arranged into outfits. The question was, which ensemble to start with?

After a minute of trying to figure out what Natalie would want him to do, Allen decided to start with the suit. It fit surprisingly well.

He emerged from the dressing room and walked to where Natalie was seated.

"Well?" he said.

Natalie looked up from her phone.

"Turn around."

Allen obeyed.

"Very nice. Though I'm not sure about the shirt."

She looked thoughtful.

"Go try on the other outfits."

Allen had been hoping for a more enthusiastic response (he thought the suit looked great) but tried not to let it bother him. A few minutes later, he emerged in a pair of charcoal pants with a light blue shirt and a blue cotton sweater.

"The blue really brings out your eyes," said Natalie, who seemed more interested in her phone than Allen. "Okay, go try on the next outfit."

Allen did as he was told, but Natalie clearly didn't like the next look, judging by her face.

"What's wrong with it?" he asked her.

"Too blah."

"I kind of like it."

"Go change into the last look."

Allen did as he was told.

Natalie approved the final outfit and told Beto they would be purchasing the suit, the two button-down shirts she had liked, the pair of chinos and the charcoal pants, and the blue cotton sweater he had tried on.

"So are we done?" asked Allen as soon as they got outside. "Can I go?"

"Are you kidding?" said Natalie. "That was just the first stop."

Allen groaned.

They arrived at Todd Snyder thirty minutes later.

The boutique, which was located near Madison Square Park on East 26th Street in Manhattan, looked like a larger version of Brooklyn Tailors. At least to Allen.

"I don't understand why we have to go to another place," Allen had said to Natalie as they rode over. "We got plenty of stuff at Brooklyn Tailors. And I have stuff at home."

"It's all about options, Whitford," Natalie had replied. "And Brooklyn Tailors and Todd Snyder are advertisers."

They walked in the door and Natalie went over to a dapperly dressed salesman.

"Ciao, Fabrizio!" she said, kissing him on both cheeks. "How are you?"

"Good, good," he said. "So is this the young man?"

Natalie nodded.

"Allen, this is Fabrizio."

"So I gathered. Nice to meet you," said Allen.

"A pleasure," said Fabrizio. "Miss Natalie gave me very strict orders to pick out only the best for you."

"Fabrizio has an amazing eye," said Natalie. "If I had the budget, I'd hire him as my assistant."

"You are too kind," said Fabrizio.

"So, is everything ready?"

"Right this way."

He led them to the fitting area.

"If you like, you can join him," said Fabrizio. "Otherwise, please take a seat, and I will get him whatever he needs."

Allen prayed that Natalie wouldn't go in with him.

"I'll wait out here," she said, smiling at Fabrizio.

Allen breathed a silent sigh of relief.

"Please," said Fabrizio, turning to Allen.

He led him to one of the fitting rooms and unlocked the door.

Allen saw several pairs of jeans, a small pile of t-shirts, two more suits, a couple of button-down shirts, two turtlenecks, and a couple of sweaters.

"Call me if you need anything."

Allen stared at all the clothes and groaned. He prayed that everything fit and that Natalie liked what she saw. Otherwise, it would be a very long afternoon.

Nearly four hours after they had begun, they were done shopping. Allen had never been so exhausted in his life. But Natalie seemed invigorated. Though maybe that was due to the two Caffè Americanos she had downed.

"Who says clothes don't make the man?" she told him as they stood outside Todd Snyder. "I can't wait to see what Paolo does with your hair. Now take these bags and don't let them out of your site!"

"Why don't you just take them?" said Allen, peevishly.

"Because I have errands to run. Just bring everything with you to the office on Monday. Order a car and charge it to Hipster." She looked down at her phone. "I have to take this. See you Monday!"

She walked quickly down the street, her phone to her ear. Allen watched, then looked down at the four large bags and wondered how he was going to hide them from his mother.

CHAPTER 9

Eric sat in front of his computer, reading through the Blind Date questionnaire. The instructions said to be honest and answer truthfully, as Blind Date's goal was to find you the perfect mate, someone you were compatible with. But surely some people (many people, he suspected) lied.

He stared at his monitor. Some of the questions were really personal. And he felt uncomfortable answering them, honestly or otherwise. Could he just leave them blank?

He clicked on the FAQ section and scrolled to where it said, "Do I have to answer all the questions?" The short answer was "No." But it said the more questions you answered, the better your odds of being matched with someone you'd want to date.

He took off his glasses and rubbed his eyes. Was Molly having as hard a time as he was? He was tempted to text her, but he didn't want to reveal which questions he was having trouble with. Mainly the ones having to do with sex.

He began to type again, then stopped. He stared at the screen, then opened a new tab and typed "best male dating profiles" into his search engine.

Over an hour later, he hit "save" on the questionnaire. He had left several questions blank, but he reasoned it was better to not answer than to lie. He would review what he had written later or the next day, then submit it. For now, though, he needed to prepare for his upcoming history seminar.

Molly took another sip of her wine. She had invited Felicity over to help her with the Blind Date questionnaire.

"Wow, some of these questions are super personal," she said, as she scrolled through them. "Favorite sexual position, really?"

"I know," said Felicity, "but trust me, they have a reason."

"If you say so," said Molly. "But what if you've never had sex?"

Felicity stared at her.

"Do not tell me you're still a virgin."

"Of course not," said Molly, a bit defensively. Though she had only been with one guy, her high school boyfriend, who she had dated for two years before they slept together.

Felicity looked at her, then read the next question.

"So how would you describe your perfect mate?"

"Well…" began Molly. "He has to be smart. And funny. But not crude funny. More witty. And he should be thoughtful. You know, considerate. Wonder what I would like. And he should be a reader. I won't date a guy who doesn't read books."

"I don't read books," said Felicity. "I mean, I do, obviously. But they're so long. I prefer magazines."

"And yet you work for a publishing company."

"In *Marketing*."

Molly rolled her eyes.

"What?" said Felicity.

"Nothing," said Molly.

"Okay, so back to the questions. What are the top traits your ideal guy should have?"

"Didn't I just list them?"

"What about good-looking and successful?"

"Is *good-looking* a trait? Besides, I don't want to sound superficial."

"It says to be honest."

"You think I'm superficial?"

"No, but most women would say that looks matter."

"Okay, I would be lying if I said I didn't care about how a guy looked. But there are plenty of good-looking jerks out there. I'd rather find an average-looking guy with a good sense of humor who really cared about me."

"Suit yourself," said Felicity. She looked at Molly's laptop. "Only twenty more questions to go!"

Molly groaned.

Felicity looked at her phone.

"I need to roll. Nick and I are meeting up with some friends of his. You good?"

"Yeah," said Molly. "I just want to review it one more time before I send it in."

"Probably a good idea."

Felicity grabbed her coat and headed to the door.

"Text me if you have any questions. Though I may not answer until tomorrow afternoon," she said with a grin.

"Have fun," said Molly.

"Oh, I will," said Felicity. "Ciao!"

Allen stared at his reflection. It was the day of the photo shoot, and he had spent nearly two hours having his hair and makeup done and trying on different outfits. Finally, Natalie had deemed him ready. Looking in the mirror, he barely recognized himself. He looked like one of those guys he and Eric made fun of in Hipster's "In Crowd" spreads.

"Not bad, right?" said Natalie, pleased with her handiwork.

Allen had to admit, he looked good, but… He frowned.

"What's wrong?"

"It feels fake."

"Fake?"

"Like it's some other guy in the mirror."

"Yeah, some totally hot guy who's going to land himself a whole bunch of dates."

Allen continued to look at himself.

"But what if women see the pictures and then meet me and think, 'that's not the guy I saw online'?"

"Listen," said Natalie. "Go on any dating site and most of the photos you see there are either edited, old, or bad. You want to attract good-looking, interesting women? You've got to look good and interesting yourself."

"But what about Blind Date? I thought the whole point of it was that how you looked on the outside wasn't as important as the kind of person you were on the inside."

"Yeah, yeah, yeah," said Natalie. "They may say that, but get real. Why else would they ask you to submit three photos along with the questionnaire? Now come along. I don't want Lucy yelling at us."

Allen took one last look at himself in the mirror. He was dressed in a pair of expensive jeans, a form-fitting white t-shirt, and a leather jacket. Paolo, the stylist, had trimmed his hair and put some product in it, to show off the waves and give it some shine. He had also applied some concealer, to hide a couple of blemishes on Allen's face, and a bit of bronzer, so Allen didn't look quite so pale.

Allen hadn't wanted any makeup, but Natalie had insisted and had assured him that no one would notice. Though Allen wasn't so sure about that.

They met Lucy in the studio, which was located in the same building as Hipster's offices, in the Williamsburg section of Brooklyn.

Allen had never before participated in a photo shoot before and was nervous.

"Just do what Lucy says and you'll be fine," whispered Natalie. Then she gave him a push.

"Allen, how nice of you to join us," said Lucy, frowning. "This is Patrick. He'll be taking the photos of you. And his assistant, Terrell."

"Hey," said Allen, looking at the two men.

"We're going to do a bunch of shots in the studio. Then we'll head outside. Sound good?"

"Sure," he said.

Patrick smiled at him.

"First time having your photo taken professionally?"

"Unless you count class pictures," said Allen.

Patrick smiled.

"Just do what Lucy and I tell you to do and you'll be fine. Now step over here, so we can do some lighting tests."

"Okay, that should do it," Lucy said a couple of hours later, after Allen had changed back into his jeans. (They had shot him in several different outfits.) "Let's head outside. Is that what you want him to wear?" she asked Natalie.

"For now," she replied. "I'll have Allison bring a couple of changes."

Allison was Natalie's intern, who was studying Fashion at FIT.

Patrick and Terrell gathered their equipment and the party headed over to Grand Ferry Park, which had spectacular views of Manhattan. Lucy arranged Allen in various poses, sitting on some rocks, leaning against a tree, and reading a book on a park bench. There were some kids playing basketball and Lucy asked them if Allen could join in, just for a few minutes. Allen had been embarrassed but didn't say anything.

One of the kids tossed him the ball and Allen dribbled it.

"Go on, take a shot," said the kid.

Allen dribbled the ball to the basket then shot a layup. The ball went in.

"Do that again," said Patrick.

Allen looked at the kids, who were watching him.

"It's cool," said the boy who had thrown Allen the ball.

Allen, feeling more confident this time, dunked the ball this time.

"Got it!" said Patrick. "Now do another layup."

Allen did as he was told, and again the ball went in. He collected the basketball, then threw it back to the kid.

"You famous or something?" asked the boy.

Allen shook his head, but the kid didn't seem convinced.

"You sure got a lot of cameras and fuss for someone who isn't famous."

"We're shooting some photos for a magazine," Natalie explained.

"Which one?" asked the kid, who looked to be maybe ten or twelve.

"Hipster."

"Never heard of it."

Allen couldn't help smiling.

"We need to go," said Lucy.

Allen waved goodbye to the boy, then followed Lucy.

The party made their way back to the studio, stopping to get some pizza along the way. When they got back, Lucy suggested they take some shots of Allen at Hipster.

"Aren't people not supposed to know where I work?" Allen had asked.

"We'll blur out anything that might give it away," said Lucy.

Natalie then had Allen change back into the suit.

As they made their way to Justin's office, several staff members whistled and hooted at Allen, which only served to make him more self-conscious.

"Ignore them," said Natalie. "They're just jealous."

But Allen found it hard to tune them out.

They arrived at Justin's office, and Natalie turned to look at Allen.

"Hey Paolo!" she called. "Can you do a quick touchup?"

Paolo instantly came over and gave Natalie a questioning look.

"Can you fix his hair and touchup his makeup?"

"No problem," he said.

"What's wrong with my hair and makeup?" asked Allen, who had forgotten about both.

"You were outside. Now we're shooting inside. Don't look so worried. It'll just take a minute."

Allen tried to sit still while Paolo fussed over him. Finally, he was done.

"Now go sit on Justin's desk," Lucy commanded.

Allen hesitated.

"Go on," said Natalie.

"But what if he comes in?"

"He won't," said Natalie. "He has a bunch of meetings with advertisers. Now go."

Allen slowly made his way over to Justin's desk.

"Lean against it," said Lucy.

Allen did as he was told but felt uncomfortable.

"You guys want to do some test shots?" Lucy asked Patrick and Terrell.

Patrick nodded. A few minutes later, he said he was ready, and Natalie, Lucy, and Patrick took turns calling out instructions to Allen.

Finally, a half-hour later, Lucy declared the session a wrap.

Thank God, thought Allen. He was exhausted.

"Can I go change now?" he asked.

Natalie nodded.

"Just give everything to Allison when you're done. Shell have it cleaned."

Allen glanced at the intern and wondered what it was like working for Natalie. Then he headed to the restroom to change. When he was done, he went to Natalie's office.

"So when can I see the photos?"

"Lucy should have them later this week."

"Do I get a say in which ones I use?"

"Maybe," said Natalie. "Now leave me alone. I have work to do."

CHAPTER 10

The next morning Allen was working on an article when Justin came by and slapped him on the back.

"I heard the photo shoot was a success!"

Allen stopped typing and looked up.

"Natalie even suggested we use some of the photos in an 'In Crowd' spread."

Great, thought Allen. Just what he wanted. Not.

"I thought we didn't want people knowing about the whole dating thing."

"Hmm… good point." Justin looked thoughtful. "I know! We can do one of those before-and-after pieces. Run it in the 'New Year, New You' edition alongside your piece." He rubbed his hands together. "The advertisers will love it!"

Allen didn't like the look in Justin's eyes.

"Come on, man, cheer up! You look like your dog just died."

"I didn't ask for the clothes or the stylist," Allen grumbled.

Justin shook his head.

"I don't get you, Whitford. Most guys would be thrilled to get a free makeover."

"I guess I'm not most guys."

"Whatever. I just need you to bring your A game to our little dating project."

"Don't worry. I said I'd do it, and I will."

Justin gave Allen's shoulder a squeeze.

"That's my man! Well, I'm off. Catch you later!"

Allen nodded, not making eye contact for fear Justin might linger. Only when he sensed Justin was no longer there did he glance around. Then he turned back to his screen.

"You wanted me?" asked Allen

Natalie had asked him to come to her office.

"Sara and I were just taking a look at your Blind Date questionnaire."

Allen had hoped she had forgotten about that. It had been two days since he had sent the draft to her, and he hadn't heard back. So much for being in a hurry. Not that he minded.

"And?" said Allen.

"And we just wanted to go over a few things before you sent it in."

"Like what?"

"For instance, you said that your favorite food is pizza," said Natalie.

"So?" said Allen.

"So it just sounds so… I don't know, boring."

She looked over at Sara.

"Don't look at me," said Sara. "I like pizza."

"What about Korean food? Korean fried chicken is all the rage, and it would be a great way to get a Korean fried chicken place to advertise on Hipster."

"Seriously?" said Allen.

"What, you don't like fried chicken?"

"It's fine, but my favorite food is pizza. And Blind Date said to be honest."

"Fine. Whatever," said Natalie. "But don't come crying to me when you don't find your dream girl."

"If she's my dream girl, she'll like pizza," said Allen.

"He does have a point," said Sara.

"Whatever," said Natalie. "Let's finish this up. I have an appointment to get to."

"Hey, I'm not the one who called this meeting," said Allen.

They continued to go through Allen's questionnaire until Natalie said she was satisfied.

"Okay, then," she said. "We just need the photos, then we should be good to go. I'll check in with Lucy."

"So, can I get back to work now?"

"This *is* work," said Natalie. "In fact, this could be the biggest story of the year for Hipster. Everyone will be talking about it on social media."

Allen frowned.

"You okay?" asked Sara.

"I just don't like the idea of people talking about me on social media."

"You'll change your mind once everyone raves about your new look and you've met your dream girl," said Natalie.

Allen wasn't so sure about that, but he didn't say anything. He just turned and headed back to his desk.

The next morning Allen was editing one of Dave's tech articles when he saw Natalie and Sara approaching. They both had big smiles on their faces. Though they stopped smiling when they saw Allen looking at them.

"You ready to see the photos?" asked Natalie, stopping at his desk.

"Are they any good?"

"No," said Natalie.

Allen looked at Sara, but she was looking down. Now he was worried.

"Please tell me we don't have to re-shoot them."

Natalie turned to Sara and the two were smiling again.

"They're amazing!" said Natalie. "Come. We'll show you."

Allen got up and followed them back to Natalie's office.

"Sit over here next to me," Natalie commanded, pulling the spare seat next to hers.

Allen dutifully sat.

"You ready?"

"As ready as I'll ever be," he replied.

She turned her monitor so Allen would have a better view.

"Lucy only sent me her top picks," explained Natalie. "Still, there are over two dozen shots. Sara and I narrowed them down. But if you don't like any of them, we can show you the other ones. But I think you'll be pleased."

Allen waited.

"Okay, here we go!"

Natalie opened a folder and Allen watched as a series of photos played across the screen.

"I really like the outdoor ones," said Sara.

Allen agreed.

"So, what do you think?" Natalie asked Allen, after they had gone through the photos.

"Do I really look like that?"

"Yup," said Natalie. "And these haven't even been Photoshopped yet."

Allen was staring at Natalie's monitor, where the last photo was displayed. He had never thought of himself as good looking. But he had to admit, the photos Patrick took were definitely the best pictures he had ever seen of himself.

"I think he likes what he sees," Natalie loudly whispered to Sara.

"Okay, I admit, they're good photos," said Allen. "But do they really look like me?"

"Who cares?" said Natalie.

"Face it, Allen. You're a good-looking guy," said Sara. "And these photos reflect that."

Allen felt himself blushing.

"You okay?" asked Sara.

"I don't know. This whole thing feels weird. You really think women are going to want to date me?"

Natalie and Sara exchanged a look.

"When women see these photos, they'll be lining up to date you," said Natalie. "You'll have to fight them off."

Allen began to feel panicky.

Sara gently placed a hand on his arm.

"Breathe," she said.

He looked down at the floor and slowly breathed in through his nose, then out through his mouth.

"Now let's decide which ones you should post on Spark and send to Blind Date," said Natalie.

After considerable back-and-forth, they selected the three photos Allen would upload to Spark and the three he would send to Blind Date. He has also asked if he could give a couple of the photos to his mother for Christmas.

Natalie and Sara had been touched and said they would arrange it. Then Allen had been dismissed.

He went back to his desk and logged into Blind Date. Then he uploaded the photos, which Natalie had sent to him, and submitted his questionnaire.

"One down, one to go," he said.

He opened the Spark app and added the photos to his profile, which he read over one last time. Satisfied with how everything looked, he pressed "submit."

A few minutes later, he received messages from both sites saying they had received his information. In the case of Blind

Date, he would be receiving his three matches within 72 hours. His Spark profile would be live within 24 hours.

He turned back to the article he had been editing, but he found it hard to concentrate. All he could think about was what Natalie had said. The last time he had tried online dating, only a handful of women had responded to his profile. Could a few professional photos and a juiced profile really make a difference?

CHAPTER 11

Eric had finally submitted his questionnaire to Blind Date. Now, in a few days, he would receive his matches. He texted Molly right after he had received the confirmation message, letting her know he had signed up. She replied with a smiley face.

"You sign up?" he wrote back.

"Yup!" she typed. "Just sent in my questionnaire and pics."

"OK. Let me know how it goes."

She replied with a thumbs-up emoji.

Eric stared at his phone for several seconds. Then he put it down and went back to reviewing his notes for class.

"I did it!" Molly said to Felicity. "I submitted everything to Blind Date."

She had gone up to Marketing first thing Friday to tell Felicity the news in person.

"Good for you," said her friend. "So which photos did you wind up using?"

"The ones you told me to. The one of me in the blue dress from my dad's fiftieth; the one at the beach—though sending a swimsuit pic to a site where looks aren't supposed to factor in seemed a bit hypocritical; and the one of me at my desk with a pile of books. Though I think it makes me seem dorky."

"More like a hot librarian," said Felicity.

"Ugh. Do guys really go for that?"

"It wouldn't be a cliché if it wasn't true."

She had a point, Molly thought. Still.

"Anyway, I should receive my matches by Monday."

"And you are to alert me as soon as you do."

"Aye, aye," said Molly, giving Felicity a salute. "You have anything that needs to go to Editorial?"

Felicity rummaged through the stack of folders on her desk.

"Here," she said, handing her one. "Give this to Constance."

"Will do," said Molly, taking it. "Catch you later."

Allen was riding the subway to work when his phone started vibrating and wouldn't stop. He took it out of his pocket and unlocked it, trying to avoid bumping elbows with his fellow straphangers. It was the Spark app, telling him he had new messages. That must mean his profile was live. He glanced around the car. It was packed. He knew he should probably wait to open the app, but his curiosity got the better of him.

Trying to shield his phone from prying eyes, he opened the app and saw that he had received over two dozen requests to connect.

"Whoa," he said, a bit too loudly.

He glanced around. Was that woman staring at him? He quickly put his phone away. Fortunately, he only had a few more stops.

As soon as he emerged from the subway station, he took out his phone and checked the Spark app again. There were now close to fifty women inviting him to chat with them. He stared at the screen. He had never gotten close to that number of replies when he had gone on U Date.

He shook his head and put away his phone.

As soon as he got to Hipster, he parked his bag under his desk, then went to get himself some coffee. On his way back to his desk, he noticed several of the women who worked there looking at him and smiling.

"Hey, Allen," said Charlotte, one of the other writers. "You do something with your hair?"

"Why? Is something wrong with it?" he asked, self-consciously running a hand through it.

Charlotte smiled.

"No, it looks good."

"Oh, uh, thanks," he said.

This was the first time Charlotte had ever said anything about his looks or had really engaged with him.

"You want to grab lunch sometime?" she said, taking a lock of her hair and placing it behind her ear.

Wait. Was she flirting with him?

Allen had always thought Charlotte cute, but she had never seemed interested in him.

"Uh, sure," he said.

"Great!"

They stood there awkwardly for several seconds.

"Well, um, I should get to work," said Allen.

"Me, too," said Charlotte. "Just message me when you're free. There's this new raw food restaurant I've been wanting to try."

"Sure," said Allen, still surprised by Charlotte's sudden interest in him.

She smiled at him again, then headed over to her desk.

As soon as Allen sat down, he took out his phone and opened the Spark app. He shook his head in disbelief. It was as if every twenty-something woman in New York wanted to connect with him.

"Hey, Whit, whatcha lookin' at?"

It was Dave.

Allen immediately turned off his screen.

"Just checking my messages."

"Uh-huh," said Dave.

"Hey, man."

The two were joined by Brian, Hipster's sports reporter.

"What's up?" Dave asked him. "You get those tickets?"

"I'm working on it," said Brian.

"If you guys don't mind," said Allen.

"Oh, sure, sure," said Dave. But he didn't move.

"Hey, I heard you were working on some dating piece," said Brian.

"Where'd you hear that?" said Allen, trying to act nonchalant.

"I overheard Sara and Natalie talking about it."

"That true, Whit?" asked Dave.

Allen looked from Dave to Brian. He wanted to lie to them, say he had no idea what they were talking about, but he had never been very good at lying to people.

"Yeah, but it's very hush-hush."

"We won't tell," said Dave. "Right Brian?"

Brian nodded.

But Allen didn't trust them to keep their mouths shut.

"So what's the deal?" asked Dave.

"According to Natalie and Sara, he's supposed to check out these two new dating sites and see if he can find his dream girl by the end of the year," said Brian.

"Ooh, his dream girl!" said Dave, batting his eyes.

Allen was not amused and scowled.

"So which sites?"

"I'm not supposed to say."

The last thing Allen wanted was for Dave to go on Spark and search for him.

"Come on, Whit. You can tell us. We won't tell."

"Sorry."

"Fine," said Dave. "Be that way."

"You can read about it in the 'New Year, New You' issue."

"You know I can hack your computer, right?"

"Isn't that, like, illegal?" said Allen.

Dave shrugged.

"Come on, dude, leave the guy alone," said Brian.

"Fine," said Dave.

Allen watched as the two went to the break room. Once they were a safe distance away, he reopened the Spark app. He still couldn't believe it. Fifty women wanted to go out with him? And it wasn't even ten o'clock! Suddenly, he panicked. Justin wouldn't expect him to go out with all fifty women, would he? And what if more women sent him requests?

He quickly searched for an FAQ page and was somewhat relieved to find out that fifty requests were the maximum within a 24-hour period. And you wouldn't receive any additional requests until you had either accepted or rejected the existing ones.

He let out his breath, not realizing he had been holding it. Then he began to go through the requests.

"Hey there."

Allen jumped.

"I didn't mean to startle you," said Sara.

"Sorry," said Allen. "I was, uh…"

Sara peered over Allen's shoulder.

"You checking out Spark?"

Allen realized he hadn't turned off the screen.

"Yeah, I got fifty invitations to connect."

"I'm not surprised," said Sara. "What's the maximum?"

"Fifty. So, do you think Justin will make me go out with all fifty of them?"

Just thinking about it made Allen feel on the verge of hyperventilating.

"I doubt that," said Sara. "Just find a few that interest you and go out with them."

"But there are so many," said Allen. "How do I choose?"

Sara smiled.

"Take your time. And if you need help, give me a shout."

"Okay," said Allen.

A couple of hours later, Allen messaged Sara: "Help!" he wrote.

He had gone through the profiles of the women who had liked his profile several times now, and he had only rejected a handful of requests.

"What's up?" she wrote back.

"I need help whittling down the list."

"You want to come to my office?"

Allen nodded.

"Be right there."

He arrived to find Natalie also there.

Allen looked at Sara.

"She wanted to help."

"So, what seems to be the problem?" said Natalie.

"I can't decide. I deleted a bunch, but there are still too many. And I don't think I can deal with going out with more than a few women."

"Show me," said Natalie, holding out her hand.

Allen reluctantly handed her his phone.

Natalie immediately began swiping.

"Just don't do anything," said Allen, worriedly.

Natalie ignored him and continued to view the profiles of the women who wanted to connect with him.

"Nope. Nope. Definitely not. Maybe."

"May I have a look?" asked Sara.

Natalie handed her Allen's phone.

Allen watched nervously as Sara began to scroll.

When she was done, she handed Allen back his phone.

"So?" he asked.

"I'd say you have a lot of good choices."

"Any of them stand out to you?"

"I'm not the one who has to go out with them."

"But how am I supposed to narrow it down?" Allen said, trying not to sound whiny.

"Just accept the ones you feel the strongest about and decline the rest," said Sara. "Go with your gut—or your heart."

"Here, give the phone back to me," said Natalie.

Allen hesitated.

"Fine," she sighed. "I'll look over your shoulder."

Allen started going through the remaining profiles. As he did, Natalie would say "keep" or "delete."

Finally, they narrowed the list of candidates down to ten.

"There now," she said. "That wasn't so hard."

"Yeah, but I still have too many. I don't think I can handle more than three at a time." And even that sounded like a lot to Allen.

"So go through them again," said Natalie, growing bored.

Allen went through the profiles one more time, holding the phone close to his chest.

"Okay, I'm down to six."

"There you go!" said Natalie. "So which ones did you choose?"

Allen showed her the profile of a cute blonde.

Natalie read the description and shook her head.

"No."

"What's wrong with her?"

"Did you read her profile? Her goal in life is to be a reality TV star."

Natalie reached over and declined the invitation. Still

holding Allen's phone, she moved onto the next profile, yet another blonde.

"She's cute. And she says she works in fashion. Ooh, I wonder if I know her."

She hit accept.

"So glad you approve," said Allen, sarcastically.

"Okay, next," said Natalie. She stared down at the phone. "Hmm…"

"May I see?" asked Sara.

Natalie handed her the phone.

"Oh, I like her," said Sara, looking at the photo of an attractive brunette with the screen name BookNerd451. "And I'm guessing from her handle she likes to read." She turned the phone around to show Allen.

"Yeah, she sounded all right."

Sara hit "accept."

"Here, I think you should pick the rest," she said, handing Allen back his phone.

"Thanks."

"Well, if you no longer need my services," said Natalie, "I'll be going."

"I should get going, too," said Allen. He paused at the door. "Do you think Justin would be okay if I only went out with three women from Spark?" he asked Sara.

Sara shrugged.

"You can always ask."

Allen lingered in the doorway.

"Well, thanks again for your help."

"No problem," said Sara. "Let me know who you end up meeting and how it goes."

"Will do," he said. Then he headed back to his desk.

He had started to edit an article when he felt his phone vibrating. It was a text from his mother, which he ignored. But while he had his phone out, he decided to open the Spark app.

He scrolled through the remaining profiles, including the ones he had agreed to connect with. There was something about FlirtyFashionista, the blonde, that seemed familiar now that he studied her photos. But he couldn't put his finger on it. He shrugged and looked again at BookNerd451's profile. She seemed like a good, safe choice.

"Okay, one more," he said, under his breath.

He went through the requests he had yet to accept or decline one more time and picked a redhead who worked as a political consultant at a grassroots organization and reminded him a bit of Molly. Then he declined the rest.

"Okay," he said, putting his phone away.

He spent the rest of the day trying not to think about the dating article and largely succeeded. It was only later, when he was checking his phone and saw that he had a message from Spark, that his heart started to speed up and he felt anxious. He opened the app and saw that FlirtyFashionista had messaged him.

"Hi WryWriter007," began the message. "Thanks for accepting my request. You want to meet for breakfast? (I figure, why not cut to the chase?) Cheers, FF"

Allen stared at his screen. He had assumed that he would message with whomever before actually meeting them. But FlirtyFashionista wanted to skip that step. He looked again at her profile. *Why not?* he said to himself.

"Sure," he replied. "Breakfast sounds good. When and where?"

He waited to see if she would reply, but after a couple of minutes he put his phone away.

He checked his phone several more times that afternoon and evening, but there was still no reply. Finally, as he was reading in bed, he received another Spark notification. He had a message waiting for him from FlirtyFashionista.

"You free Tuesday?" she had written. "If so, let's meet at Buvette at 8. Or is that too early?"

"I'll be there," Allen replied, not even hesitating.

CHAPTER 12

"I got my blind dates!" Molly informed Felicity.

She had again gone up to Marketing to deliver the news.

"And?" said Felicity.

"They all seem interesting," Molly replied. "And I like how Blind Date gives everyone pen names that reflect some aspect of their personality or interests."

"I know, right? Nick's Blind Date name was Tom Brady, which totally fit. So, who'd they match you with?"

"Derek Jeter—I'm guessing because he played baseball in college and is a big Yankees fan; Jim Morrison—an aspiring musician who's into seventies rock and I'm hoping looks like Jim Morrison."

"Or he has a serious drug problem," said Felicity.

"I thought you said they screen for that," said Molly.

"True. What about the third one?"

"His Blind Date name is Jay McInerney."

"Who's that?" said Felicity.

"You never heard of Jay McInerney?"

"Nope. Should I have?"

Molly had to stop herself from rolling her eyes.

"He wrote *Bright Lights, Big City* and a bunch of other stuff. He was super big in the Eighties."

Felicity shrugged.

"So, I'm assuming he's a writer."

"Correct," said Molly. "And his profile says he grew up in the city."

"So which one are you leaning towards? Is there an early favorite?"

Molly gave her a look, the one that said, "Really?"

"Let me guess, the writer."

"Ding, ding, ding!"

"You are so predictable," said Felicity.

"Frankly, I'm surprised they didn't match me with more writers."

"Maybe they figured you could meet writers at work."

"Not young single straight ones."

"Good point. So what about Derek and Jim? You going to give them a shot?"

"Of course! It's just, I'm not really into jocks."

"So why'd they match you with Derek? Could he secretly want to be a writer? Or maybe he wrote that he has a thing for hot librarian types."

Molly looked down, avoiding Felicity's gaze.

"I may have put down that I was a big Yankees fan."

"Why'd you do that?"

"I don't know. You told me guys like women who like sports. And it's not as though I don't like the Yankees. My dad loves them."

"Yes, but your dad's not the one looking for a hookup." Felicity sighed. "Clearly Blind Date took your Yankees fandom seriously."

"I know," said Molly. "But hopefully Derek and I have more in common than just baseball. Anyway, I'm going to send a note to all three of them and see what they have to say."

"Good girl," said Felicity. "Oh, I forgot to ask, what name did Blind Date give you?"

"Edna O'Brien."

"Edna O'Brien? She sounds like someone's great aunt from Milwaukee. 'Hey, have you heard from Great Aunt Edna? I heard she broke her hip bowling.'"

"Ha, ha, very funny. I'll have you know, she's a famous Irish writer. Philip Roth called her 'the most gifted woman now writing in English.'"

"Well, la-di-da," said Felicity. "I've never heard of her."

"It never ceases to amaze me how few famous writers you've heard of when you work for a publishing company."

Felicity ignored the comment.

"So can you ask for a new name? You can't expect to land a date writing to guys as Edna."

"I don't think Edna's so bad."

"Then how come there aren't any porn stars named Edna?"

"Seriously?" said Molly. "Also, when did you start watching porn?"

"Never mind that. Just admit that Edna isn't sexy."

"But isn't the whole point of Blind Date about looking beyond the superficial? So someone's name shouldn't matter."

"Fine, *Edna*. So, changing the subject: You have any interest in going to the launch party for Yasmin Farhi's new book?"

"Oh my God, are you kidding?" said Molly. "I love her."

"That's why I asked."

"I hear her new book is amazing. It's a love story set in the Middle East and France."

"I know," said Felicity. "I'm on the marketing team."

"Right," said Molly. "Duh."

"So, you want to attend the book launch party? It's going to be epic."

"Are you kidding? Sign me up! When is it?"

"Right before Valentine's Day."

"Of course. And where are you holding it?"

"Still working on it," said Felicity. "But it'll be someplace fabulous. Miranda was given a pretty big budget. I guess the higher-ups think this one will do even better than her debut novel."

"Which sold, like, a million copies, right?" Molly sighed. "I would kill to be a quarter as successful as Yasmin Farhi. Even a tenth! If only my life were more exciting."

"Hey, your life is plenty exciting," said Felicity.

"Oh yeah," said Molly. "The daughter of an Irish detective from New Jersey who dreams of being a writer." She sighed. "If only I had been born to an Arab mother and a Jewish father, raised in Paris, and attended Cambridge, then Harvard."

Felicity smiled.

"Well, when you put it that way. But I bet you could write a bestseller if you put your mind to it."

Molly frowned.

"Maybe. So, have you actually read the book?"

"I skimmed it," said Felicity.

Molly shook her head.

"Any way you can get me an advance copy?"

"I'll see what I can do, and I'll add your name to the guest list in the meantime. Should I include a plus one? You never know, one of these Blind Date guys could turn out to be the one."

"I doubt that."

"Have a little faith, Molly Margaret Malloy. After all, look at me and Nick."

"You still madly in lust?"

Felicity grinned.

"Madly."

"Try not to look quite so happy."

"Can't help it. Just thinking about Nick makes me smile."

"I should go."

"Thanks for stopping by," said Felicity. "And I'll put down 'plus one,' just in case!" she called as Molly headed to the elevator.

Allen opened the email from Blind Date. It contained the screen names and summaries of his three matches. The first one on the list was Grace Kelly, an aspiring actress from Philadelphia who had recently moved to New York. Allen smiled. He loved classic films and had seen several starring Grace Kelly. If this Grace Kelly was anything like the original, he'd be very happy.

His second match was Chris Evert. She loved tennis and had played in college. Allen, of course, knew who Chris Evert was, but a tennis player would not have been at the top of his list. No doubt they had matched him with Chris because he had put down "tennis" as one of his interests, a last-minute Natalie suggestion.

The final name on the list was Edna O'Brien. Allen scratched his head. The name Edna O'Brien sounded vaguely familiar. He did an internet search and discovered she was a famous Irish writer. He then read through Blind Date Edna O'Brien's profile. She was an English major who loved to read and worked for a publisher. Reading through her profile, he could see why Blind Date had matched them. They shared many interests. On the spot, he decided to send her a quick note.

He had begun typing when he sensed a presence behind him. He turned to see Sara.

"Hey," she said. "You hear from Blind Date yet?"

"As a matter of fact," said Allen, "I just did. And I was about to send one of my matches a note."

"Cool. Which one?"

"Edna O'Brien."

Sara had a funny look on her face.

"That's her screen name."

"Ah," said Sara.

"She's a writer, like me."

"Well, that explains it. What about the other two? You get three matches, yes?"

Allen nodded.

"The other two are Grace Kelly and Chris Evert."

"Let me guess. Grace Kelly is an actress and Chris Evert is a tennis player."

"Correct."

"Well, good luck," said Sara.

"Thanks."

"And don't write off the actress and the tennis player. Blind Date sent you their profiles for a reason."

"I won't. I just hope they aren't disappointed."

"Disappointed?"

"I'm not exactly the most interesting guy on the planet."

"Please," said Sara. "All of these women are lucky to be matched with you."

Allen felt his cheeks grow warm.

"Thanks," he said.

"So how are things going with Spark? You line up any dates?"

"As a matter of fact, yes. One so far."

"Well, let me know how it goes."

"Will do," said Allen.

Sara left and Allen got out his phone and opened the Spark app, to see if BookNerd451 or the redhead, whose screen name was ImWithHer2016, had messaged him. They had. He quickly replied to both, taking a cue from FlirtyFashionista and suggesting they meet. By the end of the day, he had arranged brunch dates with both of them for that weekend.

CHAPTER 13

"I got an email from Jay McInerney!" Molly messaged Felicity.

"The guy who wrote *Bright Lights, Big City*?"

"No, the guy from Blind Date."

"Oh, right," wrote Felicity. "And?"

"It was just a quick hello. But it was really sweet."

"You write him back?"

"I did."

"Great. Let me know when you hear from the other two."

"I will. Now back to reading this manuscript. Yawn."

"That good, eh?"

"It's another rom-com."

"What's wrong with rom-coms?"

"I'm just tired of reading about seemingly smart women who fall for guys who either don't know they're alive or treat them like jerks."

"Well, the public seems to think otherwise."

"Yeah, yeah, yeah. Well, back to reading. Later."

Molly closed her messaging app and noticed she had email. There was a message from Blind Date. Jim Morrison had written her. She clicked on the link and began to read.

"Hey, Edna. Thought I'd send you a note to get the ball rolling. I saw that you liked listening to music and were a Maggie Rogers fan. My band actually opened for her once. I'd tell you our name, but we're not supposed to reveal that kind of stuff. But it was pretty epic. If I could, I'd play music full time, but gotta pay the bills. So what other music do you like and what concerts have you been to? I recently saw The 1975. They were awesome. Anyway, write back whenever. Cheers, 'Jim'"

Molly reread Jim's note and smiled. She would reply to him later. For now, though, she needed to get through the rom-com manuscript.

Eric had waited until he got back to his apartment to open the email from Blind Date. As a teaching assistant/graduate student, he didn't merit his own office. Instead, he shared a space (to call it an office would have been an overstatement) with two other TAs. Which was why he rarely spent time there, preferring to work at the library or in the apartment he shared with his friend Harry, who had graduated from NYU the year before him.

Eric had suggested to Allen that they share a place after graduation. But Allen hadn't wanted to live up by Columbia and was trying to save money, so he could eventually get a place of his own. Then Harry's roommate had announced he was moving back to Texas, and Harry had asked Eric if he wanted the room.

Harry's apartment was on the Upper West Side, relatively close to the university, and the rent was reasonable (for New York). So Eric had immediately said yes. And as Harry worked in an office in Midtown during the day and often traveled, Eric often had the place to himself.

He poured himself a glass of water, then opened the email from Blind Date, which contained his three matches.

The first one was Doris Kearns Goodwin. She had grown up on Long Island, gone to college in Maine, and was currently a Ph.D. candidate in History at a university in the New York Metro area. He wondered if she was at Columbia and immediately began mentally going through all of the female Ph.D. candidates in his department. Could one of them be Doris?

He shook his head. It was highly unlikely.

He then moved onto his next match. Her Blind Date name was Diana Spencer. She was British but had attended university in the States, majoring in education, and now worked at a kindergarten in New York City.

Eric immediately conjured up an image of Princess Diana, who his mother had adored, and wondered if "Diana Spencer" was as pretty as the real Princess Di had been.

Then there was Coco Chanel, who, despite her Blind Date name, was American. Though she worked in fashion and loved all things French.

Eric wasn't sure why Blind Date had matched him with Coco, but he figured there must be a reason.

He reread all three profiles and sat back in his chair. Had Molly also received her matches? Probably. He was disappointed that Blind Date hadn't matched them. Though he knew going in that the chances of that happening were slim. Still, a part of him had hoped that the universe would bring the two of them together.

He stared at the screen another minute, saw that it was nearly six o'clock, then got up to see what there was to eat. He opened the fridge and glanced around. There wasn't much to see. Just a few cheese sticks, a half-empty bag of English muffins, an apple, and some beer. Eric sighed, closed the door, and made a mental note to go grocery shopping.

He then opened the cabinet and spied a couple packages of ramen noodles. He took one out, then put it back. Then he went to get his phone.

"You have dinner plans?" he texted Allen.

"No. Why?"

"You want to meet me at the Penrose?"

"Sure. What time?" Allen texted back.

"You still at work?"

"Yeah, but I'm about to leave."

It would take them both just over half an hour to get to the gastropub, which was located on the Upper East Side.

"How's seven?"

"Sounds good," wrote Allen. "See you soon."

"So I signed up with that dating site I told you about, Blind Date."

Eric watched to see how Allen would react, but Allen continued to sip his beer.

"No comment?"

"What do you want me to say?" Allen replied.

"I don't know. I guess I expected you to say something snarky. I know how you feel about dating sites. Though this one is different."

Allen looked at his friend. He wished he could tell him he knew all about Blind Date, but Justin had given him strict orders not to discuss the dating article with anybody.

"Maybe it is," he finally replied. "In any case, good luck."

"Thanks. So, you want to hear about my matches?"

"Sure."

"So, as I think I explained, Blind Date has you fill out this super in-depth questionnaire, and then they match you with three people based on your answers. And they give everyone famous pen names that relate to you in some way."

"Interesting," said Allen, trying to pretend he didn't know. "So, what's your pen name?"

"Bill Bryson."

"As in the crabby middle-aged guy who wrote about walking in the woods and Australia?"

"He's not that crabby," said Eric, defensively. "And he's a great writer and historian. He's also very funny."

"So, *Bill*, who'd they match you with?"

Eric scowled.

"Do you really want to know or are you just being polite?"

Allen turned and looked at him.

"I honestly want to know."

"Doris Kearns Goodwin, Diana Spencer, and Coco Chanel."

"Huh," he said, looking thoughtful. "I can understand them matching you with Doris Kearns Goodwin. And I can kind of see Diana Spencer. But Coco Chanel? You have some hidden passion for fashion that I don't know about?"

"No. But there's probably something else we have in common."

"Well, let me know how it goes."

"You know, you should try Blind Date yourself. You could even do an article about it for Hipster. I bet your boss would go for it. You could title it, 'Do looks really matter? A new dating app aims to find out.'"

"Thanks for the suggestion," said Allen, squeezing his right hand into a fist.

"You can tell Justin it was your idea. I don't mind."

Fortunately, Allen was spared having to say anything as their food had arrived.

Allen was having trouble going to sleep. He had hated lying to Eric about Blind Date, and he hadn't heard from FlirtyFashionista. He had messaged her to confirm earlier, but he hadn't heard back. Now it was nearly eleven o'clock. He checked his phone one last time and saw he had a new Spark message. He quickly opened it. It was from her.

"Sorry I didn't reply sooner," she had written. "I'm actually out of town and can't make breakfast tomorrow. Can we do it the following Tuesday? Thanks for understanding!"

Allen stared at his phone and scowled. The one date he had been looking forward to, and she had cancelled. Well, technically, postponed. He continued to scowl. He started to write her back but turned off his phone instead.

It was lunchtime, and the words on Molly's screen were starting to blur. A signal that she needed food. She hit "save" and quickly checked her email before venturing out. There was another email from Blind Date. Jay McInerney had written her back. She immediately began to read, putting aside her hunger.

"Dear Edna, thanks for the fast reply. You asked me what I write about. These days, not much. The magazine I write for is all about Top Ten lists and quick hits. Which doesn't make it a whole lot different from other ezines. My dream is to be a real writer and write a novel. I've been working on one since high school, but I kind of stalled out. I think it's because I do so much mind-numbing writing at work. But one of these days I'm going to get to it and finish.

"As for what books I've been reading, here are a few I read recently that I'd recommend."

Molly looked over his list. She had heard of or read all of them.

"I used to read a lot more," he continued. "But again, work kind of leaves me braindead.

"So let me ask you the question: What books have you read recently that you'd recommend? And what kind of book do you hope to write?"

He then signed the email "Best regards, Jay."

Hmm, thought Molly. What kind of book did she plan on writing? She had started and then deleted at least a half-dozen attempts.

She began to reply when her stomach let out a growl. *Food first, reply to Jay later*, she said to herself.

She reached into her drawer to grab her bag when she sensed someone behind her.

"How's the manuscript?"

It was her boss, Constance.

She quickly sat up, leaving her bag in the drawer.

"The manuscript's okay. It just feels formulaic. Woman's frustrated at work. Dreams of living in France. Goes on vacation there. Meets a handsome Frenchman. Falls in love…"

"Well, you know what they say," said Constance. "There's nothing new under the sun. And as your friend Felicity will no doubt tell you, contemporary romances are quite popular right now, especially ones set in France or Italy."

"I know," said Molly. "I guess I'm just a bit jaded. Though I like that it's at least set in the South of France, not Paris."

"Have you ever been?"

"To Nice?" She nodded. "My junior year, briefly."

"You like it?" asked her boss.

"I did. I hope to go back someday."

"Well, let me know when you're done reading the manuscript. I need that report by Friday. Then I have another manuscript I want you to take a look at."

"No problem," said Molly.

Constance left and Molly took out her bag and hastily made her way to the elevators to get some lunch.

CHAPTER 14

Allen usually looked forward to the weekend, but this weekend was different. He had lined up brunch dates with BookNerd451 for Saturday (today) and with ImWithHer2016 for Sunday and was feeling nervous.

He stared at his closet. What did one wear on a brunch date? When had he cared? But he was under strict orders from Natalie to look sharp. She had even created a chart that showed which shirt worked with which pair of pants, etc., so he could dress appropriately.

He grabbed the new pair of chinos and one of the button-down shirts Natalie said went with it, along with a sweater. Then, as he was checking himself out in the mirror, there was a knock on his door.

"You decent? May I come in?"

It was his mother.

"I'm decent," said Allen, smiling. "Come on in."

His mother entered the room and looked him over.

"You look nice," she said. "Are those clothes new?"

Allen nodded.

She continued to examine him.

"You do something with your hair?"

Allen nodded again.

"Going somewhere?"

"I have a date."

"Anyone I know?"

"I don't think so."

"Well, have fun," she said, sensing Allen's discomfort. "I'm heading off to yoga, then running some errands. You need anything?"

"Could you get some more peanut butter?"

Allen had always loved peanut butter. He would eat it on sandwiches or an apple and sometimes would just stick a spoon or his finger into the jar and eat it straight.

"Anything else?"

"Maybe some sharp cheddar cheese? You know the kind I like."

His mother smiled at him. To think she used to worry that Allen would waste away. Now she was constantly restocking the refrigerator. Though she didn't mind. She loved having Allen at home, and she knew he appreciated being there, at least most of the time.

"Okay," she said. "Text me if you think of anything else." She stopped and turned back. "Oh, and the Silvermans are coming over for dinner tonight. Care to join us? I can ask them to bring Dana."

Dana was the Silvermans' daughter, who was a junior at Barnard. Allen had known Dana forever, but he had no interest in dating her, and he had a feeling she felt the same way about him.

"Thanks," said Allen, "I'm good. And isn't Dana studying abroad this semester?"

"Do you want me to ask?"

"Don't bother. I may be meeting up with some of the guys later. But thanks for the offer."

He went over to his mother and gave her a kiss on the cheek.

"Have a good time at yoga."

Allen arrived at the restaurant a few minutes after eleven and looked around. Then he spied her, sitting at a table near the back, reading a book. He made his way over and stopped. As if sensing his presence, BookNerd451 put down the novel she was reading and looked up. Then she smiled.

"WryWriter?"

Allen nodded.

"I'm Cathy," she said. "Please, have a seat."

She leaned over and removed her bag from the other chair, placing it on the floor next to her.

"Nice to meet you, Cathy," said Allen, taking the now-empty seat. "I'm Allen." He glanced at the book she had turned face down. "What are you reading?"

"*The Bookish Life of Nina Hill.*"

"Is it good?"

"So far."

Allen was about to ask her another question when a server came over.

"Can I get you some coffee or a drink?"

"I'll have a coffee and a mimosa," said Cathy.

"Make that two," said Allen. He turned back to Cathy after the server had left. "So what's the book about?"

"It's about this young woman, Nina, who lives in L.A. She works at a bookstore and is really into trivia and has trouble connecting with people."

"Sounds interesting. Do you think I'd like it?"

Cathy could feel herself blushing. He was even better looking in person than in his profile pics.

"I don't know," she said. "Do you like novels about semi-neurotic females? It's very well written," she hastily added.

Allen smiled at her, and Cathy felt her cheeks continuing to grow warm.

"I confess, I'm not a huge fan of chick lit. But I like a good book."

"So what are you reading?"

"Not a whole lot," Allen replied. "Though the last book I read, *The Feather Thief*, was really good."

"I haven't heard of it," said Cathy. "What's it about?"

"It's about a young man who steals a bunch of valuable feathers from a British museum in order to make exotic flies for fishing."

"Huh. Is it fiction or nonfiction?"

"Non."

"And you say you liked it?"

"I did."

"I'll have to check it out. Anything else you'd recommend?"

"Like I said, I haven't been doing a whole lot of reading lately. Work's been really busy, and I fall asleep as soon as I read a few pages. Though one of my goals for the new year is to read more."

"I can relate," said Cathy. "I don't read nearly as much as I used to. But I always make time for a good book."

The server came over with their coffees and mimosas and asked if they were ready to order.

"I guess we should take a look at the menu," said Allen. "Will you give us a minute?"

"No problem," the server replied. "Be right back."

Allen regarded the menu, then looked over at Cathy.

"Do you know what you're going to have?"

"The French toast with a side of bacon. What about you?"

"I can't decide between the vegetable omelet and the bagel with lox."

"Tough choice," said Cathy.

Their server returned a few minutes later and took their order. Allen wound up ordering the vegetable omelet with a side of multigrain bread.

"So where were we?" said Allen, after the server had departed.

"We were discussing books and the fact that neither of us read as many as we used to."

She smiled at him and Allen smiled back.

"Right."

There was an awkward silence for several seconds.

"I actually used to have a book blog," said Cathy.

"You did?" said Allen.

She nodded.

"It was my way of keeping track of the books I read, but other people seemed to like it."

"What was it called?"

"Cathy's Book Nook. Not the most creative name, I know."

"Do you still manage the blog?"

"Technically, though I haven't posted anything in ages."

"Give me the address and I'll check it out."

He smiled at her, and Cathy felt herself starting to blush again. *Get a grip, girl,* she told herself. *It's not like he's the only good-looking guy in New York.*

"Remind me when we're done with brunch," she told him.

"Will do. So it said in your profile that you worked for a PR firm."

"That's right. It's a boutique agency that mostly handles authors. Though we also represent artists and dancers. It was kind of my dream job."

"Cool," said Allen. "So have you met a lot of famous authors?"

"A few. Mostly I write press releases and get them placed and handle a lot of the social media stuff. Though if there's a big event, say a book talk or a launch party, I usually get an invite.

"And your profile said you were a writer."

"That's right," said Allen.

"What do you write?"

"Mostly Top Ten lists and blurbs about restaurant and store openings."

"For?"

Justin had told Allen not to discuss the article with anyone, but he didn't say Allen couldn't reveal where he worked.

"You hear of Hipster?"

"You mean the online zine for the discerning city dweller?"

Was that a touch of snarkiness he detected?

"That's the one."

The conversation stopped as the server arrived with their food.

"Enjoy!" he said, cheerily.

Allen tucked into his omelet, not looking at Cathy. He always felt a bit self-conscious when talking about Hipster.

"I didn't mean to dis your mag," said Cathy, a few minutes later. "Truth be told, I often check it out when I'm searching for a new restaurant or to see what's going on in the city. It's just…"

Allen waited.

"I don't know. It just strikes me that you all are trying too hard to sound cool or hip. You know? And there are way too many Top Ten lists."

Allen didn't disagree.

"Yeah," he said. "I know it can seem a bit pretentious. But we do our research and try to provide people with helpful information."

"Like how to safely dye your dog," said Cathy, her lips forming a half smile.

"Hey, you wouldn't want people accidentally poisoning Fido, would you?"

Cathy could tell from his expression that he wasn't offended.

"Point taken."

They finished their meal and the server returned, asking if they'd like anything else.

"I'm good," said Cathy.

"Me, too," said Allen. "Just a check, please."

The server deposited their check on the table, and Allen immediately picked it up.

"How much do I owe you?" Cathy asked him.

"It's on me," said Allen.

Technically, it was on Hipster, but Allen didn't feel the need to mention that.

"Thanks."

Allen paid, and they headed outside.

"Well, it was nice meeting you, Allen."

They were standing in front of the restaurant, where there was a line to get in.

"It was nice meeting you, too, Cathy," he said. Though he hadn't felt a spark.

They stood there awkwardly for a minute.

"Oh, I forgot to ask! What's the address of your book blog?"

Cathy recited it, and Allen entered it into his phone.

"My email's on the site," she added.

"Got it," said Allen.

He smiled at her, and Cathy smiled back at him.

"Well, I should get going," she said.

"Me, too," said Allen.

They stood there awkwardly for several more seconds, then they turned and walked in opposite directions.

CHAPTER 15

Allen stared at his alarm clock. He had been out drinking with some of his high school friends and his head felt fuzzy. He thought about rolling over and going back to sleep, but he had a brunch date with ImWithHer2016 in a couple of hours and had hoped to get a run in first.

He glanced again at the clock, then dragged himself out of bed. A short time later, he was in Central Park, running around the reservoir. It was a crisp, fall morning, and the cool air woke him up.

By the time he got home, his head was no longer fuzzy, and he was drenched with sweat. He went into the kitchen to get some water and found his mother there.

"I didn't hear you come in last night."

"I was trying to be quiet."

"You have a good time?"

"Yeah."

He went over to the refrigerator and filled a glass with cold water.

"How's Matt doing?"

Matt was one of Allen's best friends from high school, who had gone to Babson.

"Making a small fortune working at JPMorgan Chase."

"That's nice," said his mother. "You know law school's still an option."

"I know," said Allen. "But I just don't see myself as a lawyer. Nothing against lawyers," he added, as his stepfather came into the kitchen.

"You go for a run?" his stepfather asked.

Allen nodded.

"You hungry?" asked his mother. "I'd be happy to fix you something."

"Thanks, but I'm good."

She gave him a look.

"Just make sure you eat something."

"I will. I'm heading out to brunch in a few."

"Another date?"

Allen nodded.

"Same girl as yesterday?"

He briefly thought about lying.

"No, different one."

"Two dates in one weekend, eh?" said his stepfather.

He was smiling at Allen, but Allen felt uncomfortable.

"I need to go take a shower," Allen said. "Catch you later."

Then he made his way to the bathroom.

Allen had thrown on a pair of jeans, a white t-shirt, and a flannel shirt for his brunch date with ImWithHer2016. He had thought about shaving, but as he was running late, he opted not to. Besides, according to Hipster, a little stubble was sexy.

He had taken the subway downtown and only arrived a few minutes late at the restaurant, a popular brunch spot located in Nolita. This time Allen was the first to arrive. He put his name down and went over to the bar, though he didn't feel like drinking. He had had more than enough alcohol the night before. That was the problem with hanging out with Matt and the guys. They tended to drink a lot.

He asked for a glass of water and scanned the room. The walls were exposed brick, and there was sunlight streaming through the large plate-glass windows.

He checked his phone to see if ImWithHer2016 had messaged him, but he had no Spark messages.

He waited another 15 minutes and was about to send her a message, saying he had left, when a slightly disheveled-looking redhead, her coat open and her hair falling out of her ponytail, came rushing through the door. He watched as she scanned the room, then went over to the hostess, who pointed at Allen.

"WryWriter?" said the redhead.

Allen nodded.

"ImWithHer, I presume?"

He smiled down at her. There was something adorable about the slightly frazzled look on her face.

"I'm Hillary," she said. "Sorry I'm late. Yoga class ran long. Then there was a line for the shower, and…"

She stopped herself, her cheeks turning pink.

"Anyway, sorry I'm late."

Allen continued to smile.

"No worries. I'm Allen, by the way."

"Allen, party of two," called the hostess.

"That's us," said Allen.

The hostess led them to a small table along the back wall and gave them each a menu.

"Just so you know," said Hillary, after she had placed her coat on her chair and sat, "I'm not usually late. In fact, I pride myself on being on time."

"Like I said, it was no big deal." Even though he had started to get annoyed. "I was a few minutes late myself."

Hillary visibly relaxed.

"So where do you do yoga?"

"At a place called Mindful Yoga. Why? Do you do yoga?"

"No, but my mom does."

"Yoga's great," said Hillary. "Total de-stresser."

"Are you usually stressed?"

"When you work in politics, things are always stressful."

"That's right, your profile said you were a political consultant."

Hillary nodded.

Their server appeared, asking if they'd like something to drink. They each ordered a cappuccino.

"So, I have to ask," said Allen. "Were you a big Hillary supporter?"

"However could you tell?" said Hillary, somewhat sarcastically, though she smiled as she said it.

"Well, your Spark name was kind of a giveaway."

"I worked for her campaign in college. I've kind of always been interested in politics. I was in student government throughout high school. Then I got a job helping Democrats around the country get elected when I graduated."

"Sounds pretty hardcore."

"Not really. I'm just trying to make this world, or at least this country, a better place. I mean, who isn't for education and healthcare for all and equal rights?"

"You clearly don't watch Fox News," said Allen.

Hillary smiled.

"Anyway, I like to think I'm doing my bit. The only downside is work doesn't leave a lot of time for dating or relationships."

Allen understood.

"But enough about me," said Hillary. "You said in your profile that you're a writer."

"That's right."

"Who do you write for?"

"Hipster."

"I know Hipster!" She leaned across the table. "So does

everyone there wear flannel shirts and have beards?" she said, eyeing him.

"Only the guys."

Hillary leaned back and smiled.

"Funny. So did you always want to be a writer?"

"Pretty much. I wrote for the literary magazine in high school and minored in Creative Writing at NYU."

"What was NYU like?"

Allen looked thoughtful.

"Good. I liked most of my professors and made a bunch of friends. And I liked being in the city. But it's not for everyone."

"I thought about applying, but I got into University of Chicago, and that was it. I would have loved to have been there when Barack Obama was, but..."

She shrugged.

"You major in Political Science?"

"Yup."

The server brought over their cappuccinos and asked if they were ready to order. They said they needed a minute and quickly scanned the menu.

"So do you plan on staying at Hipster for a while?" Hillary asked, after they had ordered.

"At least for a couple of years, probably. Though I really need to work on my novel."

"Ooh, a novel! What's it about?"

"It's about a young man whose parents are killed during 9/11 and how that affects him."

"Sounds deep."

"I don't know about deep."

"So were you here when 9/11 happened?"

Allen nodded.

"My father was a firefighter. He was killed trying to save people."

Hillary froze.

"I'm so sorry."

"Not your fault."

"That must have been rough, though."

"It was. But my mom's really strong."

"Do you have any siblings?"

Allen was about to say "no."

"Two stepbrothers."

"Judging by your expression, I gather you don't get along."

"They weren't Cinderella evil stepsister level, but let's just say they weren't always nice to me."

"I totally get it," said Hillary. "I have a stepsister who likes to pretend I don't exist."

Allen nodded his head.

They continued to make small talk through brunch. When they were done, Allen asked for the check.

"Which way you headed?" Hillary asked Allen, once they were outside.

"Uptown," Allen replied.

"Me, too."

"You taking the six?"

"I am. I'm meeting a friend at Bloomingdale's. In fact, I should probably text her, let her know I'm on my way."

Allen waited, glancing around the street as Hillary typed on her phone.

"You didn't have to wait," she said, after she had put her phone away.

Allen shrugged.

They made their way to the subway and stood next to each other on the platform.

"I enjoyed brunch," said Hillary.

"Me too," said Allen.

"We should do it again sometime. Or maybe grab a drink after work?"

"Sure," said Allen.

A wind swept through the station and they could hear the train coming. The train was crowded, but they found a place to stand. As they approached 59th Street, Hillary turned to Allen.

"Well, this is where I get off. Thanks again for brunch."

She smiled at him, then hurried through the doors, making it just before they closed.

CHAPTER 16

Allen had just started editing an article when Sara stopped by.

"So, how did your Spark dates go?"

"Good," he replied.

"You going to ask either of them out again?"

"Maybe."

He really didn't want to discuss either date, but he knew from Sara's expression that she was looking for more than monosyllabic answers.

"They were both nice, but…"

"But?"

"I didn't feel a spark with either of them."

Sara groaned at the pun, which Allen hadn't realized he'd made.

"It was only one date, though," she said. "And if you liked them, why not ask them out again, get to know them better?"

"Under other circumstances, I might. But there's less than two months until the Hipster New Year's Eve Bash, and what if I spend a lot of time getting to know them and still feel the same way? Then I'm back to square one with Justin breathing down my neck."

She opened her mouth to say something, then saw the look on Allen's face and decided not to press the issue.

"So, do you have other dates lined up?"

Allen nodded.

"I have a breakfast date tomorrow. The one originally scheduled for last Tuesday."

"That date number three?" Allen nodded. "Well, maybe the third one's the charm," said Sara.

"I hope so."

Allen had been nervously looking forward to his rescheduled breakfast date with FlirtyFashionista. He had written her back that that Tuesday was fine, and she had sent him a bunch of happy emojis in response. But he hadn't heard from her since. He had also finally figured out who she had reminded him of: Eric's sister Emily. He had actually thought about asking Eric if his sister was back in New York, but he worried that could lead to Eric asking him uncomfortable questions.

"And how's Blind Date going?"

"Good," said Allen.

"You been communicating with your three matches?"

Allen nodded. In truth, he had mainly been communicating with Edna, only exchanging one or two emails with Grace and Chris. Which was fine with him. But he didn't want word getting back to Justin.

"Well, I'll leave you to it," said Sara, seeing Allen looking over at his computer. "Just let me know how it goes."

"Will do," said Allen.

"So?" said Felicity.

She was looming over Molly.

"So what?" said Molly.

"You hear any more from your Blind Dates?"

"I told you about Jim Morrison, right?"

"That his band opened for Maggie Rogers?"

Molly nodded.

"He have anything else to say for himself?"

"We've only exchanged a couple of emails."

"What about Derek Jeter? You ever hear from him?"

"Just a quick note letting me know he was on the road and would write more when he could."

"Well, that's something."

Molly shrugged.

"Frankly, I don't really care. He was my least favorite."

"Though you don't really know him. He could turn out to be a great guy."

"Maybe."

"So, who's in the lead?"

Molly smiled.

"I know that smile," said Felicity. "Let me guess, it's that writer."

"There's just something about him. I can't put my finger on it, but he feels… familiar, like I know him."

"So what does he have to say for himself?"

"He's working on a novel."

Felicity rolled her eyes.

"Of course. Does he know you're an editor?"

Molly nodded.

"But he doesn't know where I work."

"I just hope he's not using you."

"I doubt that."

"So what do you two talk about?" asked Felicity.

"Books, music, stuff. We've also been sending each other puns."

"Puns?"

"We're both English majors. Puns are our language."

"Whatever."

"What did you and Nick talk about when you were corresponding?"

"Sports, TV, music. Nick's a big reality TV fan, like me.

Though he prefers *Survivor* to *The Bachelor*. But it gave us loads to talk about."

Molly smiled.

"Well, I must be going," said Felicity, picking up the stack of folders she had left on Molly's desk. "Keep me posted."

Eric had written to all three of his matches soon after he had received them. Both Doris and Diana had written him back within 24 hours. Coco, however, had taken longer, replying that she had received his email and would write him back when she wasn't so crazed. He assumed she was still crazed as she hadn't written to him again. Though that was fine by him. She had seemed an odd choice to begin with, and he was happy with Doris and Diana.

He had been dying to ask Doris where she was getting her Ph.D. But he knew it was against the rules. Instead, he asked her what area of History she was studying, and she had replied American. That had led to several back-and-forths about American history versus British history, Eric's area of study. And Eric was quite enjoying their exchanges.

He was also enjoying corresponding with Diana, asking her questions about her life in England and what she thought of America and New York.

Finally, that evening, he received a message from Coco.

"Bonjour!" she had written. "Or should I say, bonsoir? Sorry I didn't write sooner. I'm actually typing this as I'm waiting to board my flight. I'm heading to Paris for a couple of weeks for work. I love Paris, though I'll be stuck in meetings most of the time. Still, they can't keep me locked up the whole time, right?

"Anyway, I'm sorry I haven't written. Like I said, I've been crazy at work, preparing for this Paris trip. Have you ever been to Paris? It's one of my favorite places. If I could, I'd live there. Maybe one day.

"Let me know what grad school is like.

"Au revoir!"

As Eric stared at the computer screen, visions of Paris popped into his head. He had visited Allen there when they were studying abroad, and the two had walked all over, going to the Eiffel Tower, Notre Dame, the Pompidou Center, the Luxembourg Gardens, and Montmartre.

One day, he hoped to go back.

He began to type a reply but wasn't sure what to say. Well, she had asked him about graduate school. So he could write her about that. But compared to Paris, grading papers sounded so boring. So he stopped.

He was about to close his email when he received a new Blind Date message. It was from Doris. He began to read it and smiled.

CHAPTER 17

"You seem distracted," Allen's mother said to him at dinner Monday. "Is everything all right?"

"I'm fine, Mom," he replied. Though, in fact, he was not. He had once again messaged FlirtyFashionista to confirm their breakfast date, and she had yet to reply.

His mother continued to look at him.

"Is everything okay at work?"

"Yes, I'm just really busy."

They continued to eat.

"You go on any more dates?" she asked him a few minutes later.

Allen put down his fork and knife and turned to face her. He knew she meant well, but he wasn't in the mood to talk about his love life.

"Can we please change the subject?"

His mother and stepfather exchanged a look.

"So how's the writing coming?" asked his stepfather. "Have you been working on your novel?"

Yet another topic Allen didn't want to discuss.

"It's okay. I just haven't had much time."

"They been keeping you busy at work?"

Allen nodded. (Hadn't his stepfather heard him when he said he was busy?)

"Writing lots of articles?"

Allen nodded again.

"They give you a feature yet?" asked his mother.

Allen sighed. It was clear his parents weren't going to leave him alone.

"Yes, but I'm not allowed to talk about it. It's going to be part of our 'New Year, New Edition,' and Justin thinks it's going to blow up."

"Oh, Allen, that's wonderful!" said his mother.

"Yeah, I guess."

"You don't sound very excited," said his stepfather.

"It's on a topic I'm not particularly comfortable writing about."

"Well, you know what I always say," said his mother. "If you want to be a good writer, you need to challenge yourself. No one's ever won an award for playing it safe."

Allen was quite familiar with his mother's philosophy, as were her students. She was always telling them to challenge themselves.

"Anything you can tell us about?" asked his stepfather.

"I'm working on a piece on where to get the best haircut for under fifty bucks and another on where to find the best tacos."

"And this is what young people are interested in these days, cheap haircuts and tacos?"

Allen knew that his stepfather was old-fashioned and didn't think much of Hipster or those who read it and tried not to let his comment irritate him.

"It is if you don't make a lot of money and live in New York City," he replied.

He placed his napkin on the table and got up. He had had enough questioning.

"I have some work to do," he said. "Thanks for making dinner."

He picked up his plate and headed to the kitchen.

"Help yourself to apple pie!" called his mother.

Allen scraped his plate and placed it in the dishwasher. The apple pie was sitting out on the counter. He thought about not taking a piece, then immediately changed his mind.

"I see you found the pie," said his mother, upon entering the kitchen.

Allen had helped himself to a piece, which he had topped with a scoop of vanilla ice cream.

"Okay if I take it back to my room?"

"As long as you remember to put your plate in the dishwasher afterward."

Allen tossed and turned in bed that night. He still hadn't heard back from FlirtyFashionista by the time he had turned off his phone, and he wondered if she had forgotten. Finally, around six, he got up. It was still dark outside, but he knew he'd feel better if he went for a run.

As he jogged around the reservoir, he tried not to think about her. Instead he focused on Edna. The two had continued to email, and at times it felt as though he knew her. Though he knew that wasn't possible. But they had so much in common, both wanting to be writers and loving books. And they had both gone to college in the New York Metro area. Clearly, Blind Date's matchmakers had done their research. Though he still wondered why they had matched him with Chris.

They had exchanged a couple of emails, but neither of their hearts seemed to be in it. They just didn't seem to have much in common.

He slowed down to check his phone. It was time to head back. He completed his second circuit around the reservoir, then jogged home.

His mother was in the kitchen when he stopped in to get some water.

"Good run?"

Allen nodded.

"I made coffee if you want some."

"Thanks," he said.

"So, you going to tell me what's up?"

His mother had always been able to tell when something was on his mind.

Allen thought about lying and saying he was fine, but he was tired and thought maybe she'd have some advice.

"So I'm supposed to be meeting this woman for breakfast this morning, but I haven't heard from her. And last week she cancelled on me last minute."

"Ah," said his mother.

Allen waited for her to say more.

"That's it, just 'ah'?"

"What were you hoping I would say?"

"I don't know, maybe, 'I'm sure she'll show'?"

His mother looked up at him.

"Would it make you feel better if I said it now?"

"Not if you don't believe it."

"You said she cancelled on you last week?"

Allen nodded.

"She said she was called away last minute and asked if we could do this Tuesday instead."

"And you haven't heard from her since?"

Allen shook his head.

"Did you call her?"

"I don't have her number."

"Then how were you communicating?"

"Through a messaging app."

"Did you message her?"

"I did."

"And?"

"Nothing."

"Well then, it seems to me you have two choices: either you can go there and hope she shows up, or you can send her a note explaining that as you didn't hear back from her, you decided not to go."

As usual, his mother's advice was quite sensible. And if it wasn't for the stupid article and his inexplicable need to see FlirtyFashionista in person, he probably would have blown off breakfast. But a part of him hoped that FlirtyFashionista was just not a good correspondent and would be there. So he thanked his mother for the advice and then went to take a shower and change.

Allen made his way down to the West Village, to Grove Street. It was a little past eight o'clock when he entered Buvette. He knew there was a high likelihood that FlirtyFashionista wouldn't be there, but he still hoped he was wrong.

He glanced around the restaurant. There were a handful of people, but FlirtyFashionista was not one of them.

"May I help you?" asked the hostess, smiling up at Allen. (He had taken pains to look his best, even though he was uncertain his date would be there.)

"I'm supposed to be meeting someone," he replied. "But I don't see her."

He glanced around the restaurant again.

"Would you like to wait at a table?"

"Sure," he said.

He ordered a coffee and tried to distract himself by reading a newspaper someone had left on a nearby table.

At eight-thirty, he decided she was a no-show and signaled to the server. Then he felt his phone vibrating. He had a Spark notification. He opened the app and saw there was a message from FlirtyFashionista.

"OMG! I'm so sorry!" she had written. "I just got your message. I was out of town all weekend and had zero coverage and got back late last night and overslept. Can we reschedule?"

She had inserted several prayer emojis.

Allen scowled. It would have been nice if she had written to him when she got back instead of waiting until now. But she seemed genuinely sorry.

He sighed and replied "Sure." Though as soon as he had sent the message, he regretted it. He didn't want her to think he was desperate.

A minute later, his phone buzzed again. She had written him back.

"Thank you! To make it up to you, how about drinks later this week, my treat?"

Allen started to reply, then shook his head and turned off his screen, pocketing his phone. The server was standing there, and Allen asked if he could get a muffin and another coffee to go.

Allen arrived at work a little before nine-thirty and was immediately accosted by Dave.

"Just rolling in?"

"Can it," snapped Allen.

"Someone's a little touchy this morning."

He examined Allen's outfit and hair.

"My you look nice. Got a hot date later?"

"Let it go, Dave. I mean it."

Dave held up his hands and backed away.

Allen removed his messenger bag and his coat. Then he turned on his computer. He checked his email and saw he had a message from Blind Date. Both Grace and Edna had written to him.

Grace had been auditioning for commercials. She had told Allen how grueling the process was, and Allen had been glad he wasn't an actor.

Emailing with Grace had reminded him of Sophie, who he hadn't heard from since she had moved to L.A. He wondered if they knew each other.

Grace had told him she was more interested in movies than television. But she had been auditioning for ads at the advice of her agent, who said some work was better than no work.

She had written to Allen about her plans for the week and had asked him what he was up to.

That was the other nice thing about Grace, she always asked about him. Not that he could tell her much. But he appreciated the interest.

Next he opened the email from Edna. She wanted to tell him about a book she had just read that she thought he would like and about a group she had just been turned onto (by Jim, though she left that part out). And, as had become their M.O., she closed the email with a joke.

"Why did the doughnut go to the dentist?"

"I don't know," said Allen. Then he scrolled down.

"To get a new filling!"

Allen groaned, though he was smiling.

He hit "reply" and began writing her back. When he was done, he looked for a joke to send her, perusing the various online joke sites, of which there many. He smiled as he found one he thought she'd appreciate.

"Why did the bee get married?" he typed.

He hit "enter" several times, then typed the answer.

"He'd finally found his honey!"

"Hope you have a sweet day!" he added. Then he pressed "send."

"What are you smiling about?"

It was Sara.

"I was just exchanging jokes with Edna."

"Edna?"

"One of my Blind Dates."

"Right. So, you two send each other jokes?"

"I figured it was a good way to break the ice."

Sara smiled.

"So how was your breakfast date? You look very nice, by the way."

"Thanks. She stood me up."

"You don't seem that unhappy about it."

"Oh, I was. Believe me. But emailing with Edna helped."

"Well, that's good."

Allen turned back to his computer, but Sara didn't move.

"So have you lined up more dates?"

Allen turned to look at her.

"I was hoping I wouldn't have to."

"You went on, what, two dates?"

Allen knew what was coming.

"You should go on a few more."

"What if I don't want to?"

Sara looked at him.

"Fine. I'll go back on Spark."

"Good man."

CHAPTER 18

Allen reactivated his Spark profile and was again stunned by the number of invitations he received. Were there that many twenty-something women in New York in search of a date? It certainly hadn't seemed that way the last time he had tried online dating less than a year before. He wanted to believe his new-found popularity had nothing to do with the photos Patrick had taken, or his new expensive clothes, or his new look. But he had never been good at lying to himself. He just hoped these women weren't expecting some kind of supermodel or Prince Charming. If so, they'd be disappointed.

Allen took a deep breath and ran a hand through his hair. There were a lot of profiles to get through. But at least he had some practice now.

As he started to scroll, he remembered what Sara had said about giving Cathy and Hillary another chance. He had liked both of them. So it wouldn't be that big a deal to ask either of them out on a second date. Though neither of them had reached out to him again. And wasn't the whole point of Spark that the women were in charge? So maybe they weren't interested in going out with him.

He scowled, then glanced around to make sure no one was looking over his shoulder. The coast was clear, or as clear as it could get in an open office. Then he continued going through the profiles of the women who had reached out to him.

It had taken him until the late afternoon, but he had finally whittled his new prospects down to three, the number of women he felt could handle dating in a week. Mission accomplished, he went back to his article on where to find the best tacos in New York.

Like most New Yorkers, Allen had eaten his fair share of Mexican and Tex-Mex food, more so since he had turned 21 and could legally drink—many Mexican places being known for their pitchers of margaritas or sangria. However, he didn't consider himself a taco connoisseur. So he had asked Hipster readers to weigh in and identify their favorite taquerias in the city.

He had been stunned by the number of responses he had received—New Yorkers apparently being as opinionated about tacos as they were about pizza. And he had been in the process of winnowing the list down to a manageable number of places he could personally check out. Still, the idea of having to go to at least a dozen taquerias felt overwhelming. Fortunately, he knew at least two people who wouldn't say no to a free meal, especially if it involved beer.

He sent a group message to Eric and Molly, asking if they would be game to go on a taco crawl with him, paid for by Hipster. Less than a minute later, his phone began vibrating. But it wasn't either of them. It was a message notification from Blind Date.

He opened the email and saw that he had a message from Chris Evert, the tennis player. She was writing to let him know she was getting back together with her boyfriend, her former mixed doubles tennis partner, and removing her profile from Blind Date.

Allen sat back in his chair. His first thought was relief. One less person to deal with. Then he started to panic. What if Justin made him ask Blind Date for a new match? Well, he would just have to keep Chris's defection a secret.

He quickly wrote her back, saying he understood and wished her luck. A part of him wished he could remove his profile, too, though he knew that wasn't possible.

He turned off the screen on his phone and went back to reading reviews of taco places. But a few minutes later, his phone started buzzing again. He picked it up and saw that Eric had replied to his message.

"I'm in!" he wrote. "When?"

"Thursday?" Allen replied. The article was due Monday, but he wanted to give himself time.

"Thursday works," Eric messaged him back.

He waited to see if Molly would chime in, but she didn't. She was probably in a meeting or engrossed in some manuscript. Allen sighed thinking about what it would be like to spend one's day reading books. He had thought about applying for jobs in book publishing, having always loved to read and figuring it might help him get his own book published. But in the end, he was offered the first job he had applied for, at Hipster.

He had resumed reading reviews of taco places when again his phone began vibrating. He picked it up and saw that Molly had finally replied.

"I'm in!" she wrote. "Where should we meet up?"

"I'll get back to you," Allen replied.

He scanned the list of taco places he had written down. They were mostly in Manhattan and Brooklyn. (He had made the decision not to include Staten Island as he deemed it too far. And none of the top taco places were located there.)

As he was going over the list, he felt a presence looming over him. He looked up to see Justin peering over his shoulder.

"Whatcha workin' on there, Whit-man?"

"The taco story."

"How's it going?"

"Good. I'm going to visit places Thursday."

"Just make sure to include only the best!"

"That's the goal."

"So, how's the dating piece coming along?"

"Good."

"You line up a bunch of dates?"

"I'm working on it."

"Tick-tock," said Justin, tapping his watch. "The Hipster New Year's Eve Bash is just around the corner."

"I know," said Allen.

Justin gave a little sigh.

"I envy you."

"You do?"

Allen couldn't imagine Justin envying anyone, especially him.

"Absolutely! You're young, not bad looking, able to date whomever you want. The world is your oyster!"

Allen stared at him.

"Well, keep me posted," said Justin, gazing at something or someone a little ways away. Then he turned back to Allen. "So, uh, care to share photos of your dates?"

Allen had no desire to share pictures of his dates with Justin, but he could tell from the way Justin was looking at him that he wasn't going to leave until Allen did.

He opened the Spark app on his phone and pulled up the list of dates he had accepted.

"Here," he said, handing his phone to Justin.

"Very nice. Very nice, indeed," he said, gazing at the women.

Allen wanted to grab his phone back, but he sat on his hands.

"Hmm. This blonde looks familiar."

Allen looked up.

"May I see?"

Justin turned the phone around. There was the photo of FlirtyFashionista.

"I just know I've seen her somewhere before. Have you gone out with her yet?"

"Not yet. We're supposedly getting drinks tomorrow."

"Maybe I should tag along."

He was grinning at Allen, but Allen wasn't smiling back. The last thing he wanted was Justin tagging along on one of his dates.

Justin slapped him on the back.

"Don't look so worried, Whitford! I was kidding. I have plans tomorrow. Though let me know how things go between you and the blonde."

Allen nodded, not knowing what to say.

A few seconds later, Justin departed.

All the next day Allen felt anxious. After having asked him out for a drink that Wednesday (today), FlirtyFashionista had disappeared again. He debated whether or not he should message her, to see if they were still on. Finally, around three, he did. Nothing.

By six he had decided she was blowing him off again and turned off his computer. But as he was headed to the elevator, he felt his phone vibrating in his pocket. He took it out and saw that he had a Spark notification. FlirtyFashionista had messaged him back.

"I'm so sorry!" she had written. "Another crazy day, and I've got to work late AGAIN. Raincheck?"

Allen knew he should probably write her off, tell her

thanks but no thanks. But he found himself unable to.

"No worries," he replied, disappointment mingling with anger. "I was just about to write to you, saying that I had to work late and needed to reschedule."

It was a lie, and he hated lying, but he didn't want her thinking he was pathetic.

"Oh good," she replied a couple of minutes later. "Not good that you have to work late, too. I mean good that you're not upset. I hate canceling on people, especially last minute."

Was she for real?

"I'll message you tomorrow to arrange a makeup date," she continued. "Thanks for being so understanding!"

Allen stared at the message, then closed the app and shoved his phone in his pocket. The elevator had come and gone, so he pressed the button again. But before it got there, his phone had started vibrating again. It was the Spark app. He wondered if FlirtyFashionista had sent him another message, but it wasn't from her. It was from BlondeAmbition2018, one of the women whose invitation to connect he had accepted earlier.

"Hi!" she had written. "I know this is totally last minute, but do you want to grab a drink tonight? I was supposed to get together with a friend, but she blew me off. I probably shouldn't write that, but I'm pissed, and I could use a drink, and I figured what the heck."

Allen smiled. He appreciated her honesty and found her message amusing.

"Hi back," he wrote. "Where do you want to meet?"

A minute later, she replied.

"Oh, wow! I didn't really think you would answer. You want to meet me at Attaboy? Or you can pick a place."

"Attaboy's fine," Allen wrote back. "When?"

"6:45? 7?" she replied.

Allen looked down at his phone. It's was nearly twenty after six. Attaboy was on the Lower East Side, not that far away, but he wasn't sure how he would get there or how long it would take.

"Let's say 7."

Molly was staring at her screen. She had typed and then deleted her latest note to Jay at least a half dozen times now. Why was she having such a hard time?

"You're still here."

Molly looked up to see her boss, Constance, standing next to her desk.

"You have any guy friends who'd be interested in reading a manuscript?"

"Maybe," said Molly. "Why?"

"I just got a new one in, and I want someone unbiased to take a look at it. It's a male coming-of-age story."

Molly immediately thought of Allen. But he was so busy with Hipster and his own novel, he probably didn't have time to read a manuscript. Then it hit her. Jay! He'd be perfect. Assuming he had the time.

"As a matter of fact, I think I know the perfect person."

"Great. See if he's interested. If so, have him sign a standard non-disclosure agreement."

Molly frowned.

"Something wrong?"

"No. It's just…"

Constance looked at her.

"It's fine. I'll send him an email, see if he's interested. What's the title?"

"It's called *Growing Up New York*. Though we may change it."

Molly jotted it down.

"Got it."

Constance stayed a few seconds more, then headed back to her office.

As soon as she was out of sight, Molly opened the email she had started typing to Jay.

"How would you feel about reading a manuscript?" she began.

Eric was working on a paper, but he was having trouble concentrating. He had checked the Blind Date app several times that afternoon, but there were no new messages. He had sent emails to both Diana and Doris that morning and had hoped to have received a reply from at least one of them. They were probably both busy he told himself.

He reread his last exchange with Doris. Of his three matches, she was the one he felt he had the most in common with. But he was enjoying his exchanges with both of them.

He decided to send Doris another note.

"You ever suffer from writer's block when working on a paper, even when you know the topic cold? I've been working on this paper for days, and for some reason I just can't put my thoughts into words. Usually, when I've done this much research, the writing comes easily. But this time, I don't know. Maybe it's a case of too much information. Got any advice? If so, let me know."

He hit "send," then went back to staring at his computer screen.

CHAPTER 19

Allen ducked into the bathroom and stood in front of the mirror, checking his teeth and wondering if his hair looked okay. Then he chided himself. When did he start obsessing about his looks? Not that he was obsessing. He just wanted to make sure he didn't have anything stuck in his teeth or that he didn't look too disheveled.

He ran a hand through his hair, in an attempt to tame it a bit. But his curls had a mind of their own. Finally, he gave up and left.

The train was crowded, but Allen found a spot to stand and tuned out all the ambient noise, listening to Mumford & Sons on his earbuds.

He arrived outside the bar a little before seven and pulled up BlondeAmbition2018's profile. She reminded him of a young Rachel McAdams, though blonder and bustier. He swiped through her photos and wondered if they were legit. So many people used heavily edited or old photos these days. And her photos seemed almost too good. Though he knew he shouldn't talk. After all, he had had a stylist and a makeup artist and a professional photographer helping him with his profile pics.

He put his phone back in his pocket and entered the bar. The place was crowded but not packed, it still being relatively early. He immediately spied her, leaning over the bar and chatting with the bartender. She looked like her photos, a pleasant surprise, and was quite animated about something.

He made his way to where she was seated.

"Hi there," he said.

She ignored him.

He gently tapped her on the shoulder.

"What?" she said, turning and glaring at him. Then, seeing who it was, she softened. "Oh. Sorry about that."

"That's okay," said Allen, smiling at her. "I get that a lot."

"You must be WryWriter."

Allen nodded.

"Allen," he said, holding out a hand.

"I'm Carly," she said, taking it. "Here, have a seat."

She removed her bag and coat from the stool next to her.

"I didn't mean to snap at you. I was just telling Sam here how lame some people are about keeping dates. Just because you start dating someone doesn't mean you should drop your friends, right?"

"Can I get you a drink?" Sam asked Allen.

"What do you have on tap?"

Sam rattled off the names of a dozen beers, and Allen ordered a Brooklyn Lager. Then he turned back to Carly.

"So, I take it your friend blew you off for some guy?"

"Yup. Third time she's done it this month."

"And you're still friends?"

"I'm hoping it's just a phase."

Sam deposited Allen's beer in front of him.

"Thanks," he said.

He took a sip. He could sense Carly watching him.

"So, WryWriter, tell me about yourself."

"What do you want to know?"

"Well, you said in your profile that you grew up in New York City. What was that like?"

"Good, I guess. I don't really have any place to compare it

to. I went to private school. My mom teaches there, so I got free tuition. Then I went to NYU. I guess you could say I'm a city kid, but most tourists do more in a week here than I probably have in twenty-two years. What about you? Your profile said you were from Chicago."

"Technically just outside, a town called Wilmette."

"You go to school there?"

"I did. I went to New Trier High School and then Northwestern University. My mom got cancer, and I wanted to stick close to home."

"Sorry to hear that," said Allen. "Is she okay?"

"Fortunately, yes. They caught it early, and she responded well to chemo. She's in remission now, which is why I decided to come to New York. It's been my dream since forever. I actually applied to NYU, but when Mom got sick…"

"I understand," said Allen. "I'm glad she's doing better."

"Yeah. My sister's still out there. She's married and is expecting her first kid. So mom's happy. You have any siblings?"

"Two stepbrothers."

"I take it from your expression you're not close."

"Nope. They were both your stereotypical jocks who picked on me and anyone else who couldn't defend themselves."

"Ah."

"But we learned to tolerate each other. You get along with your sister?"

"Most of the time. She's a lot older than me. I was kind of an accident. But yeah, we get along."

"Must be nice," said Allen. "So why was it your dream to come to New York?"

"Promise you won't laugh?"

"Promise."

"So my mom was a huge *Sex and the City* fan, and I'd watch it with her. I used to imagine myself being just like the women on the show, living in New York, eating in stylish restaurants, going shopping. It became kind of a goal. Then I found music, and I knew New York was where I had to be."

Allen smiled.

"So, has it lived up to your expectations?"

"Sort of. I didn't realize how expensive everything was. I mean, I knew, but… I realized too late that all these women you see living it up here either have trust funds or rich husbands."

Allen nodded. He understood. New York was a tough city to live in if you didn't make a lot of money or have parents who let you live with them rent-free.

"So you said on your profile that you're a musician. What instrument do you play?"

"Guitar and piano, but I'm mainly a singer."

"You have a regular gig?"

"Not yet. I played around Chicago, but New York is tougher to break into. I've done a few open mics, but I'm still waiting to be discovered."

"Do you think it'll happen?"

"If the right person hears me. I also have a YouTube channel. Hey, you mind if I order some food?"

"No, go right ahead."

Carly asked for a menu and ordered a burger. Allen did the same.

"So what do you do when you're not playing music?" Allen asked.

"I take care of a little boy part-time and walk people's dogs. Brook, she owns the place where I live, is pretty understanding. The apartment was a graduation present from her folks, and she only has to pay maintenance and expenses, which she, Danielle, and I split. Danielle is our other roommate. She works at a gallery in Chelsea."

"And Brook?"

"She's an accountant. We joke that she's the only one of us who has a real job."

"How did you guys meet?"

"College. We were sorority sisters. Brook is from New York, and Danielle's from Connecticut. But enough about me. Tell me more about you."

Carly then peppered him with questions until their burgers arrived.

"So, can I interest the two of you in dessert or coffee?" Sam asked when they were finished.

Allen looked at her.

"Do you do cappuccinos?" she asked Sam.

He nodded.

"I'll have a decaf cappuccino then."

"Make that two," said Allen.

A few minutes later their cappuccinos arrived.

As they sipped and talked, Allen glanced around. The place had really filled up.

"Everything okay?" asked Carly.

"Sorry. Just noticing how crowded it's getting."

"You want to roll?"

Allen nodded and signaled for a check. When it arrived he pulled out his wallet.

"How much do I owe?" asked Carly.

"It's on me."

"You sure?"

"Gotta support the struggling musicians," he said with a smile.

Carly smiled back at him.

"Well, thank you. This evening turned out way better than I thought it would."

Allen had to agree.

He paid the bill, and the two of them made their way outside.

"Thanks for inviting to have a drink," said Allen.

"Thank you for accepting," said Carly.

They stood there, neither moving, for another minute until Carly said she should go. She had only taken a couple of steps when Allen stopped her.

"Hey," he called. "Could I get your number?"

She stopped, turned, and smiled at him.

"How about you give me *your* number?"

He watched as Carly entered it into her phone. Then she got up on her toes and gave him a kiss on the cheek.

"Thanks again for cheering me up."

She then turned and walked away.

CHAPTER 20

"I may never eat another taco," said Eric, after they had visited their fourth taqueria.

"I'm amazed you could even eat that many," said Molly, who had begged off eating any more tacos after the third place.

"We still have one more place to try," said Allen, whose gastrointestinal tract was already complaining.

"Can it wait?" asked Eric. "If I eat one more taco, I think I'm going to explode. And I have to teach tomorrow."

Allen looked down at his notes. He had already consumed eight tacos, two at each stop.

He had hoped to make it to five places that evening. But he had to agree with Eric. One more taco and he might explode.

"I guess we can finish up tomorrow."

"We?" said Eric.

Allen gave him his best sad puppy dog look.

"Oh no," said Eric. "Don't look at him, Molly! He's giving us the look."

"The look?"

"It's the look he would give his mom or his teachers when he wanted something or to get out of being punished."

"Did it work?"

Eric nodded, shielding his face with his hand.

Molly looked over at Allen. He did look rather sweet and forlorn.

"I'll go with you tomorrow."

"No!" said Eric. "I can't believe you fell for it!"

Allen turned and looked at Eric, his hands pointed up in prayer.

Eric clenched his teeth.

"Must. Not. Give. In."

"Please? If not for my sake, do it for Molly."

"Okay, fine! You win," said Eric. "I'll come, too. But I'm busy tomorrow."

Allen grinned, while Eric scowled.

"You free Saturday? We could go during the day."

"Saturday's okay," said Eric. "But after that, I am never eating another taco again."

"Molly?" said Allen, turning toward her.

"What time?"

"How's noon?"

"Noon's good."

Allen looked at Eric.

"I'm good with noon, too. I'll just leave myself a note to not have breakfast that morning."

"Then it's settled."

They made their way outside. The cool, crisp night air felt good.

"Well, see you guys Saturday," said Allen. "I'll text you where to meet me."

"Sounds good," said Molly.

They started to head to the subway when Eric pulled Molly aside.

"You got a second?"

"Sure, what's up?"

Allen stopped and turned around.

"You guys coming?"

"You go ahead," said Eric. "I need to ask Molly something."

Allen didn't move.

"It's personal," said Eric. "And doesn't involve you."

Allen looked at Molly.

"Like you guys tell me everything," she said.

"Fine," said Allen.

He cast a glance at Eric, then turned and headed toward the subway.

Eric waited until Allen was out of sight, then turned back to Molly.

"So?" asked Molly. "What's so hush-hush that you didn't want Allen to hear?"

"You want to grab a coffee or something?"

Molly looked at him.

"Fine. Where do you want to go?"

"I saw a place a couple of blocks over, on our way here. Let's go there."

Eric led the way to the place he had seen, which turned out to be a little Italian café, and they grabbed a table for two and ordered cappuccinos and a plate of biscotti.

"So, what's with all the secrecy?" asked Molly.

"I just didn't want to discuss Blind Date in front of Allen. You know how he feels about online dating."

"Did you tell him you signed up?"

"I did."

"And?"

"He wished me good luck."

"Well, better than the alternative."

"Anyway, you and I haven't really talked in a while, and I wanted to know how things were going. You good?"

"I'm good. Been busy at work."

"How's the whole Blind Date thing going?"

"Good. It's kind of weird not being able to see who you're writing to, but the guys all seem okay so far. What about you?

You like who they matched you with? How's grad school treating you?"

"Let's just say I have a whole new respect for teaching assistants."

Molly smiled.

"What about the people in your program? Are they nice?"

"I guess. We don't really hang out together. I've made a couple of friends, but frankly I've been so busy with research and grading papers…"

"Sounds kind of lonely."

"It's okay. I don't mind. There's a department mixer next week I was thinking of attending."

"You should go! So, speaking of mixing, how are you doing with Blind Date?"

"Good, I think. I've been corresponding pretty regularly with two of my matches. The third left me for Paris."

"Paris?"

"She works for some fashion company and left to go there right after we were matched."

"Do you know which company?"

Eric shook his head.

"Can't ask, and I don't really care."

"I'd love to go to Paris," said Molly, wistfully.

"It's okay," said Eric.

Molly stared at him, then shook her head.

"So tell me about your other matches."

And he did. When he was done, Molly peppered him with questions.

"Any idea where Doris is getting her Ph.D.? It would be pretty funny if she was at Columbia. Maybe you should ask the women at the mixer if any of them are on Blind Date."

"Like they would tell me."

"Hey, you never know."

Eric thought about it, then discarded the idea.

"So tell me about your Blind Dates."

"Well, there's Jim Morrison. He's in a band that opened for Maggie Rogers."

"Wow. You'd think a guy like that would have no problem landing dates. He must be hideous."

Molly scowled.

"Sorry. Go on," said Eric.

"Then there's Jay McInerney. He's a writer. Of the three, he's probably the one I have the most in common with. He was an English major, like me, and we've been sending each other jokes."

"Jokes?"

"You know, puns and stuff. It started out as kind of a way to break the ice, then became kind of a thing."

She smiled as she thought about the last joke Jay had sent her.

"And then there's Derek Jeter. I haven't heard much from him. He seems to travel a lot."

"You think he could be a baseball player? Maybe he plays for the Yankees."

"I doubt it."

They finished their cappuccinos and asked for the check.

"It was nice catching up," said Molly, as they stood outside.

Eric nodded.

"Well, see you Saturday."

"See you Saturday," he said. Then they went their separate ways.

Molly checked her email as soon as she got home. Lo and behold, there was a Blind Date message from Derek Jeter.

"Hey, sorry I've been kind of incommunicado," he had

written. "I've been traveling for work and super busy. But I didn't want you to think I was blowing you off. To answer your question, yes, I like to read. I just don't do a whole lot of it these days. Maybe you could recommend something. You know of any good books having to do with history and/or sports?"

Nothing immediately sprang to mind. Then again, she wasn't exactly a big sports fan. But she liked a challenge. She made a mental note to do some research in the morning and get back to him.

She let out a yawn and headed to the bathroom to get ready for bed.

All the way uptown, Eric thought about Molly.

You should tell her how you feel, a little voice inside his head told him.

Why bother? You know she doesn't think of you that way, said another voice.

Eric held his head in his hands. Too many voices. Clearly, he had had too many beers—and too many tacos—as his head and his stomach both hurt.

He was so lost in thought that he nearly missed his stop and just made it out of the car before the doors closed. When he emerged from the subway station, a sharp wind buffeted him, but the cool air felt good. He took a deep breath, then walked the two blocks to his apartment.

He poured himself a glass of water, then took out his phone and checked his messages. There was an email from Blind Date. Doris had written to him.

"UGH!" said the email. "Sorry to bitch, but I had an absolutely awful day and need to vent. I had to take over a class at the last minute and was totally unprepared. I felt like an idiot. I pride myself on being prepared, but I had no time. And I got flustered. Has that ever happened to you? Anyway, thanks for letting me vent. I owe you."

Eric nodded his head. He knew exactly how Doris felt. He occasionally had nightmares about showing up to class unprepared. Though it hadn't happened yet.

He wrote her right back.

"I bet it wasn't as bad as you say, but I can totally relate. I have nightmares about showing up to class unprepared and in my underwear. But knowing you, I bet you did better than you thought. At least you were dressed, right? Anyway, I hope tomorrow's a better day. And feel free to vent anytime."

He reread what he wrote, then hit "send."

CHAPTER 21

Allen spent most of Friday editing articles. He had taken an editing workshop in college, but he felt odd about editing the work of actual writers. Though most of the freelance writers who Hipster hired weren't much older than him. Still, he made sure to double-check spelling and grammar, as they weren't his strong suits (much to his English teacher mother's consternation).

He had wondered why Hipster didn't have a copy editor. But Justin had explained that they didn't need one as most of the writers had been English majors. Which wasn't actually true. But Allen had kept his mouth shut and did his best to make sure the articles he edited didn't have any glaring mistakes.

In between articles, he would check his phone. He and Carly had been messaging each other since their date. And Allen had invited her to join him, Eric, and Molly on their taco crawl that Saturday. She couldn't make it, but they would be getting together that Sunday.

He sent her another message, just to see what she was up to. Then he got up and went to the kitchen to get an energy drink.

When he got back, he checked his phone again. But Carly hadn't replied.

He stared at his phone for several seconds, then turned back to his computer.

The afternoon seemed to drag by until it was finally five. He was just finishing going over Dave's latest tech column when he saw Sara.

"Hey, Sara!" he called. "You got a sec?"

She stopped and came over.

"What's up?"

"Question for you."

"Shoot."

"So, I think I may have met someone."

"That's great."

"Yeah," said Allen. "She's a singer but very down to earth. It's still early days, but…"

Sara waited.

"The thing is, I told Justin I would go out on more Spark dates. But my heart's not really in it."

"I see," said Sara.

Allen waited for her to say more.

"So what do you think I should do?"

"Well…" she said. "If you told Justin you'd go out on more Spark dates, you probably should."

Allen frowned.

"What about Blind Date?" asked Sara. "You still communicating with your three matches?"

Allen didn't want to tell her one of them was no longer on Blind Date, but he hated to lie. So he just nodded.

"Any of them float your boat?"

"I don't know about floating my boat, but one of them, Edna, and I seem to have a lot in common and have been writing pretty regularly."

"That's good! And the others?"

Again, Allen didn't know what to say.

"They're good."

Sara regarded him.

"I think you should go on a couple more Spark dates."

Allen scowled.

"Who knows if the singer will work out? This way, you have a backup."

"Fine. But I really think the singer could be the one."

He could already picture Carly at the New Year's Eve Bash, dressed in something slinky.

"Well, I need to shove off," said Sara. "Have a good weekend."

"Thanks," said Allen.

As soon as Sara was gone, he took out his phone and opened the Spark app. Then he sent a message to BrownieLover411, one of the women whose invitation to connect he had accepted. According to her profile, she was a food stylist.

"Hi there," he wrote. "Sorry for not getting back to you. Been a crazy week. I know it's last minute, but are you free at all this weekend?"

A short time later, as he was getting ready to leave, she wrote him back.

"You free for brunch on Sunday?"

He had made plans to get together with Carly Sunday afternoon, but he figured he could do an early-ish brunch.

"Would you be okay meeting at 11 or 11:30?" he wrote her back. "You can pick where."

As he was waiting for her to reply, he received an email from Blind Date. He had a note from Edna waiting in his inbox.

"Hey there." she had written. "I didn't hear back from you re the manuscript I mentioned. Could you let me know if you're interested?"

Allen had spaced, or maybe he had unconsciously blown it off. A part of him had panicked when he read that someone else was working on a coming-of-age story set in New York. What if it was better than his or covered the same territory?

He knew he was being a bit irrational, but he had been feeling guilty about not working on his novel.

"Sorry," he typed. "Been slammed at work. Can I get back to you this weekend?"

He then put his phone in his pocket and grabbed his bag.

Molly hadn't noticed Felicity standing there.

"What are you still doing here?" Felicity asked her.

"Just finishing up some stuff," said Molly. "What brings you to Editorial so late on a Friday?"

"The boss lady needed me to pick up something."

Molly looked around.

"I think everyone's left."

"Not Lisa. Miranda told her she was not to leave until she had signed off on the routing folder."

"I take it she just signed off."

Felicity nodded.

"That's why I'm here. Lisa said she had to run, so Miranda sent me here to retrieve it."

"Well, don't let me stop you."

Felicity didn't move.

"So, what are you doing tomorrow night?"

"Why?" asked Molly.

"One of Nick's buddies just moved to the city and doesn't really know anyone here. And we thought it would be nice to take him out and show him around. Nick suggested I invite you along."

"Why?"

"What's with the suspicious look?"

"You know why. What's wrong with him?"

"Nothing," said Felicity.

"Uh-huh," said Molly.

"Honest," said Felicity.

"But why me? Why didn't Nick ask one of the women he works with or one of *his* female friends to go out with you guys?"

"Because he knows you're my bestie, and he thought you and Finn would hit it off."

"Have you met Finn? Wait, is he Irish?"

"No, and I believe so," said Felicity.

Molly had a soft spot for Irish guys, at least the ones from Ireland.

"Look, check out his Instagram if you want to learn more about him."

"What's his handle?"

Felicity told her.

Molly grabbed her phone and opened the app.

"Okay. I'll admit he's cute."

Felicity grinned.

"And he's not dating anyone?"

"Nope. At least not as far as I know."

Molly continued to go through Finn's feed.

"Okay. When and where tomorrow?"

"Nick made us a reservation at Brunetti at seven."

"Fine," said Molly.

Felicity clapped her hands.

"Yay! You won't regret this."

"I better not," said Molly.

"Okay, I'm off to collect the folder. See you tomorrow."

Molly, Eric, and Allen had resumed their taco crawl. Their first stop for the day was Gueros, a place in Crown Heights, Brooklyn, that Hipster readers had raved about. They could taste why.

"So, I have a question for you," said Molly, between bites.

"Shoot," said Allen and Eric simultaneously.

Molly smiled.

"What kinds of books do you guys read these days?"

"Doing some research?" asked Allen.

"Yeah, Constance thinks we need to publish more books aimed at twenty-something males. She thinks they're an underserved market."

"I don't disagree," said Eric.

"So, what books have you read recently?" she asked them.

"Recently?" said Allen. "Uh…"

"What about in the last six months?"

"I just reread *A Song of Fire and Ice*," said Eric.

"*A Song of Fire and Ice*?"

"*Game of Thrones*," Eric clarified. "That's what the HBO series was called, but the book series is called *A Song of Fire and Ice*."

"Ah," said Molly.

"I read *Good Omens*, by Terry Pratchett and Neil Gaiman," said Allen. "And I like Christopher Moore. His books are funny. Kind of dark, but funny. I read *Noir*, his latest, over the summer."

"What about sports or history books?"

"I'm not that into books about sports," said Eric. "But there are a lot of great history books. Do you want a recommendation?"

"There was that book, *Unbroken*, about this former track star who survived a plane crash in the Pacific and then was captured by the Japanese during World War II," said Allen. "Angelina Jolie directed the movie. Powerful stuff."

"I had forgotten about that!" said Molly. "Thanks. Anything else spring to mind?"

They proceeded to list a few more. Then Molly said she was good.

"So, you ready to hit the next place?" asked Allen.

"Lead on," said Eric.

"I don't think I will ever eat another taco again," said Molly, as they emerged from their third taco joint.

"I feel you," said Eric.

"Only one more place to go," said Allen.

He looked over at Eric, sensing he was wavering.

"Fine," said Eric. "But after this, I'm done. And I'm not responsible for any bodily emissions."

"Ew," said Molly.

"Thank you," said Allen. "And duly noted."

"Well, it's been fun, but I'm gonna roll," said Molly. "I've got a date."

Allen and Eric both stared at her.

"What?" she said.

Eric opened his mouth to say something, then shut it. (He was going to mention Blind Date but thought better of it.)

"Do you find it so surprising that I have a date?"

Allen and Eric both shook their heads.

"Anyone we know?" asked Allen.

"No. He's a friend of Felicity's boyfriend. Just moved to the city. We're meeting up at Brunetti."

"Mmm, Brunetti," said Allen. "I haven't been there in ages."

"Me neither," said Eric.

"Hey, you feel like grabbing some pizza later? What time did you say you were going to be there?" Allen asked Molly.

"I didn't," said Molly, becoming annoyed.

"I'm game," said Eric.

"I thought you were full," said Molly.

"I can always eat pizza," Eric replied.

Molly glared at them.

"You two are not going to Brunetti tonight."

"It's a free world," said Allen. "And I could really go for some pizza."

Molly continued to glare at them.

"Methinks we hath annoyed the lady," said Eric.

"Fine. We shall go to Brunetti another time," said Allen.

"Thank you," said Molly. "Hope you two clowns have fun downing more tacos."

She grabbed her bag and left.

"Is it just me or did she seem a bit P.O.'d?" asked Allen.

"Just a bit," said Eric.

"Well, we should head out. You ready to eat a couple more tacos?"

"Not really."

Allen took him by the arm.

"¡Vamonos!"

CHAPTER 22

Molly stared into her closet, trying to decide what to wear for her date. Brunetti wasn't fancy, but she wanted to look nice.

She grabbed her phone and called Felicity.

"What's up? You're not backing out, are you?"

"No," said Molly. "What are you wearing tonight?"

"Jeans and this new sweater I got. Why?"

"I can't decide what to wear."

"You've been to Brunetti before. Don't overthink it."

"But I haven't gone out with Finn before, and I want to make a good impression."

"You'll make a good impression no matter what you wear."

Molly twisted her lips.

"So you think it's okay to wear jeans?"

"As long as they're not mom jeans."

"I don't think I own any mom jeans."

"Then you should be fine."

"Okay," said Molly.

"I need to finish getting ready," said Felicity. "See you in a bit."

She ended the call, and Molly went over to her chest of drawers. She pulled out a pair of skinny jeans and rummaged in her sweater drawer.

"Hmm," she said, not loving any of her options.

She closed the drawer and went back to her closet. She took out a button-down shirt that fell to her hips. She then slipped on the jeans and the shirt and looked at herself in the mirror.

"Okay," she said, checking out her reflection. Then she went into the bathroom to apply some makeup.

When she was all done, she again looked at herself in the full-length mirror.

She had added a sweater on top of the shirt, in case it was cold out, and had pulled on a pair of cowboy boots.

"Gotta go," she said to her reflection.

Brunetti was hopping when she arrived, and she was glad Nick had made them a reservation. She was about to give the host her name when she spied the three of them in the corner, immersed in conversation.

She made her way to the table, stopping beside it.

"Hey," she said.

The three of them looked up.

"Hey!" said Nick, smiling up at her. "Glad you could make it. Molly, this is Finn. Finn, Molly."

Molly smiled at Finn. He looked just like his Instagram photos, but better, with thick dark hair, green eyes, and a cleft chin.

How this man didn't have a girlfriend was beyond her.

"Nice to meet you, Molly," said Finn, holding up a hand.

"Nice to meet you, too."

Felicity got up."

"Here, sit between me and Finn."

Molly squeezed in and took a seat.

"So, what were you all discussing?"

"We were just asking Finn what he thought of New York City," said Felicity.

"And I was telling them it's a bit overwhelming. Amazing, but overwhelming. I haven't actually gotten to see that much of it since I moved. They've kept me quite busy at work. In fact, this is the first weekend I've had off since I got here."

"Wow," said Molly. "That's harsh."

"It is what it is. I knew when they hired me that it would be long days and nights. But hopefully it'll be worth it. I just feel a bit bad not going home over Christmas and New Year's."

"You're not going home for Christmas?" said Molly.

He shook his head.

"Who doesn't get Christmas off?"

"I have the actual day off, but I decided to stay in the city rather than go up to Hingham. And my folks said they'd be happy to come to New York for a day or two. They wanted to go to Midnight Mass at St. Patrick's, but tickets are already sold out."

"Oh well. At least you'll get to see them."

"I love Christmas in New York!" said Felicity. "All the lights and the cool Christmas displays in all the department store windows. And ice skating at Rockefeller Center."

"Well, I hope to get to see some of those things," said Finn.

"I'll make sure you do," said Nick.

Their server came over and asked if they'd like something to drink. Nick ordered a bottle of prosecco.

"We're celebrating," he announced.

Everyone looked at him.

"I got that promotion."

"That's great, man," said Finn.

"How come you didn't tell me?" said Felicity, playfully hitting him.

"I only found out yesterday."

The server returned with the bottle of prosecco and

poured some into each of their glasses.

Finn raised his up.

"To Nick's promotion!"

"To Nick's promotion!" echoed Felicity and Molly.

They drank, then put their glasses down.

"So, does it come with a raise?" asked Felicity.

Nick nodded.

"And a big move."

Felicity's smile turned into a frown.

"To the twenty-second floor," said Nick, grinning.

Felicity hit him.

"Ow!" he said.

"I'd like to make another toast," said Finn, raising his glass.

They raised their glasses once again.

"To good friends," he said. "And to meeting Molly, the first Irish rose I've seen since coming here."

Molly could feel her cheeks turning pink.

"To Molly!" said Nick and Felicity.

They clinked glasses and drank. Then Felicity leaned over and whispered in Molly's ear.

"I think he likes you."

Molly glanced over at Finn. He was smiling at her.

Molly got home a little after ten. Nick, Felicity, and Finn had tried to persuade her to come bowling with them after dinner, but Molly had begged off. She was full and tired and had just wanted to go home and go to bed. Though she had enjoyed dinner, despite not eating much. (She was still full from all the tacos she had consumed that afternoon.)

Finn had chatted her up the whole evening, asking her about her family and school and what it was like reading books for a living. And she had asked him about his family and school and what it was like working for a big accounting firm.

It turned out the two had a lot in common, both being Irish and having two older sisters.

Molly finished brushing her teeth, then climbed into bed.

She was about to shut off her phone when she got a text from Felicity.

"Finn can't stop talking about you!"

Molly smiled.

"I think he's going to ask you out again."

A second later, she received a text from an unknown number.

"Hey, it's Finn," read the message. "I had a really great time tonight. I know we just saw each other, but I was wondering, would you like to have brunch with me tomorrow?"

Molly thought for a minute. Would she like to have brunch with Finn tomorrow?

Most definitely.

"Sure," she wrote back. "What were you thinking?"

"Let's say noon. I'll message you where in the morning."

"Sounds good," typed Molly.

Finn replied with a smiley face emoji and wished her a good night.

"He asked me out!" Molly texted Felicity.

"I knew it! When?"

"Tomorrow, for brunch."

"OK. Let me know how it goes."

"Will do," Molly texted. "I'm turning off my phone. Goodnight."

CHAPTER 23

Allen arrived at the restaurant right on time and immediately
spied her. She was seated at the bar, reading a book, her brown
hair pulled back in a braid. He walked over and gently tapped
her on the shoulder.

She jerked, then turned around and gazed up at Allen.

"WryWriter?"

Allen nodded.

"Allen," he said, extending a hand.

"Hannah," said the young woman.

Allen glanced around. The restaurant was busy, and there
appeared to be a wait for tables.

"Did you put your name down?"

"I did," said Hannah.

She hopped off the barstool and headed over to the
hostess stand. Allen hung back, watching as Hannah said
something to the hostess, who nodded and looked his way.

Then Hannah went to get him.

"Come on," she said.

Allen followed her back over to the hostess, who was
holding two menus.

"This way," said the hostess, leading them to a table for
two near the back.

"Thanks, Vic," said Hannah.

"No problem," said the hostess, depositing the two menus

on the table and glancing again at Allen. "Your server should be right over."

"You know her?" Allen asked Hannah after they had sat down.

"She's my roommate," said Hannah. "Well, technically, my apartment-mate."

"Ah," said Allen.

"She's actually an actress," Hannah continued. "She's been in a couple of commercials. And she's up for a role in some pilot. It could be her big break. She's heading to L.A. to test this week. I hope she gets it, but I'll miss her."

Allen wondered if Hannah was nervous or always talked this much.

"So, in your profile you wrote that you loved to bake and were a food stylist," said Allen.

"That's right," said Hannah.

"So what exactly does a food stylist do?"

"Lots of things. I style food for photo shoots and TV shows, so it looks good, like you'd want to eat it."

"And do you make the food, too?"

"Sometimes. It depends."

"You style a lot of brownies?"

Hannah smiled.

"Brownies, cakes, cookies. You name it, I've probably styled it."

"Sounds like fun."

"It can be," said Hannah. "It's also a lot of hard work. Spending three hours trying to make a chocolate cake glisten without melting under hot lights can be a challenge."

"I bet," said Allen. "So what are some of your favorite things to make? I assume from your handle that brownies are one of them."

Hannah tilted her head and scanned his face.

"Are you really interested in food or are you just being

polite? It's fine if it's the latter. I just don't want to bore you with food talk."

"No, I'm truly interested. My mom loves to cook, and we watch baking shows together."

"Which ones?"

Truth be told, Allen hadn't watched any baking shows with his mom in a while. He thought for a minute, then remembered.

"*The Great British Baking Show*. Mom loves that. And I like it, too," he quickly added.

"I love *The Great British Baking Show*," said Hannah. "If I lived in the UK, I'd apply."

"I think there's an American version. You could always apply to be on that."

"It's not the same."

"So, have you always been into baking?"

"Oh yeah. I—"

She was interrupted by their server, who deposited two mimosas on the table.

"We didn't order these," said Allen.

The young man smiled.

"They're on the house."

"Must be from Vic," said Hannah. "Tell her thanks."

The server nodded.

"Can I get the two of you anything else?" he asked them.

"I'll have a coffee," said Allen.

"And I'll have a cappuccino," said Hannah. "Thanks."

She held up her mimosa.

"To new friends," she said, smiling.

"To new friends," said Allen.

They clinked glasses and drank.

"So you were about to tell me all about your baking career."

Hannah eyed him again.

"You really want to know?"

"I wouldn't ask if I didn't."

"Okay," she said. "Just remember, you asked."

She continued to look at him. He seemed like he was interested, unlike most of the guys she had gone out with recently, who mostly wanted to talk about themselves.

"My mom tells people I started baking as soon as I could hold a spoon. But I think she exaggerates a bit. But I made my first batch of cookies when I was six. And I haven't stopped baking since."

"Six, eh? That's pretty young. I assume your mom helped you."

"According to her, I made them all by myself. I'm sure they were dreadful. But she ate them anyway."

"Good mom," said Allen.

"She is," said Hannah. "She's a caterer and would let me help her in the kitchen as she was preparing stuff. When I got older, she'd even let me make some of the desserts. I was very popular in elementary school."

"I bet. I would have loved to have had a friend who was into baking."

The server reappeared with their coffees.

"You two ready to order or do you need a few more minutes?"

Hannah and Allen exchanged a look.

"Could you give us a few minutes?" said Hannah.

"No problem," he said.

They studied their menus.

"You know what you're going to have?" Hannah asked Allen.

"I'm thinking the lox plate."

"Good choice."

"And you?"

"The Belgium waffle with berries and a side of bacon."

"Sounds good."

"It is. It's my go-to, here. Their Belgium waffles are the best."

"Maybe I'll switch my order."

"No, get the lox plate. I'll give you a bite of mine."

Hannah signaled to their server. He came over and took their order.

"So, tell me about you," said Hannah. "It said in your profile that you're a writer."

"I am."

"What do you write about?"

"Things to do in the city, style trends, food."

"You write for a magazine?"

Allen nodded.

"You ever hear of Hipster?"

"Who hasn't?"

She glanced at him, tilting her head and squinting.

"What?"

"You just don't seem like the Hipster type."

"And what type is that?"

"The kind who wears skinny jeans, ironic t-shirts, and Doc Martens, has a beard or a soul patch, and wears glasses even though he doesn't have to."

"Well, you will be disappointed to know that no one actually dresses like that at Hipster, except for maybe Dave. He's our tech reporter and a total gamer. And probably dresses like that because he's lazy."

"I'm disappointed. So why Hipster?"

"They had a job opening, and I applied."

"And do you like it?"

"For the most part. I'm getting a lot of experience writing and editing. Not everyone straight out of school gets to do that. And I figured it would look good on my resume. But I have to admit, writing Top Ten lists gets old fast."

"I bet. So you working on anything interesting?"

Allen couldn't tell her about the dating story, though a part of him wanted to.

"I'm doing a piece on the best taco places in the city."

"I bet the research was fun," said Hannah.

"A little too much fun," said Allen, who still felt a bit gassy from the day before's taco binge. "I must have eaten over a dozen tacos."

"Ouch. I once had to taste over a dozen chocolate chip cookies for a recipe I was testing. Pretty sure I went into sugar shock after the fourth one. The things we do for work, right?"

Allen smiled.

"Tasting chocolate chip cookies? Now that's an assignment I'd happily take on."

"Next time I'm testing a recipe, I'll let you know."

"So you test recipes, too?"

"Oh yeah. One of my many gigs. I help cookbook authors."

"Nice," said Allen.

"It can be."

"Here you go!"

It was the server with their food.

"Can I get you anything else?"

Hannah looked over at Allen.

"I'm good," he said.

"Me, too," said Hannah.

"Enjoy!" said the server, then he quickly departed.

They ate in silence for several minutes.

"So, you plan on staying at Hipster for a while?"

"I haven't really thought about it," said Allen. "I mean, I don't think I'll be there forever, but probably for at least a year, maybe two."

Hannah took another bite of her waffle.

"What about you? Do you plan on styling food and testing recipes forever?"

"No. I'd love to open my own bakery, but…"

"But what?"

"Do you know how much it costs to rent space in the city? Plus there are the permits." She shook her head. "I don't think I'm ready. One day though. So do you write anything besides Top Ten lists?"

"Actually, I've been working on a novel."

"You're writing a book? Very cool. What's it about?"

"It's kind of a coming of age story, about a boy whose parents are killed in 9/11 and how he struggles with all sorts of stuff as a result."

"Sounds deep," said Hannah.

"I don't know about *deep*. My father died during 9/11."

"Oh, I'm sorry."

"It's okay. It wasn't your fault. He was a firefighter. He died rescuing people."

"You must be proud of him."

"I guess. Mostly, I just miss him."

Hannah didn't know what to say.

"Sorry. I didn't mean to bum you out."

Hannah looked up at him.

"You didn't bum me out. It's just sad. My dad died when I was little, too."

"What'd he die from?"

"Heart attack."

"How old were you?"

"Eight."

"That must have been rough."

"It was. But my mom was amazing. She had been one of those stay-at-home moms. But right after dad died, she became a caterer. She had always loved to cook and needed to find a way to put food on the table. Catering was a no-brainer. And she's been doing it ever since."

"Wow," said Allen. "You ever think about joining her?"

"Sometimes. But catering is hard work. And I'm more into cooking than serving. What about your mom? What did she do after your father died?"

"She's a teacher. High school English. She taught before my dad died and just continued teaching afterward."

"She remarry?"

Allen nodded.

"You like your stepdad?"

"He's okay."

"Any stepsiblings?"

"Two stepbrothers."

"You get along?"

"We tolerate each other. What about you? Did your mom remarry?"

"No, she never did. Dad was the love of her life, and she says she's married to her business. But maybe one day."

"Any siblings?"

"One, an older brother."

"Is he into cooking, too?"

"Not at all. Though he loves to eat."

Allen smiled.

They finished their food and pushed their plates away.

"Can I get you two anything else?"

It was their server again.

"I'm good," said Hannah.

"Me, too," said Allen. "Just the check."

A minute later the server returned with the bill.

"No hurry," he said

Hannah reached for her wallet.

"I got this," said Allen.

"You sure?" asked Hannah.

"Yeah," said Allen, pulling out his wallet.

He paid with his credit card and pocketed the receipt.

It was nippy outside, and Hannah was rubbing her arms.

"I should get going," she said. "Thanks for brunch."

"Thanks for inviting me." He paused. "Could I have your number?"

Hannah smiled.

"In case you need an emergency supply of brownies?"

Allen smiled back at her.

"Actually, I was thinking I could hook you up with Dorian, Hipster's food critic. That is if you're interested."

"I'd love that!"

Allen thought she had a nice smile.

Hannah recited her number, and Allen typed it into his phone.

"I'm throwing one of my tasting parties next weekend if you're interested," she informed him.

"Tasting party?"

"It's when I test a bunch of recipes and invite my friends over to try them. You should come if you're free."

"Sounds like fun."

"Tell you what. Why don't you give me your number and I'll text you the details."

He immediately did so.

"Well, I've gotta run," said Hannah. "Hope to see you next weekend at the party!"

Allen watched as she practically skipped down the block and smiled. He had gone into the brunch thinking he would just eat and make small talk and then write her off. But now that he had met BrownieLover411, he looked forward to seeing her again. Then he remembered: Carly. He glanced down at his phone and saw she had left him two messages.

CHAPTER 24

Allen yawned and polished off his coffee. It was Monday, and he was actually grateful to be back at work. The weekend had been exhausting. He couldn't remember the last time he had gone out so much. Probably not since his junior semester abroad.

After he had had brunch with Hannah, he had met Carly at a movie. Then they had hung out afterward.

Hannah and Carly.

They were so different, yet he liked both of them. Carly was an extrovert, who knew what she wanted and wasn't afraid to go for it. Whereas Hannah was more like him, more reserved. Yet he had enjoyed spending time with both of them. Though when he was with Carly, he felt he disappeared a bit, like she was lead vocals and he was just a backup singer. He also couldn't help noticing how men looked at her.

And then there was Edna. They had continued to exchange emails, and he would tell her things he wouldn't normally share with a stranger. But there was something familiar and safe about her, as though she knew him.

He had asked Edna if she could tell him a bit more about the manuscript she wanted him to read, fearing the plot might mirror his own. But she had demurred, saying he would have to sign an NDA first.

Allen had asked her how that would work, since they

weren't supposed to divulge their real identities, and Edna said she would get back to him. So did this mean he was interested? He was. Though he confessed his concern about his own novel. To which Edna had replied that she would be happy to take a look at it when the four weeks were over.

That had given Allen pause. He knew Edna worked in publishing. But the idea of her reading his work…

And then there was Grace. Was she ghosting him? He had sent her several emails, asking how work was going and other things. But she had barely replied. Actresses. Were they all so self-absorbed and bad at replying to email? He realized it was an unfair statement. But a part of him still smarted from his breakup with Sophie, and Grace seemed just like her.

So who would he take to the Hipster New Year's Eve Bash? Carly? Hannah? Edna?

Justin would probably love Carly. Though Allen wasn't sure if that was a good thing or a bad thing. And Carly would probably be thrilled to be invited. The Bash was like something right out of *Sex and the City*.

And what about Hannah?

Although he didn't know her well, he couldn't imagine her really enjoying the party. And he knew it was important that he and his date make a good impression.

Then there was Edna. He had no idea what she looked like, but he could imagine spending several hours chatting pleasantly with her regardless. Still, it might be too big a risk inviting her.

Allen was lost in thought when a shadow fell over his desk. "Ahem."

He looked up and saw Natalie standing there.

"Oh good," she said. "You're back."

Allen looked confused.

"Back?"

"You looked a million miles away."

"Just a couple," said Allen, smiling.

"So?" said Natalie.

"So?" Allen repeated.

Natalie sighed.

"How were the dates?"

"Good," he said.

"Good? That's it?"

"Hey, it's better than the alternative."

Natalie made a face.

"What do you want to know?"

"Any keepers?"

"Actually, two."

"Do tell."

"One's a singer. The other's a food stylist."

"Go on," said Natalie.

"Not much else to say. Carly, she's the singer, we've been out a couple times now. She has a great smile, and we've been messaging pretty frequently. As for Hannah, we only just met, but I'm probably going to see her again this weekend. She seems very down to earth."

"Excellent!" said Natalie.

"I guess."

"You guess? You have half the women in New York fawning all over you, and the best you can muster is, 'I guess'?"

"I wouldn't say half the women."

"You know what I mean."

Allen yawned.

"The ladies keeping you up?"

Natalie was grinning, but Allen was not amused.

"I'm just tired. I had a busy weekend."

Natalie continued to grin.

"Not that kind of busy."

Natalie sighed.

"You'd never last on *The Bachelor*."

As if he would ever apply.

"So, which one are you leaning toward?"

"It's too early to say."

"What about the Blind Dates?"

"They're going okay."

"You keeping good notes?"

He nodded. He had been making notes after each of his dates, but it felt wrong. And he worried what the women he had dated would think when his story was published. Hopefully, none of them were regular Hipster readers.

"Well, I just wanted to check in. Keep me posted. I'm off to check out a new designer. Ta."

"And what are you smiling about?" asked Felicity.

She was back on the Editorial floor.

"Nothing," said Molly, quickly turning off the screen on her phone.

"That nothing wouldn't happen to be named Finn O'Brien would it?"

Molly turned and looked up at her.

"I have no idea what you are talking about."

But she couldn't help smiling as she said it.

"I knew it!" said Felicity. "I knew you two would hit it off! So...?"

"So...?" said Molly.

"Come on," said Felicity. "I know you saw him again yesterday."

"I did," said Molly, smiling again.

"And?"

"And we had brunch and then went for a walk."

"That's it?"

"That's it. Though he just texted to tell me what a nice time he had this weekend."

Felicity eyed her.

"Did you at least kiss?"

"Maybe."

She was grinning again.

"I take it he's a good kisser."

Molly nodded. Her cheeks were turning pink.

"I knew it," said Felicity. "You could totally tell."

"How do you know if someone is a good kisser just by looking at them?"

"Trust me. You know. So, are you going to see him again?"

Molly nodded.

"We talked about getting together after work Thursday."

"Excellent," said Felicity. She turned to go. "Any more from Blind Date?"

"Actually, I exchanged emails with Jay, Jim, and Derek over the weekend."

"You hussy!"

"Hey, you were the one who told me to sign up. Just because I met Finn doesn't mean I'm blowing off Blind Date. Besides, I want Jay to read this new manuscript Constance is expecting."

"Oh?"

"It's a coming-of age-story by a new writer she's hot on. She asked me to find a twenty-something guy to vet it, and I thought Jay would be perfect."

"And how are you going to swing that?"

"I'm working on it."

"Well, good luck," said Felicity. "So, you going to tell Finn about Jay and your other Blind Dates?"

"No," said Molly. "Why should I?"

"Wouldn't you want to know if Finn was dating someone else?"

"That's different."

"How?"

"I'm not actually dating any of the Blind Date guys."

"Well, you seem pretty cozy with Jay."

"We're just friends."

"If you say so," said Felicity.

"I do."

"Okay. I need to head back. Catch you later."

"Bye," said Molly. Then she unlocked her phone, so she could read Finn's message again.

CHAPTER 25

The week flew by and before Allen knew it, it was Thursday. Carly texted him to confirm that he would be going to her open mic the following night. She had managed to get a slot not too late, at nine-thirty, and had told him to feel free to invite his friends.

Allen had frowned at that. He had hoped to have Carly to himself. Though he realized that was ridiculous. There would be dozens of people at the venue.

He knew it was important to Carly for lots of people to show up, and he thought about sending a group message, letting people know about the gig, but he stopped himself. How would he explain his connection to Carly? No one was to know about the dating article. He also didn't want to risk one of his friends scooping her up. Finally, he decided he would just invite Eric.

"Hey, you want to go to Pianos with me tomorrow?" Allen texted him.

"Maybe," Eric replied. "Who's playing?"

"A new singer I heard about. She's on at 9:30."

"What's her name?"

"Carly Carrera."

"Never heard of her."

"Like I said, she's new. Though she has a bunch of clips on YouTube."

There was no reply from Eric.

Allen messaged him again.

"We could grab a bite beforehand. My treat."

Finally, Eric wrote back.

"Well, if you're paying. :-) What time?"

"Let's plan on meeting at 8. I'll find a place to eat nearby. We can meet there."

"OK. You invite anyone else?"

"Nope, just you."

"OK. See you tomorrow."

Allen was standing outside the Clinton St. Baking Company. It was a bit nippy, and he had his hands in his pockets to keep them warm. Finally, Eric showed up.

"Sorry, I'm late. The train took forever."

"No worries," said Allen.

They went inside and grabbed a table. Around nine, they headed to Pianos.

Allen didn't know why he felt nervous, but he did.

"You okay?" Eric asked. "You seem a bit on edge."

"I'm fine," Allen replied.

But Eric wasn't buying it. He could read Allen's moods like a clock.

Pianos was packed, but Allen spied a couple of free chairs at a four-top.

"Okay if we join you?" he asked the couple seated there.

"Sure," they said simultaneously, then laughed.

"I'm Dale," said the man, "and this is Laurie."

"Allen," said Allen, taking a seat.

Eric introduced himself and followed suit.

"How's it been?" Allen asked the couple.

"Good," said Dale. "Though we only got here at eight-thirty."

"I liked the guy who just played," said Laurie.

"He was all right," said Dale. "So, you two visiting or do you live here?"

"We live here," said Allen. "Where are you from?"

"Ohio," said Dale. "This is our first trip to New York."

"Actually, I was here in high school," said Laurie. "But this is our first trip here together."

"Well, welcome," said Allen.

A server came over, and Allen and Eric each ordered a beer.

Finally, it was Carly's turn to go on. There was a smattering of applause and some cheers as her name was announced. Allen thought about waving to her but remembered that he wasn't supposed to know her. So he just politely clapped.

Then she began to sing.

Allen gazed up at her. He had watched a handful of her videos. But she was even better in person. She had a kind of Sara Bareilles/Maggie Rogers vibe and everyone in the club was quiet as she sang.

She had started with a bunch of covers, then played some original stuff. When she was done, just over half an hour later, several men were standing and whistling. Allen was one of them. He hadn't even realized he was standing until Eric tugged on his shirt. Then he quickly sat down.

"You must really like her," said Eric.

Allen could feel his cheeks grow warm. Or maybe it was because the room suddenly felt crowded and hot.

He watched as Carly smiled and stepped off the stage. She walked over to a table where a group of people around their age was sitting. No doubt her friends. She chatted with them for a minute, then looked around. She caught Allen's eye and smiled at him, then gestured for him to come over.

"Is she gesturing at you?" said Eric, looking surprised.

Allen was still looking at Carly.

"Come on," he said.

He took a step, then turned back to Dale and Laurie.

"It was nice meeting you. Enjoy the rest of your stay in the Big Apple."

"You made it!" said Carly, beaming at Allen. She turned to her friends. "Everyone, this is Allen!"

"Hi Allen," said a chorus of voices.

Eric cleared his throat.

"And this is my friend, Eric," said Allen.

"Hi Eric," said the chorus.

"Nice to meet you, Eric," said Carly, smiling at him. "So over there, that's Brook and Danielle," she said, pointing to the two women. "And that's Ham and Gil," she said, pointing to the two men.

"Hi," said Allen and Eric.

"Move over, guys, so Allen and Eric can squeeze in."

"That's okay," said Allen. "It doesn't look like there's any room."

"Nonsense," said Carly. "Ham, grab that empty two-top behind you and a couple of chairs."

Ham did as he was told.

"There now," said Carly. "Have a seat."

Allen and Eric sat.

"You were great," said Eric.

"Thank you," said Carly.

"So how come I haven't heard of you before?"

Carly smiled.

"I just moved to New York this summer. And I'm still trying to get the word out."

"Hey, Carly!" called the emcee.

"I'll be back in a minute," she told the group.

Allen watched as she made her way over to the stage.

"So, you're Allen," said Brook.

"Hmm?" said Allen. His attention had been focused on Carly.

"The guy Carly found on Spark," Brook continued.

Eric looked at Allen.

"Um," said Allen.

"Carly said you're a writer," said Danielle.

"That's right," said Allen, avoiding Eric's gaze.

"Who do you write for?" asked Ham.

"Hipster.

"Cool," said Gil.

"So how do you all know Carly?" Eric asked them.

"Danielle and I live with her," said Brook. "And Gil here is Danielle's brother."

"And I'm a friend of Gil's," said Ham.

An awkward silence followed.

Finally, Carly reappeared. She was beaming.

"Good news?" asked Brook.

Carly nodded.

"I got a gig!" she said, practically bouncing on her toes. "It's just once a week, on Wednesday nights, and it doesn't pay much. But if I bring in a good crowd, they'll consider moving me to a better night."

"That's awesome!" said Danielle.

"I like Wednesdays," said Ham. "I'll come hear you."

"Me, too," said Gil.

Allen saw how the two men were looking at Carly. Did she have any idea they were into her? He suddenly felt insecure.

"Congrats," he said.

As Carly chatted with her friends, he looked at his phone. It was getting late.

"We should get going," he said to Eric.

Carly looked disappointed.

"So soon? I was hoping you could join us for a drink to celebrate."

"It's been a long week," said Allen.

"But it's Friday," said Carly. "Just one drink?"

"Come on, Allen," said Eric. "We can stay for one little drink."

Allen scowled at him.

"Fine. One drink."

Carly beamed.

"Yay! Let's order."

She signaled to a nearby server.

"You okay?" Carly asked Allen, after they had ordered.

"I'm fine," Allen lied. "Just tired. And feeling a bit claustrophobic."

Carly glanced around.

"I understand. Places like this can feel that way. But you get used to it."

She placed a hand on his thigh and smiled at him.

"But I'm really glad you came."

Carly's touch was like a jolt of electricity. He looked down at her hand. She was smiling at him and gently caressing his leg in a way that made his pants feel a bit tighter.

"I'm glad I did, too," Allen said.

CHAPTER 26

"Was this what love felt like?" Molly wondered.

She had just gotten home from her date with Finn, her third since she had met him a week before, and she was practically floating around her apartment.

He was so charming and considerate. And good-looking. (She had always been a sucker for men with dark hair and light eyes.) And he understood what it was like growing up in a loud Irish family and having two bossy older sisters. But this couldn't be love, could it? Not after just three dates. They barely knew each other. But when she was with him, she couldn't help smiling. And she felt all bubbly inside. Of course, it could have just been lust.

She and Finn had kissed and fooled around. Though they hadn't slept together. Molly had a strict rule about not sleeping with guys until they had been together at least a month and she was sure the guy wasn't just interested in getting laid. Which was probably why she had only slept with one boy, her high school crush, who she had dated for two years before they had sex. They had broken up before heading off to college. Or rather he had suggested they break up as who knew when they would see each other again. And Molly had lamely agreed.

She checked her phone, to see if Finn had texted her, and saw she had a new email from Blind Date. There was a note from Jay in her inbox. She opened it and smiled.

His messages always made her smile, and not just because of the jokes.

She didn't feel the same way about him as she did about Finn, but she still felt a strong connection, as though maybe they had known each other in a past life. Though she knew that was silly.

She had thought about telling Jay she was seeing someone and telling Blind Date to freeze her account. But she hadn't. Although she liked Finn—more than liked—she wanted to keep her options open. At least for a little while longer. And she really wanted to see what Jay looked like. (In her mind, she had pictured him looking like a young version of the real Jay McInerney.)

Well, only two more weeks, and then she would find out. Assuming Jay wanted to meet her.

In the meantime, there was Thanksgiving to get through.

While she loved her family dearly, sitting around the table with them for several hours was not something she was looking forward to. Like many families nowadays, the Malloys had different (often strong, clashing) opinions when it came to politics, religion, and other issues. And making matters worse, her sister Fiona had recently gotten engaged, so much of the talk would be around her wedding, another subject Molly had no interest in discussing.

It was bad enough when her eldest sister, Siobhan, got married. That had been a relatively quiet affair, Siobhan being not-so-secretly pregnant. A scandal in her traditional Irish Catholic family. Fiona's wedding, however, would not be so restrained, and Molly could just envision the hideous bridesmaid dress she'd be forced to wear.

Just thinking about Fiona's wedding, which would be the following May, made Molly shiver. Though, she mused, maybe this time she would have an actual date, a handsome, successful Irish man of her own. She pictured Finn dressed in a suit and couldn't help smiling.

Then she shook her head.

Take it easy, girl. You've only been going out a week, and May is six months away.

Still, it was a pleasant thought.

She went into the bathroom and began brushing her teeth. But she couldn't help thinking of Finn. Maybe she should have let him come upstairs. She shook her head. No. She had pledged to take things slow and not give in. But that kiss he had given her...

"Good date?"

It was her roommate, Becca.

Molly spit toothpaste on the mirror.

"Sorry, I did knock."

"I guess I was lost in thought," said Molly.

She rinsed her mouth, then wiped it on a hand towel.

"So?" said Becca.

"So?"

"Come on. Give."

"I don't want to jinx it."

"Yeah, yeah, yeah. But you must like the guy if you've gone out with him three times in just over a week."

"You counting?" said Molly.

"Come on, Moll. Just admit it. You like this guy. And I assume he likes you."

Molly smiled, remembering the kiss.

"That good, eh?" said Becca.

"I don't know. He's just..."

"Well, while you're in la-la-land, may I use the sink?"

"Oh, sure," said Molly, stepping out of the way.

Becca grabbed her toothbrush and put some toothpaste on it.

"So, you going to see him again?"

"I hope so."

"Well, just make sure I meet him before you two elope."

"We are not eloping," said Molly.

Becca shrugged and finished up.

"Well, see you in the morning," she said when she was done.

"See you in the morning," said Molly.

"I heard this really cool singer at Pianos last night," Eric wrote Doris the next morning. "Her name's Carly Carrera. You ever hear of her? She has some videos on YouTube, if you're interested."

He paused, then continued typing.

"So, what are you up to this weekend? I'm working, sadly. Got a bunch of papers to grade, then have to work on some other stuff."

He paused again.

"You ever wonder what you'll do after you get your degree? I've been thinking about that a lot lately. I mean, the obvious thing is to go teach somewhere. But I'm not sure I'm cut out to teach. Maybe it's because of this class I'm teaching. The kids are totally apathetic. Maybe I'll have a better group next section and will change my mind. But I prefer doing research to teaching. Anyway, let me know your thoughts."

He reread what he had written, then hit "send."

Allen woke up Saturday morning in a bad mood. He had dreamed that Carly had become a big star and had invited him to one of her concerts. But when he had gone backstage to see her afterward she was surrounded by a bunch of people he didn't know, and they all started laughing at him.

He knew it was just a dream, but he couldn't shake the bad feeling it had given him. And when he was feeling that way, there was only one thing to do: go for a run. He went to the bathroom, splashed some cold water on his face, threw on some running clothes, and headed to Central Park. An hour later, he was back, sweaty but feeling much better.

He almost always felt better when he went for a run. But since he had started working, it had been harder to motivate himself.

He downed a glass of water in the kitchen, then went to take a shower. When he got out, he turned on his phone. There were messages from both Carly and Hannah. He opened Hannah's first.

"Just checking to see if you're still coming to the tasting party tomorrow."

Allen's stomach rumbled. He wished the party was now, as he was starving.

"I'll be there," he wrote her back.

"Yay!" she replied a minute later. "Don't eat anything beforehand. I'm making a ton of food."

"I won't," he typed. "What are you making?"

"It's a surprise."

"Can I bring anything?" Allen asked.

"Just your appetite. :-)"

Next, Allen opened Carly's text.

"Thanks for coming to my open mic. Eric seems very nice. And Danielle and Brook both thought you were cute. :-)"

"ANYWAY," she continued. "I know we just saw each other last night, but I feel like we barely talked. If you're not doing anything today, you want to get lunch or go see a movie, just the two of us?"

Allen thought. Did he have plans? If he did, he'd cancel them.

"Happy to see a movie and/or grab a bite to eat," he replied. "You decide."

He hit "send" and got dressed.

"How about we meet for brunch at noon?" Carly had texted him back.

Yet another brunch date.

"Sure. Pick a spot and I'll meet you."

"Why don't you pick?" Carly suggested. "Since you work at Hipster."

"Where do you live?" asked Allen.

"In the East 20s, but I'll go anywhere. Pick a spot, and I'll meet you."

Allen checked the Hipster hot list for brunch spots. There was one in her neighborhood, on Irving Place.

"How about Friend of a Farmer?"

"I love that place!" wrote Carly. "See you there at noon!"

"Great," typed Allen. "Whoever arrives first puts their name on the list."

Carly sent him a thumbs-up emoji.

"Thanks for the recommendation," Doris wrote to Eric. "I hadn't heard of Carly Carrera, but I just checked out a couple of her videos. She's good! She reminds me a bit of Maggie Rogers. Let me know if she plays there again. Maybe I'll go."

Eric instantly imagined the two of them going to hear music together and smiled. Then he continued reading.

"As for what I plan on doing after I get my degree, my secret desire is to discover or uncover some lost scrap of history. Kind of like Nicholas Cage in the *National Treasure* movies. Though I am against selling historical artifacts. But if that doesn't work out, I'll probably just teach, assuming I can get a job."

Eric smiled. The more he learned about Doris, the more he liked her.

He started to type a reply when his phone began ringing. The caller ID said it was his sister.

"Hey, is everything all right?" Eric asked.

His sister only ever called him when something was up.

"Everything's fine," said Emily. "I'm just calling to make sure you didn't forget about tomorrow."

Tomorrow? wondered Eric. *What was tomorrow?*

He could hear his sister sighing.

"It's dad's birthday, potato head. And mom's whipping up something special for dinner. You will be there, won't you?"

"Of course," said Eric. "What time again?"

Emily sighed a second time.

"Six o'clock, and don't be late."

"I'll be there," said Eric.

"You better be," said Emily. Then she ended the call.

CHAPTER 27

Allen arrived at the restaurant a few minutes early and put his name down on the list. The hostess, a pretty brunette probably in her early twenties, smiled up at him and said it shouldn't be more than thirty minutes. Allen thanked her and said he'd be outside.

There was no sign of Carly, so he decided to take a walk around the block. Hopefully, a brisk walk would lessen some of the nervousness he was feeling. As he approached the restaurant, he spied Carly and waved.

She smiled and waved back at him.

"You just get here?"

"No, I got here a little early and put my name on the list," he replied. "Then I took a walk around the block. Should only be another fifteen minutes or so."

"Oh good," she said. "I'm hungry."

They glanced at the restaurant. There were at least a half-dozen people waiting for tables.

"Care to go for another walk around the block?" Carly asked him.

"Sure," he said. It was a crisp autumn day, and he enjoyed looking at all the tree-lined streets and ivy-covered brick buildings that made up Gramercy Park.

Carly smiled up at him and looped her arm through his.

"I love this neighborhood," she said, as they made their

way up 19th Street. "It's how I imagined New York looking."

As they walked, they discussed some of their favorite things about the city. Then they returned to the restaurant, going inside to check on their table.

"Hi there," said Allen to the hostess.

The young woman looked up and smiled.

"Is our table ready?"

"Allen, right?"

"Good memory," he said.

The hostess looked behind her at the crowded restaurant, then back at Allen.

"It should only be a few more minutes."

Allen looked around. There was no space to wait inside.

"We'll be just outside."

"No problem," said the hostess. She smiled and tilted her head slightly, placing a piece of hair behind her ear. "I'm Amy, by the way."

Was she flirting with him?

"Thanks, Amy."

He could hear someone clearing a throat behind him. He turned and saw Carly with an unpleasant look on her face.

Was she jealous?

He led her back outside.

"Amy said it would just be a few minutes."

"So I heard."

"Is something wrong?" he asked her.

"You tell me," she said. "You seemed pretty cozy there with Amy. Maybe you'd rather have brunch with her."

Allen looked surprised.

"I was just being polite."

"Yeah, well, I didn't like the way she was looking at you."

Allen couldn't believe it. Carly *was* jealous. He wanted to smile but he didn't. No woman had ever been jealous over him before.

"How could I possibly look at another woman when I'm with you?" he told her.

Carly studied him, trying to assess if he was pulling her leg or not.

"Okay," she said. "I'm just cranky because I haven't eaten and didn't sleep so well last night."

"No worries," said Allen. "I get the same way when I don't sleep or eat."

"Just do me a favor and let me know if you start seeing someone else," she said. "The last guy I dated cheated on me, and it still hurts."

Allen immediately thought about Hannah's tasting party and swallowed.

"By the way, in case I didn't mention it, you were really great last night," Allen told Carly after they had ordered.

She smiled.

"Thanks. I was pretty nervous."

"Well, it didn't show. Listening to you, it was like hearing someone on the radio. I mean it. You sounded as if you'd been singing and playing guitar your whole life."

"That's because I have. But performing live in front of an audience is different from strumming a guitar in your room for YouTube."

"I bet. Which do you prefer?"

"Oh, performing live, definitely. You really feed off the energy in the room. Of course, if the energy sucks... But it was a good crowd last night."

"So, do you have any other gigs lined up?"

"A couple. Though now that I'll be playing at Pianos on Wednesdays, it takes some of the pressure off."

"Well, keep me posted."

Carly smiled.

"I'll put you on my mailing list."

"You have a mailing list?"

"Yeah, though not a lot of people know about it. I need to work on my website over Thanksgiving."

"I should introduce you to Celine."

"Dion?"

Allen smiled.

"No, Celine Hipster's music critic."

"That would be amazing!"

Allen noticed a young man at the next table staring at Carly. He stared back at him and the young man turned away. But a few minutes later, Allen saw him looking at Carly again.

"Do you have a problem?" Allen asked him.

The young man looked embarrassed.

"Sorry, I don't mean to stare. It's just… she looks like this singer I follow on YouTube."

He snuck another glance at Carly.

"What's the singer's name?" Carly asked him.

"Carly Carrera. She's really good. Has this total Maggie Rogers vibe, though she's her own person."

Carly smiled.

"Thank you."

The young man gaped.

"So it really is you?" He turned to his friend. "I knew it!" Then he turned back to Carly. "Could I get your autograph?"

Carly beamed.

"I'd be happy to. Do you have a piece of paper?"

The young man fumbled in his pockets.

"Here," said his friend, looking amused.

She handed Carly a pen and a piece of paper.

"What's your name?" Carly asked the young man.

"Marcus," he said. "Marcus Avery."

Carly smiled at him and proceeded to write on the piece of paper.

"Here you go!" she said.

Marcus looked like he was going to faint.

"Thank you!"

He showed the paper to his friend, then turned back to Carly.

"So, you have any gigs coming up?"

"I play at Pianos on Wednesdays," she informed him.

"Cool! Anywhere else?"

"Not right now."

Allen gave him a warning look.

"Well, it was nice chatting with you," said Marcus. "Good luck!"

"Thanks," said Carly. "Hope to see you at one of my gigs."

The young man finally turned around and was chatting with his friend. Allen breathed a sigh of relief. Though was this how it was going to be if he and Carly dated? The thought left him feeling unsettled.

"You around over Thanksgiving or are you going home?" Allen asked Carly after they had finished their meal and were back outside.

"I promised my mother I'd come home. It'll mean missing my gig at Pianos, but they said it was normally dead the Wednesday before Thanksgiving anyway."

"When will you be back?"

"The Saturday after. What about you?"

"I'll be home. But for me that's here. We typically have Thanksgiving at our place. My mom loves to cook. So there will be a ton of food. And my stepbrothers and their dates will be there."

"Sounds nice," said Carly.

"It's okay."

"Just okay?"

"Let's just say there are a dozen things I'd rather do than spend three hours with my stepbrothers."

"That's right. You said you guys didn't really get along."

"Things are a bit better now that we're all adults. But they can still be jerks."

"Well, I hope you survive Thanksgiving."

"Me, too."

Just then Carly's phone began to ring. She pulled it out and swiped.

"Gotta run," she said. "I promised Danielle I'd go check out a new art exhibit with her across town." She paused. "You want to tag along?"

Allen thought about it for a second, but art wasn't really his thing.

"You go ahead without me."

"You sure?"

She took two steps toward him, then placed her hands on either side of his face and pulled it down so his lips touched hers. Before he knew it, they were kissing in the middle of Irving Place.

"You sure you don't want to come with me?" she asked him again when they had stopped.

She smiled up at him coquettishly. Allen was tempted, but he shook his head.

"You go."

"Okay," she said.

She stayed looking up at him for a few more seconds, in case Allen changed his mind, then she turned and left.

CHAPTER 28

Allen could smell Hannah's apartment before he could see it. It smelled like... He inhaled. Was that barbecue?

He knocked on the door and someone called out that it was open.

He let himself in and saw several women, drinking and chatting amongst themselves. He scanned the room for Hannah but didn't immediately spy her.

One of the women broke off and came up to him.

"I'm Jorie," she said. "You must be Allen."

Allen nodded.

"Hannah's in the kitchen," Jorie informed him. She turned and shouted, "Hey, Hannah, Allen's here!"

Allen winced.

"Sorry," said Jorie.

A few seconds later, Hannah appeared, wearing a Food Network apron.

"You made it!"

"I make it a policy to never turn down free food," Allen said, smiling at her.

"I see you met Jorie."

Allen nodded.

"And that's Monique and Kim," she said, pointing.

"Where's Vic?" he asked, looking around.

"In L.A."

That's right, Allen remembered. He was going to ask if there would be any other guys there when the doorbell rang.

"It's open!" she called.

The door swung inward and two beefy-looking young men, who reminded Allen of his stepbrothers, entered.

Hannah smiled up at them.

"Glad you could make it!"

"Here," said the slightly taller one, handing Hannah a six-pack of beer.

"Thank you, Jason." She turned to Allen. "Allen, this is Jason and his roommate, Scott."

"Hey," said Allen.

The two men said hey back.

"Jason and Scott live down the hall," Hannah explained.

"We'd probably starve if not for Hannah," said Jason.

Scott nodded.

Hannah glanced around.

"Okay, I think that's everyone. Everyone!" she called out. "If you would gather round."

The six of them made a semi-circle around Hannah.

"As many of you know, today's theme is urban barbecue, which, let me tell you, was one of my biggest challenges to date, especially in this kitchen. But I think I pulled it off. There are pulled pork sliders, barbecued chicken sliders, brisket bites, jicama slaw, coleslaw, cornbread, and biscuits. And for dessert, I made a peach pie and peanut butter chip brownies."

"I think I died and went to heaven," said Scott.

"Just give me a minute to set out everything. Then you can dig in."

"Do you need some help?" Allen asked her.

"If you're volunteering," she replied.

Allen followed her to the kitchen and watched as Hannah arranged everything on platters or in bowls. Then they placed everything (except for the desserts) on two foldout tables.

"You made all of this?" he asked her, as he placed the last platter on the table.

"Yup."

"It looks incredible."

"Thanks."

Allen hadn't eaten anything that morning, and he was starving.

Hannah ducked back into the kitchen to grab paper plates, napkins, and serving utensils.

"Okay, everyone, take a plate and a napkin and help yourselves!"

There was practically a stampede.

"You really outdid yourself, Hannah," said Jorie, as she piled her plate with food.

"Do you want us to rate everything like we usually do?" asked Kim, after she had helped herself.

"Thanks for reminding me," said Hannah.

She raced into her bedroom and came back with a small pile of paper and a handful of pens, which she placed on a coffee table.

"When you are done, people," she called out, "please fill out the survey and rate each dish."

Allen picked up one of the surveys.

"I give these to the cookbook authors, to let them know how the recipes went over," Hannah explained. "I have a separate one that I fill out, to let them know how easy or hard it was to make each dish."

"Wow, who knew?" said Allen. "What happens if people hate something?"

"It depends. I'm not the only recipe tester. But if several testers get the same result, the author usually scrubs the recipe or revises it."

"And how many recipes do you typically test?"

"I don't know, maybe a dozen a week? It varies."

She looked over at the table.

"You better go help yourself, before everything's gone."

Allen loaded up his plate and looked for a place to sit, but the couch and two chairs were already occupied, so he just stood.

"Oh, let me get you a chair!"

Hannah headed back to her bedroom, but Allen stopped her.

"That's okay," he said. "I really don't mind standing."

"But I mind," said Hannah. "And I have a couple of folding chairs in my closet. Be right back."

She returned a minute later and unfolded the two chairs.

"Sit!" she commanded.

"What about you?" said Allen.

"I'm too nervous to sit."

Allen sat and proceeded to eat his food. Everything was delicious.

He glanced over at Hannah, who was watching everyone. He could just picture Hannah and his mom cooking together.

"Oh my God," said Monique, her mouth half full. "These pork sliders…"

Kim and Jorie nodded their heads.

"And what did you call these?" asked Scott, holding up a brisket bite.

"Brisket bites," said Hannah. "The idea is to serve stuff people can eat with their hands or with just a fork. Finger food. Though definitely use a fork for the jicama slaw and the coleslaw."

When everyone had sampled the savory food and helped Hannah clear, Hannah brought out the peach pie and the peanut butter chip brownies, along with a big container of vanilla ice cream.

"Oops! Almost forgot the plates," she said and dashed back into the kitchen.

She returned with a stack of dessert plates, more forks, a big knife, a pie server, and a scoop for the ice cream. Then she carefully cut the pie and placed a slice on each plate, topping each piece with a scoop of vanilla ice cream and placing a brownie to the side.

"Come on up and grab a plate!" she called.

Jason and Scott were first in line, taking the plates with the biggest pieces. Allen hung back, waiting for the rest of the group to serve themselves.

He stood near the kitchen and dug into the pie, making sure to get a little ice cream. The peaches tasted so fresh. And the ice cream melted on his tongue.

"Wow," he said, after swallowing. "This is amazing."

He took another mouthful.

Hannah beamed.

"Can we have seconds?" asked Jason, who had already finished his pie and brownie.

Hannah smiled.

"If there's any left." She turned to Allen. "Be sure to try the brownie."

Allen dutifully obeyed.

"Oh man," he said, savoring the gooey chocolate and peanut butter. "This is sick."

Hannah looked pleased.

"That's why she's the brownie queen," said Jorie.

"No one makes brownies like Hannah," said Kim.

"I keep telling her she should open a bakery," said Monique.

Jason and Scott nodded.

"We'd be the first in line."

"Yeah, yeah, yeah," said Hannah. "So now that you're done, I need you to fill out your surveys."

Allen picked up a survey and a pen and gave each dish a ten. Then he listed his three favorites. When he was done, he placed his survey back on the table.

When everyone was done filling out the surveys, Hannah moved to the center of the room.

"Well, that concludes today's tasting. Thank you all for coming."

"When's the next one?" asked Jason.

"Sometime between Thanksgiving and Christmas," said Hannah. "I'll let you know."

"You going home for Turkey Day?" Jorie asked her.

"No, I'm staying here. I'm working over at the food pantry Thanksgiving morning, then answering calls on the turkey helpline."

"You're so good," said Monique.

"Or she can't stand spending Thanksgiving with her family," said Kim.

Hannah swatted her.

"You know that's not true. Mom's just working, and my bro won't be around. So why go home? Besides, I like feeling useful and feeding the homeless—and helping people with their Thanksgiving dinners."

"You're welcome to come to our place for Thanksgiving," said Allen.

Where had that come from?

Hannah smiled at him.

"That's very sweet of you, Allen. But I wouldn't want to impose."

"It wouldn't be an imposition. My mom would love you."

Allen really had no idea what had gotten into him. The food must have gone to his head.

"Well, thank you," said Hannah. "Can I get back to you?"

Allen nodded.

"We'd invite you to have Thanksgiving with us," said Jason, "but I think my mom would kill me if I invited more people. We're already up to twenty-four."

"Wow," said Allen. "You have twenty-four people over for Thanksgiving?"

Jason nodded.

"I'm one of four, and my older sister and brother both have families. Plus there's my mom's sister and her family, and Scott here."

"It's too far for me to go home," said Scott.

"Don't worry about me," Hannah told everyone. "I'll be fine."

Kim and Monique gathered their things and went up to her.

"Thanks for having us over," they said, giving her a peck on the cheek.

"My pleasure," said Hannah.

Soon after, everyone had departed, except for Allen.

"Phew," said Hannah, plopping down on the sofa.

"Thank you for including me," said Allen, not sure if he should stay or go.

"My pleasure," said Hannah. "Hey, you wanna grab a couple of beers from the fridge?"

Allen headed to the kitchen.

"There's a bottle opener in the drawer to the left of the fridge," Hannah called.

Allen found it and opened both bottles, then brought them back to the living room.

"Here you go," he said, handing her a bottle. "Cheers."

"Cheers," said Hannah.

CHAPTER 29

Allen wound up staying at Hannah's for another hour, chatting with her as they cleaned up. Hannah was easy to talk to, especially as she did most of the talking. But Allen didn't mind. He found her amusing.

When they were done, Hannah thanked him, then told him she needed some alone time, to recover from the party. Allen understood. He would have felt the same way.

He headed to the door, then Hannah stopped him.

"I'm really glad you came," she said.

"I am, too," he replied. "Your friends seem nice."

"They are."

They stood there for a few more seconds.

"Well, see ya," said Allen.

"See ya," said Hannah.

He left, and Hannah closed the door behind him.

On his way home, he realized he hadn't said anything about getting together with her again. He would send her a text later—and ask his mom if it was okay to have Hannah join them for Thanksgiving. She'd probably be thrilled.

He passed by an attractive blonde as he got off the subway and his mind flashed to Carly. She would probably be pissed if she found out about Hannah, even though he and Carly weren't officially dating. And what Allen felt for Hannah was more friendship than lust.

He unlocked the door to his apartment. The place was dark and quiet.

"Anybody home?" he called. There was no answer.

He went to his room and took out his phone. There was an email from Blind Date. Edna had written to him again.

It was a short note, asking him about his weekend and if he had seen any good movies lately. She then concluded the message with a joke.

"Did you hear about the cheese factory explosion in France?" she had written. Allen scrolled down. "Da brie was everywhere!"

Allen smiled. He would have to ask her if she had ever been to France.

He opened his laptop and started to write her back.

"Hi there. Thanks for the note. Weekend's been okay. I saw this really cool singer at Pianos Friday. Her name is Carly Carrera. She sounds a bit like Maggie Rogers and has a bunch of videos on YouTube. You should check her out. And I went to a tasting party earlier today. That's where people taste different recipes. I hadn't heard of it before. But apparently it's a thing. Have you ever been to one? I think it would be cool to be a recipe tester. That is, if you liked to cook.

"Are you into cooking?" he asked. "If so, what do you like to make?

"As for movies, I haven't seen a lot recently, though I did see *Venom* and *Bad Times at the El Royale*. Anything you'd recommend?"

He then searched for a good joke to include, then reread the email. He thought about deleting the part about Carly and the tasting party, then decided to leave them in. Then he hit "send."

Molly was smiling as she sat down to brunch with her friends. She had just received a text from Finn.

"Someone's in a good mood," said her friend Tabitha.

Molly could hear her phone buzzing. She was tempted to check it, but after Finn's last message, she didn't want anyone looking over her shoulder.

"You have something you want to tell us?" asked Alexandra.

"I don't want to jinx it," said Molly. "But…"

Her three friends leaned in.

"I met someone."

"As in a guy?" said Virginia.

"As in a guy," said Molly.

"So?" asked Virginia. "Tell us about him."

"Well," said Molly, seeing three sets of eyes glued to her. "He's an accountant."

Virginia fake yawned.

"And he's Irish."

"Of course," said Tabitha.

"And he's very cute," Molly continued.

"Where's he from?" asked Alexandra.

"The Boston area," said Molly. "He's a friend of Felicity's boyfriend, Nick."

"You got a picture of him?" asked Virginia.

Molly hesitated.

"Come on," said Virginia. "Does he have an Instagram?"

"I don't want you guys stalking him. We've only been seeing each other a couple of weeks, not even."

"Well, let us know if things get serious," said Tabitha.

"I will."

"So are you seeing him this week?" asked Alexandra.

Molly nodded and smiled.

"Looks like love to me," said Virginia.

"Just don't do anything crazy," said Tabitha.

"Like what?" said Molly.

"Like elope," said Virginia.

"Please," said Molly. "I just met the guy."

"I have a friend who eloped," said Alexandra.

"You do?" said Virginia.

Alexandra nodded.

"Her parents didn't approve of the guy, so they went and got married on their own."

"Wow," said Virginia. "My father would kill me if I eloped."

"I don't know," said Tabitha. "He'd probably be happy to be rid of you."

"Hey!" said Virginia.

"She was just kidding, Virginia," said Alexandra.

But Virginia was in a huff.

"Can we please change the subject?" begged Molly. "Tell me what's up with you all? I feel like it's been ages since we all got together."

When they had finished their brunch, they asked for the check.

"Well, it's been fun," said Molly. "But I need to roll. Gotta finish reading a manuscript."

"On a Sunday?" said Virginia.

"I don't mind," said Molly. "I actually like this one."

"Can you tell us about it?" asked Alexandra.

"Not yet," said Molly.

They each left money on the table, then headed out.

"Make sure we get to meet this mystery man before things get too serious!" called Virginia, as they went their separate ways.

Molly just waved.

When she got home, she saw she had an email from Blind Date. There was a message from Jay. She immediately opened it.

"A tasting party sounds like fun," she wrote back. "As for cooking, I like it, though I don't have that much time or energy to do it these days. But maybe you and I could do our own tasting party and share some of our favorite recipes after we meet. :-)

"And I'll definitely check out Carly Carrera, if you say she's good. Hadn't heard of her, but I love Maggie Rogers, as you know. Thanks for the tip."

She added a few other thoughts, then searched online for a joke.

"Since we're on the subject of food, and you're a writer, I thought you'd appreciate this pun: 'I just made synonym buns!' texted my neighbor. I texted her back, 'You mean like grammar use to make?' I haven't heard from her since."

She read over her note, smiled, then hit "send."

Eric arrived at his parents' place a little after six.

"You're late," said Emily, upon opening the door.

"Blame the subway," said Eric. He took a sniff. Something smelled good. "What's Mom making?"

"Pot roast."

It was one of their father's favorites.

"Smells excellent."

"Is that Eric?" called his mother from the kitchen.

"It is," shouted Emily.

"Where's Dad?" asked Eric.

"Eric, there you are!" said their father, coming out of his study. "Glad you could make it."

"Of course," said Eric. He looked around.

"Something wrong?" asked their father.

"Where's what's-his-name?" said Eric, peering around.

His father and sister looked confused.

"You know, the guy you were seeing," said Eric, looking at his sister. "I assumed he followed you here from L.A."

"You know what happens when you assume," said Emily.

"Yeah, yeah, yeah," said Eric. "So what happened to him? Did he dump you?"

Emily gave him a frosty look.

"No, *I* dumped him," she corrected. "I told him I wasn't interested in a long-distance relationship. Besides, Bruce was beginning to get on my nerves."

"Finally," mumbled Eric.

"You say something?" said Emily, squinting at him.

"Nope."

"Come on, you two," said their father. "Let's go into the kitchen and see if your mother needs some help."

After dinner, Emily took Eric aside.

"So, I have kind of a weird question."

Eric looked at her and waited.

"You know your friend, Allen?"

"I'm familiar with him, yes," said Eric.

"Do you happen to know if he's on Spark?"

Where had Eric heard that name before?

"It's a newish online dating site," explained Emily.

Eric waited for her to go on.

"I know it's probably ridiculous, but I was on there the other day and happened to see this guy who looked like him."

"And you're telling me this why? Please tell me you didn't ask him out."

Emily glared at him.

"So what if I did?"

Eric glared back at her.

"What's your question?"

"My question is, was it Allen?"

"Why didn't you just ask him?"

"That would have been weird."

Eric rolled his eyes.

"So?" said Emily.

"So?" said Eric.

"Is Allen on Spark?"

"If he is, he didn't tell me. Allen hates online dating."

"Well, tell him he has a doppelganger."

"I'll be sure to let him know."

Eric paused.

"What did you say the name of the app was again?"

"Spark."

Then Eric remembered. Carly's roommate had referred to Allen as the guy she had met on Spark.

Eric looked at his sister.

"So for argument's sake, let's say it was Allen you saw. Would you have actually asked him out?"

"Maybe," said Emily. No way was she now going to admit to her brother she already had.

"Even though he's, like, my best friend."

"What's that got to do with anything?"

"Uh, hello."

"Since when do you get to decide who I date or don't date?" asked Emily, hands on her hips.

"Fine. Whatever." Eric had had enough. "I'm going."

"Don't let me stop you."

He grabbed his coat from the front-hall closet.

"Bye Mom, bye Dad," he called. Then he left.

CHAPTER 30

Allen arrived at Pianos bearing a small bouquet of roses. Carly's first set started at eight, but he had gotten there early in hopes of seeing her beforehand. He had thought about inviting a friend but had decided against it after last time. Though he knew Carly's roommates would probably be there.

He walked in and immediately spied Danielle, Brook, Gil, and Ham. And there was a good crowd. Clearly, word had gotten out.

"Have a seat," said Ham, sliding out an empty chair. Though the look he gave Allen wasn't particularly friendly.

"Where's Carly?" Allen asked, looking around.

"Backstage," said Danielle. "Those for her?"

Allen nodded.

"You think it's okay if I go give them to her?"

"Carly said she didn't want to be disturbed," said Brook.

"Why not?" asked Allen.

"She's going through her ritual," said Danielle.

"Ritual?" said Allen. "She sacrificing a chicken to the music gods?"

Brook rolled their eyes.

"No, she's meditating."

"Isn't it kind of noisy to meditate?"

"Carly just tunes it out," said Danielle.

A server came over and asked Allen if he wanted a drink. He nodded and ordered a beer.

He glanced around the room. A couple was just walking in, and he thought the woman looked familiar. Though with the low lighting and all the people, it was hard for Allen to get a good look at her. He craned his neck, but they had taken a table across the room, on the other side of the stage. Then the lights dimmed, and the emcee got on stage.

After a brief introduction, Carly came out with her guitar and smiled at the audience. There was polite applause, then she said a few words and began to sing. People continued to talk in low voices for a few minutes, but as Carly's voice soared, the room went quiet. You could tell by her face and the way she strummed her guitar that she intensely felt the lyrics she was singing, and the people in the room seemed to be feeling them, too.

When her set ended just under an hour later, there was loud clapping and whistling. Carly was glowing. She exited the stage and a minute later came to join Allen and the group at their table.

"You were amazing," said Danielle.

"Thanks!" Carly said. "You really think I was okay?"

"You were better than okay," said Brook. "You slayed it."

"What did you think, Allen?"

"I think you were incredible," he said. And he meant it.

He held out the flowers.

"These are for you."

Carly beamed.

"For me?"

Allen nodded.

"I wasn't sure what kind you liked. So…"

"They're perfect," said Carly. "I love roses."

She lowered her head and inhaled.

Their server returned and asked Carly if she wanted something to drink, and she ordered herbal tea.

"Gotta soothe the vocal cords!"

Ham turned to her.

"You should have someone film you while you're playing and post it on YouTube. I bet it'd get lots of views."

Gil nodded.

"I'll check with Bernie," said Carly. "He's the manager."

"Tell him it'd be good publicity for Pianos," said Ham.

Carly smiled, but she doubted posting a video from her gig would make a difference as the club was pretty well-known. Though it might help her get some other gigs.

"When's your next set?" asked Allen.

"At ten."

"You want to go for a walk?"

"I should really stay."

The server brought over a pot of hot water and a mug with a teabag.

"Thanks," said Carly. She poured the water over the teabag and let it steep. "So, how's your week been going?"

"Okay," said Allen, watching the steam rising from the mug.

"Working on any good articles?"

Allen really didn't feel like talking about work.

"Some."

Carly tilted her head.

"Everything okay?"

Allen was looking around the room. He saw the couple he had seen earlier. They had just gotten up and were heading toward the exit. He stared at the woman. What was it about her? She was quite attractive, but it was more than that. He didn't recognize the man.

"Sorry?" said Allen.

"I asked if everything was okay. You seem distracted."

"Sorry. Long week, even though it's only Wednesday. And confined places always make me edgy."

Carly sipped her tea. Then Ham asked her something and the friends began chatting amongst themselves. Allen tried to pay attention, but it was hard with all the ambient noise. Finally, Carly got up.

"I should go prepare for my next set," she said. She looked at Allen. "You want to grab a bite to eat afterward?"

"Thanks," he said. "But I have to get up early tomorrow."

"I'm staying," Ham immediately said.

"Me, too," said Gil.

Carly smiled at them, which annoyed Allen.

"You free this weekend?" Allen asked her.

"I think I can fit you in," she said, now smiling at him. "Text me tomorrow."

She took a last sip of her tea then headed backstage.

Molly had enjoyed listening to Carly. She would have to tell Jay she had taken his advice and had gone to hear her.

Finn had enjoyed the music, too. Or maybe it was Carly he enjoyed. Molly could tell by the way Finn looked at her that he found her attractive. Molly tried not to feel jealous, but it was hard.

Finn had asked her if she wanted to stay for the second set (he clearly wanted to), but she was tired and had a busy day the next day. So Finn had asked for the check.

They stepped outside into the cool November evening. Molly shivered a bit, having opted for fashion over warmth. Finn rubbed his hands over her arms to warm her. It felt good.

"Thanks for tonight," said Molly.

"My pleasure," said Finn. "You want to come back to my place? It's not far from here."

Molly looked up at him, staring at the little cleft in his chin.

"Thanks, but I should probably just go home."

Finn took a step closer and wrapped his arms around her. He felt warm.

"You sure?"

She felt herself wavering, especially when Finn leaned down and began gently running his tongue over her ear. She shivered, though this time it wasn't from the cold.

"I'd like to," she said, her eyes closed. "But I need to get up early."

Finn continued to nuzzle her, working his way down her neck.

"I need to get up early, too," he breathed into her ear.

Molly felt her resistance slipping. Then a car honked its horn, and she gently pushed Finn away.

"Another time," she said.

Finn sighed.

"You make me crazy, you know that?"

Molly smiled.

"You make me a bit crazy, too."

Finn made to pull her back in, but Molly stood her ground. Then she glanced around, debating whether to hail a cab or head to the subway.

"Let me get you an Uber."

"Thanks," said Molly. "But I'm good."

"I insist," he said, taking out his phone. "A car will be here in two minutes," he informed her a few seconds later.

Molly rubbed her arms, and Finn pulled her close again.

"I could always go back with you to your place," he whispered.

Molly didn't reply. She was too distracted by Finn nibbling on her ear.

Out of the corner of her eye, she saw a black car pull up.

"I think my ride's here."

Finn looked at the license plate, then checked his phone.

"You're right."

Molly went to open the door, but Finn grabbed her hand.

"You sure you don't want me to come home with you?"

Again, Molly felt tempted, but she shook her head.

"What about tomorrow?" asked Finn.

Molly smiled and nodded.

"Text me," she said.

Finn held the door for Molly, then closed it after her. As the car pulled away, she glanced back, but she couldn't see him.

The next morning, Allen received a message from Edna.

"Hi there!" she had written. "I went to hear Carly Carrera last night at Pianos. Thanks for the recommendation! You're right. She definitely has a kind of Maggie Rogers/Sara Bareilles vibe. I really enjoyed her. Anyone else you recommend?

"By the way, I just spoke with my boss. That manuscript she wanted you to read is going to be delayed. And as our four weeks will be up by then, it shouldn't be a problem. That is, if you're still willing to vet it."

Allen stared at the message. Edna had been at Pianos last night? He envisioned the room, trying to guess which woman she could have been. Was she the cute blonde sitting with a bunch of her girlfriends? (He could have sworn they were all checking him out.) Or maybe she was that brunette at the next table he saw eyeing him?

He wished he had known she would be there. Then again, they weren't technically supposed to meet until early December. But...

"Anyway, I need to go. Busy day. But I wanted to send you a quick note. Oh, and here's my joke of the day."

Allen smiled as he read it. Then he began typing a reply.

"Loved the joke," he wrote. "I was at Pianos, too. Who knows? We could have been seated next to each other.

"As for bands or musicians I'd recommend, I've been

listening to The 1975 and Vampire Weekend lately. I also like jazz, especially Brazilian jazz. My mom played it all the time when I was growing up, and I guess it sort of grew on me. Helps me to relax.

"I have a pretty busy couple of days, too. I'm looking forward to Thanksgiving next week. Not the actual day, just having some time off. What are you doing for Thanksgiving?

"Now here's my joke. (Try not to groan too much.) John and Sue are having lunch, and John mentions that he got hit with a book the night before. Sue asks him, how did you get hit on the head with a book? And John replies, I only have my shelf to blame.'"

He smiled as he read over his note, then sent it off.

Eric had been in a bad mood since Sunday evening. He kept thinking about what Emily had said. He had gone onto Spark when he got home, but he had no way of knowing if Allen was on the app.

Well, there was only one way to find out. He got out his phone and sent Allen a text, asking if the two of them could grab a beer later.

"What's up?" asked Allen, after they had gotten their beers.

"So, I had this totally weird conversation with Emily at my dad's birthday dinner Sunday."

"Emily's back in New York?"

Eric nodded.

"For now. Anyway, she's convinced she saw you on some dating site. At first, I thought that was ridiculous. But then I remembered what Carly's roommate said, about you two meeting via Spark."

Allen had hoped Eric hadn't registered that.

"Hey, you want to get some food?" asked Allen.

"Sure," said Eric.

Allen looked around for their server and signaled to him.

"Could we get some menus?"

The server brought over menus and Allen held his in front of his face, like a shield.

"So are you on Spark?" asked Eric.

Allen sighed and put down the menu.

"You know I'm not a fan of online dating."

"That's what I told her," said Eric. "But she insists she saw you."

"Is *she* on Spark?"

"I would assume so if she saw someone who looked like you there."

Allen hadn't seen Emily in years, but his mind instantly formed an image of her. It looked a lot like FlirtyFashionista. Could FlirtyFashionista and Emily be one and the same?

Eric was still looking at him, and Allen knew he couldn't lie to his best friend.

"Okay, I may have *briefly* been on Spark. But it was only for a few days."

Eric was smirking.

"What's with the face?"

"I can't believe you went on a dating app without telling me," Eric said.

"It was just for a few days. Justin wanted me to check it out. Spark's a new advertiser."

He bit his tongue. The article was supposed to be top secret.

"Speaking of dating apps, how's Blind Date going?"

"Okay, I guess."

"Just okay?"

"I'm pretty sure two of my matches dumped me."

"Dumped you?"

"I think Diana met someone. And Coco's been MIA."

"But you and Doris are good?"

"We are, but I'm worried she's going to dump me, too."

"You can always request new matches."

Before Eric could reply, their server came over and took their order.

"So, what are you doing for Thanksgiving?" asked Eric.

"The usual," Allen replied. "Mom will be in the kitchen, preparing a lavish feast for my two horrible stepbrothers and Leighton's fiancée."

"Leighton's engaged?"

"Apparently. I just found out. They were keeping it a secret, at least from us. Though it was all over Instagram."

"Have you met her?"

"Not yet. Though I saw her photo on Instagram. She's exactly what you'd expect from Leighton: blonde, big boobs, fake."

"Well, if you want to escape, you can always come over to our place. You know my mom loves you."

Allen smiled.

"Thanks. I may take you up on that. Will Emily be there?"

Eric gave him a suspicious look, and Allen regretted asking.

They ate their meal in near silence, then got the check.

CHAPTER 31

Allen had never been so grateful for a Friday. He was exhausted. Work was tiring enough. But now that he was seeing two women and corresponding regularly with a third, he just wanted to go home and go to bed. Though he had made plans to see Carly that evening, as she was heading back to Chicago that weekend.

He still couldn't believe how much his life had changed in just a few weeks. He had gone from having no girlfriend to potentially having three if you included Edna. Though he didn't think of any of them as his *girlfriend*. At least not yet.

Allen put his head down on his desk.

"Everything okay?"

Allen looked up to see Sara looking down at him.

"Just tired."

"Rough week?"

Allen gave a small nod.

He knew that most of his friends, well, except for Eric, had far more active social lives and seemed just fine. But for him, it had been a rough week.

"I guess I'm not used to dating."

"Didn't you date people when you were in college?"

"That was different. I wasn't dating three at the same time and having to lie about it."

Sara smiled indulgently.

"So, how's the dating going?"

Before he could respond (not that he wanted to), Natalie joined them.

"What are you two talking about?"

"I asked him how the dating was going," said Sara.

"And?"

"The boy's done worn out."

Natalie grinned.

"I knew they'd be going crazy over you. So, how many dates have you been on this week?"

"Enough."

"You been keeping notes?"

Allen nodded. He had been, but he hated it. It felt like a betrayal. Though he had told himself it was just like keeping a journal, something he had done when he was in middle school and high school.

"So, you know which one you're going to take to the Hipster New Year's Bash?" Natalie asked him.

Allen shook his head. It was still too soon.

"At least give me something."

Allen sighed.

"It's down to three."

"And they are?"

"If I tell you, will you leave me alone?"

"For now."

They eyed each other.

"Two are from Spark. One's a singer, the other's a food stylist. Then there's the editor from Blind Date."

"What happened to the fashionista?"

Of course, Natalie would remember that one.

"She blew me off."

"Her loss. Well, keep me posted. See you both Monday."

She sauntered off, but Sara stayed behind.

"If you want to talk, my door is always open."

"Thanks," said Allen. "But I'll be fine as soon as this whole dating experiment is over."

Allen had made a reservation for himself and Carly at a little place in the West Village that Dorian, Hipster's food/restaurant critic, had suggested. He had looked at Hipster's list of the top romantic restaurants in the city (which had been written before he had started working there), but he hadn't known which one to pick. So he had asked Dorian. And Dorian had suggested Amélie.

He had consulted Natalie's clothing chart and had dressed in a pair of black jeans, a white collarless shirt, and his blue sweater and had made sure his hair wasn't sticking up, as it was prone to do.

When he got to the restaurant he looked around, but Carly had yet to arrive. So he waited at the bar and ordered a drink. Fifteen minutes later, she raced in.

"I'm so sorry I'm late!" she said. "I got turned around. I'm still trying to figure out the Village."

Allen understood. For those not familiar with New York, the Village was a bit of a maze, unlike the rest of Manhattan, which was on a grid.

He looked at her and smiled. Despite her slightly frazzled expression, she looked beautiful, her blond hair cascading over her shoulders.

"You want to check your coat?"

She noticed he was still wearing his leather jacket.

"I'll just keep it." She glanced around. "Is our table ready?"

Allen went over to the maître d' to let him know that his date had arrived, and they were taken to a table for two.

"This place is adorable," said Carly, looking around. "It reminds me of one of those cute French bistros you see in movies or on TV."

Allen agreed. There was something intimate about the place, with the banquettes and dim lighting. And something smelled incredible.

"You smell that?" he asked Carly.

She took a sniff.

"Mmm…" she said.

They eyed the food on the surrounding tables.

"Just looking at all that yummy food is making me hungry," said Carly.

A minute later a waiter came over.

"Good evening," he said. "May I get you both something to drink?"

"Could we see a wine list?" asked Allen, though he knew next to nothing about wine.

"It's right there, sir," said the waiter, pointing down at the wine list that had been left on the table.

"Right," said Allen, embarrassed. "Could you give us a minute?"

"Of course," said the waiter.

Allen looked across at Carly.

"Should we order a bottle?"

"Up to you," she said. "I'd also be fine with a glass."

Allen didn't know what to do. It had been a while since he had gone to a romantic restaurant with a woman. The last time having been with Sophie. And she had broken up with him shortly thereafter. Just thinking about that made Allen want to drink.

"Let's get a bottle."

"Why not?" she said, smiling at him.

Allen signaled to the waiter.

"Can you recommend a bottle?"

"Would you prefer red or white?" the waiter asked him.

Allen looked over at Carly, but she just shrugged.

"What were you planning on having this evening?"

Allen continued to look at Carly. He had no idea what they were having.

"Could you give us a minute?" he said.

"Of course," said the waiter.

"Let's decide what we're having," Allen said to Carly once the waiter left. "Then I'll order the wine."

"I'm thinking the lamb," said Carly, gazing at her menu.

"And I'm thinking the duck or else the steak frites. Do you want to share something first?"

"Sure," she replied.

They decided to get a vegetable terrine, then signaled to the waiter.

"Have you decided?" he asked them.

Allen and Carly nodded and gave him their order.

"Since you are both having meat, may I suggest a cabernet sauvignon? We have a lovely one from France."

He pointed it out to Allen. It wasn't ridiculously expensive, but it was still far more than he was used to spending on wine. It was a good thing Hipster would be reimbursing him.

"That sounds fine," Allen said.

The waiter took the wine list and departed.

"So how's the rest of your week been?" Allen asked.

"Pretty good," said Carly. "I was actually supposed to babysit Dylan tonight, but Danielle said she'd sub for me."

"I didn't mean to take you away from Dylan."

Carly smiled.

"He'll survive. Besides, I'd much rather be here with you."

She placed her hand on top of Allen's and squeezed it.

A minute later, the waiter returned with their bottle. He showed the label to Allen and Allen nodded, not knowing what else to do. Then the waiter poured a little into Allen's glass.

Allen picked up the glass and gently swirled it. Then he sniffed. Finally, he took a sip.

"Very good," he said. Though he felt like a poser.

The waiter smiled and poured some into Carly's glass, then filled Allen's the rest of the way.

Allen raised his glass and Carly followed suit.

"Here's to you getting more gigs—of the musical variety."

"And here's to you finishing your novel," said Carly.

They clinked glasses and drank.

By the time they were done with their main course, Allen had relaxed. They had drunk most of the wine, and he and Carly had chatted about music and shows and movies they liked and about their college years and families.

Allen liked how Carly's face lit up when she talked about something that excited her, like her music, and how she didn't roll her eyes or look bored, like Sophie used to, when he talked.

"Would you like some dessert or coffee?" asked the waiter.

"What do you have?" asked Carly.

"We have an excellent chocolate mousse, a house crème brûlée, and a tarte tatin. That's a French apple pie. And all of our desserts are made in-house."

"Hmm," she said, scrunching her face. "It all sounds good." She looked at Allen. "You want to share something?"

"I'll give you a minute," said the waiter.

"What did you have in mind?" asked Allen.

"What sounds good to you?"

Allen thought for a minute, though he knew which one he wanted.

"The chocolate mousse?"

Carly smiled.

"That's what I was thinking."

The waiter came back over and they ordered.

The chocolate mousse had been delicious, and they had polished it off in just a few minutes. Then Allen had asked for the check.

"Thank you, for dinner," said Carly when they got outside. "I really enjoyed it."

Allen smiled.

"My pleasure. If you like good food, you should come to my place. My mom loves to cook, and she's really good."

Carly smiled at him.

"I love that you and your mom are so close."

"Well, she raised me."

"I know, but some guys would chafe living under the same roof as their parents."

"We get into it sometimes," said Allen. "But I appreciate everything she and Jonathan have done for me, allowing me to live there while I save money to get my own place."

Carly came closer.

"Well, I think they're lucky to have a son like you," she said.

She got up on her toes and kissed Allen on the cheek.

The spot where she had kissed him felt warm.

"I should probably get going," she said.

She made to go but Allen stopped her.

"Come back here," he said.

He reached for her hand and pulled her towards him. Then he took her face in his hands and gently kissed her on the lips. She opened her mouth, and Allen slid his tongue inside.

Allen had no idea how long they stood there kissing. It wasn't until someone shouted, "Get a room!" that they stopped.

They stood there grinning at each other.

"I should go," Carly finally said.

Allen nodded, but they continued to hold hands.

Carly smiled.

"I'll text you from Chicagoland."

"You promise?"

She nodded and let go of his hand.

"How are you getting home?" Allen called. "Do you want me to get you a ride?"

"I want to walk for a bit. It's such a beautiful night. And I love the Village."

"What if you get lost?"

"I can always check my phone."

Allen was going to offer to walk with her, but he sensed she wanted to be on her own.

He watched her walk away, then headed to the subway.

CHAPTER 32

Allen slept late the next morning, not getting up until nearly ten. He hadn't slept that late in ages. Must have been the wine and all the rich food.

He had made no plans, determined to spend the day working on his novel. But first, he would need coffee.

He went into the kitchen and saw that the coffee pot was half full. He poured himself a mug, then took it back to his room.

He opened his laptop and pulled up his novel. He started to read, then stopped and opened his email.

"You will be happy to know that I am spending the entire day working on my novel," he wrote Edna. "It will be painful, but it's been too long. Maybe when I have a first draft, your editor will take a look? No pressure. Just figured I'd ask.

"Oh, and I'm going to see *A Star Is Born* tomorrow. Have you seen it yet? I'm not a big Lady Gaga fan, but I hear she's great in it."

He searched for a joke online.

"Well, I'm off to write," he concluded. "But before I go, here's a joke I thought you'd like."

He reviewed what he had written, then hit "send."

Molly opened the new manuscript Constance had asked her to take a look at. It seemed like every weekend she was reading manuscripts. Not that she minded, most of the time. She loved getting to be the first person, or first editor, to read a potential bestseller.

This weekend's reading was yet another contemporary romance, this one set in Paris. As Molly began to read, she couldn't help thinking that you could stock an entire bookstore with books by women about women who dreamed of living in Paris. Did the world really need another one? Yet Constance knew a trend when she saw one, and as long as those books kept selling, she'd keep publishing them.

Molly had put her phone on the coffee table, and it had started to vibrate. She picked it up and saw she had an email from Blind Date. It was a message from Jay. She opened it on her laptop and began to read.

She thought about replying right away, then closed her browser. She would reply later.

She turned back to the manuscript, but after just a few minutes went back to Blind Date and opened Jay's message.

"I'm thrilled to hear you are working on your novel," she began. "I'd love to read it when you're done. And if it's as good as I bet it is, I'll pass it along to my boss.

"I am also spending the day working. I'm reading a new manuscript. Yet another contemporary romance set in Paris. Yawn.

"Let me know if you liked *A Star Is Born*. I'm a big Bradley Cooper fan. And I like Lady Gaga, too. Will probably go see it anyway but value your opinion."

She went online and searched for a joke, smiling as she found one she thought Jay would appreciate.

"Now here's your joke: Why did Shakespeare write with a pen?" She hit enter a few times, then typed the answer. "Because he found pencils too confusing! 2B or not 2B?"

She signed the email "xo, Edna," then sent it.

"All righty then," she said aloud. "Now back to Paris."

Allen looked at the screen. He had managed to write two chapters. Of course, it had taken him the better part of the day. But it was better than nothing. Part of the problem was that he kept rereading and tweaking what he had just written.

In college, his creative writing instructor had told the class that perfection was the enemy of good—and to not edit what they had written until they had completed a first draft. Otherwise they would never be done. But Allen found it incredibly difficult not to edit himself. Especially now that he was editing other people's work daily. But he convinced himself he was doing less rewriting than he used to.

He glanced one more time at the document, then hit "save" and closed it. He got up and stretched, then went into the kitchen to forage.

"Hey there, stranger," said his stepfather. "What are you doing home on a Saturday?"

"Working on my novel," said Allen, getting some water from the refrigerator.

"Ah," said Jonathan. "How's it going?"

"Slowly. It's been too long since I looked at it and only managed to crank out two more chapters."

"No one said writing was easy. If it was, everyone would be a writer. Though I wish some of the lawyers I worked with were better writers. You should see some of their briefs."

Allen hadn't read any briefs when he had interned at Jonathan's firm, but he didn't doubt what his stepfather said was true.

"Just keep at it," said Jonathan. "You'll get there."

"Thanks," said Allen.

"So, about Thanksgiving."

Allen waited, though he had a feeling, judging by the look on his stepfather's face, that he wouldn't like what Jonathan was about to say.

"Leighton asked if he and Tiffany could stay here while they're in town. It seems his mother doesn't want them cohabitating under her roof."

Allen didn't particularly want them cohabitating under his roof either, but he didn't say anything.

"They're flying in from L.A. Tuesday and leaving Friday," Jonathan continued.

"Will Liam be staying here, too?"

"No, he'll be staying with his mother."

Allen breathed a silent sigh of relief.

"You probably won't even see Leighton and Tiffany," Jonathan said. "Just for Thanksgiving. According to Leighton, they have a very busy schedule."

Good, thought Allen.

"That's fine," he said aloud.

They stood there awkwardly.

"So, you have any plans later?" asked his stepfather. "Your mother and I are going to the Met to check out some new exhibit, then having dinner. You're welcome to join us."

"Thanks, but I'm good," said Allen.

"You have another date?"

"No."

Then he remembered that he had invited Hannah to join them for Thanksgiving and hadn't told his mother and stepfather yet.

"So, um, I kind of invited someone to join us for Thanksgiving."

"I'm sure your mother won't mind. Who?"

"You don't know her."

"One of the women you've been dating?"

Allen nodded.

"Well, just be sure to mention it to your mother."

"I will," said Allen. "Assuming she comes. She's working at a local food pantry that morning, then answering turkey hotline calls."

"Sounds like a selfless young woman."

"She loves to cook, and it's her way of giving back."

Jonathan looked at his watch.

"Well, let me know if you change your mind about going to the Met. I need to run."

Allen reiterated that he was fine hanging out by himself, then fixed himself some lunch.

Eric had thought about not going to the History department mixer. He knew most of the people in his program and didn't have a burning desire to spend his Saturday night with them. But he had nothing better to do, and his friend Rob would be there.

"Think of it this way," Rob had told him. "At least there'll be free booze and food."

It had been hard to argue with that kind of logic, especially when Eric's refrigerator was bare. So he changed into a pair of corduroys, a turtleneck, and his tweed jacket—may as well look the part, he thought, half-jokingly—and headed over to campus.

He was surprised by the number of people there, especially with Thanksgiving less than a week away. He knew many students had already left, although the university wouldn't officially close for the holiday until Wednesday.

He saw Rob talking to one of their professors and made a beeline for him.

"Hey," he said.

"You made it," said Rob. "I wasn't sure if you'd show."

"I couldn't resist the lure of free beer," he said, eyeing Rob's glass.

"Over there," said Rob, pointing a little ways away.

"Thanks," said Eric.

He headed over to where a makeshift bar had been set up. There were a few people in line ahead of him.

"Hey, Tim," said Eric, addressing the student in front of him.

"Hey," Tim replied.

Neither said more.

In front of Tim was a woman Eric didn't recognize.

"A glass of white wine, please," she said to the bartender.

Eric thought she had a nice voice.

The bartender, a graduate student Eric vaguely knew, handed her a glass of wine.

"Thank you," she said.

She turned and nearly collided with Eric, spilling a bit of her white wine on him.

"Oh, I'm so sorry!" she said.

Eric looked at her. She wasn't conventionally pretty, but there was something about her that caught his eye. She was maybe a couple of inches shorter than him, with soft brown eyes and light brown hair. And, like Eric, she was dressed in a pair of corduroys, a turtleneck, and a tweed jacket.

"Nice outfit," said Eric, smiling at her.

She looked at Eric and smiled back at him.

"I hope I didn't spill any wine on you."

"Nah, I'm fine. Besides, it's just white wine. No one will notice."

"You want something to drink?" asked the bartender. Eric hadn't realized it was his turn already.

"Sorry," he said.

He asked for a beer, which the bartender handed him, then stepped aside.

The woman in the matching outfit had waited for him.

"Are you here with a friend?" he asked her. "I don't think I've seen you around."

"Nope, I'm a student. I just tend to spend most of my time in the library."

Eric nodded.

"I'm Eric, by the way."

"Caroline," said the young woman. "But everyone calls me Caro, which is kind of funny, considering."

Eric looked confused.

"Caro," she said. "As in Robert Caro, the author?"

Eric still looked confused.

"Because I'm studying American history."

"Oh," said Eric. "I get it now. Robert Caro. Got it."

He felt like an idiot.

"So, you're studying American history."

Caro nodded.

"I am. I've had a passion for it since I can remember. My grandmother is a DAR. That's Daughter of the American Revolution. And my family goes way back. So, what are you studying?"

"British history," Eric replied. "I hope that doesn't make us enemies."

He smiled at her, and she smiled back.

"Last I checked, England and America were on good terms," said Caro.

"The special relationship," said Eric.

They stood there, sipping their drinks, smiling stupidly at each other, when Rob came over.

"Hey, I was starting to think you got lost or something," he said to Eric.

He glanced over at Caro.

"Caroline," he said, frostily.

"Robert," said Caro.

Eric looked from one to the other.

"You two know each other?"

"In a manner of speaking," said Caro. "What's the matter, Rob? No frosh to bone?"

"I thought I'd take the night off," said Rob. "Let them recover."

Again Eric looked from one to the other.

"Sorry, am I interrupting something?"

"No, Rob was just leaving," said Caro. "Weren't you, Robert?"

"Can't we be adults, Caroline? We're both in the same department, after all."

"Maybe you should have thought about that before you screwed Amanda."

Eric looked from Caro to Rob. It felt a bit like watching a tennis match.

"Have fun with the Ice Queen," said Rob, patting Eric's shoulder. "I'll be over there if you need me."

He watched as Rob went to talk with some other grad students.

"So, um, you and Rob…" began Eric.

"We went out at the beginning of the year," said Caro, stealing a glance at Rob.

"Was it serious?"

He had no idea Rob had been seeing someone, at least seriously.

"Apparently not to Rob."

"Sorry," said Eric, watching as Rob chatted up a pretty brunette.

"It's not your fault," said Caro, turning back to look at him.

Again there was an awkward silence.

"Well, I should go speak with my professor," said Caro. "It was nice meeting you, Eric."

"Same," he said.

He watched her make her way across the room, wishing he was better at making cocktail conversation.

CHAPTER 33

After spending all day Saturday inside, working on his novel, Allen was looking forward to getting out and seeing a movie with Hannah. It was raining when he woke up, and he thought about blowing off his run. Instead, he dragged himself to the gym. When he got back, he found a message waiting for him from Carly. She had made a short video of herself playing her guitar and had pasted the link.

"Check out my new video!" she wrote. "Miss you!"

Allen clicked on the link.

Carly was sitting on her bed in her room, surrounded by stuffed animals, her guitar on her lap. She introduced the song, then began to play.

He watched the video a couple of times, then closed the app.

"I like the song!" he wrote her back. "Did you just write it?" He thought about what else to say. "You'll be happy to know I spent all day yesterday working on my novel. It still needs a lot of work, but it felt good to write something for me again."

He stared at his phone. He didn't want to mention that he was going to see a movie with Hannah, so he just typed "Miss you." Then he went to take a shower.

As he stood under the water, his eyes closed, he thought about Carly and their goodbye kiss. He hadn't wanted to stop kissing her and had been disappointed when she said she wanted to walk home by herself.

Then he thought about Hannah. Which made him think about food. His stomach rumbled in response.

He dried himself off, then went to his room and glanced at Natalie's chart. Though did he really need to dress up to go see a movie? After all, he'd be sitting in the dark.

He opened his drawers and pulled out a pair of jeans, a turtleneck, and a sweater.

As he was checking himself out in the full-length mirror, wondering if he should change, there was a knock on the door.

"May I come in?" called his mother.

"Door's open," Allen called back.

His mother poked her head in.

"You can come in," said Allen.

She entered the room and looked him over.

"You look nice."

"You always say that."

"Because it's true."

Allen took another look at himself in the mirror, his lips pulling to one side.

"Can't decide what to wear?"

Allen nodded.

"Another date?"

Again Allen nodded.

"We're going to see *A Star Is Born*, then grabbing a bite to eat afterward."

"Let me know how you like it." She got a faraway look in her eyes. "I remember when Bradley Cooper was in *Alias*. Now he's a big star."

Allen looked confused.

"*Alias* was a TV show starring Jennifer Garner. Before your time."

"Ah."

"So who's the girl?"

"Her name's Hannah."

"Is she the one Jonathan told me about, who you invited over for Thanksgiving?"

Allen nodded again.

"What does she do?"

"She's a food stylist, and she also tests recipes."

"I like her already. And she's not going home for Thanksgiving?"

"Her mom's a caterer and is working that day, and Hannah said she'd rather stay here and help out at a food pantry."

"Very admirable."

"Yeah," said Allen.

"Well, have fun," said his mother. "And by all means, have Hannah join us for Thanksgiving."

Allen had liked the movie, but he didn't love it. And he suspected that Hannah felt the same way. They were now seated at a pizzeria close to the theater.

"So, what did you think?" he asked her.

"I thought Bradley Cooper was great, but…"

"But…"

"But I didn't love the movie. I mean, it was okay. I didn't hate it, but… I prefer the older version."

"You mean the one with Barbra Streisand and Kris Kristofferson?"

"No, the one with Judy Garland and James Mason."

"I've never seen that one," said Allen.

"You should watch it," said Hannah. "It's classic. So what did you think of the movie?"

"I felt the same way as you. Didn't love it. Didn't hate it."

They continued to eat their pizza.

"So I meant to ask you the other day, where are you from? I know you said your mom was a caterer and you weren't going home for Thanksgiving."

"Guess," she said, taking another bite of pizza.

"Hmm," said Allen, studying her.

"Well, you don't have an accent, at least one I can detect." Hannah took a sip of her beer.

"And as you said you're not going home for Thanksgiving, that probably means you're not from New York or nearby."

Hannah tilted her head.

"Ohio?" guessed Allen.

"Eh!" said Hannah, making a buzzer sound.

"Well, you don't have a New England or a Southern accent."

"I could be hiding it. And not everyone from New England or the South has an accent."

"True," said Allen, carefully listening to her. "California?"

"Eh!" said Hannah, making the buzzer noise again.

"Washington?"

"Eh!"

"Illinois?"

"Eh!" said Hannah, clearly enjoying herself.

"Just tell me," said Allen. "Please."

"Oh, all right," she said. "I'm from Philly. Just outside. And before you ask, I went to Johnson and Wales in Providence, to study culinary arts and nutrition, and got an internship with the Food Network afterward. They liked me, so they kept me on. Then I decided to go freelance. Does that answer your questions?"

Allen smiled.

"Thank you."

"You're welcome," said Hannah, smiling back at him.

"And where's your brother?"

"Still in Philly."

"And your mom's catering company is in Philly?"

Hannah nodded and took another bite of pizza.

"Any other questions?" she asked when she was done.

"Not right now," said Allen.

They got a box for the remaining pizza and their server asked them if they'd like some dessert.

"What do you have?" asked Hannah.

"We have tiramisu, cannoli, tartufo, and biscotti."

"Do you make them here?"

"We do."

Hannah looked thoughtful.

"Allen?" she said, turning her eyes on him.

"Hmm?" he said. He had been spacing out.

"Do you have a preference?"

"They all sound good. Which one do you want?"

Hannah looked up at their server.

"Which one do you recommend?"

"They're all very good," she said. "But the tiramisu is my favorite."

"Okay, one tiramisu," said Hannah. "Two forks."

The woman nodded.

"Would either of you like some coffee?"

"I'm good," said Hannah.

Allen thought about ordering a cappuccino or an espresso but decided against it. He wanted to get a good night's sleep.

"Nothing for me, thanks."

"Be right back with your tiramisu," said the server, then she headed off to the kitchen.

Allen looked down at the now empty plate. Despite the size of the tiramisu, which had been enormous, they had eaten every last bite.

"I need to make tiramisu," said Hannah.

"But you just had tiramisu."

"I know, which is I want to make it."

Allen looked confused.

"Occupational hazard," she explained. "When I eat something I like, I want to see if I can make it myself, put my own spin on it."

"Of course," said Allen.

"Can I get you anything else?" asked their server. "Maybe a little limoncello?"

Hannah shook her head.

"Just the check, please," said Allen.

The server placed their check on the table. Hannah reached for her bag, but Allen stopped her.

"I got this," he said.

"You got it the last time. I should pay."

"It's okay. I don't mind." Especially as Hipster would be reimbursing him.

Hannah didn't look convinced.

"Please, allow me."

"All right," said Hannah, squinting at him. "Hipster must pay better than I thought."

If only she knew. But Allen kept his mouth shut.

He paid and they went outside.

The temperature had dropped, and it had become rather chilly.

"Well, thanks for dinner," said Hannah. "And the movie."

"My pleasure," said Allen.

Hannah hesitated.

"I guess I should be heading off. Big day tomorrow."

"You styling some food?"

"I am. I've got an all-day shoot, and I'm responsible for making the food, too."

"Doesn't seem fair right before Thanksgiving."

"Hey, gotta take the work when you can get it. And I don't mind. Pays the bills."

"Speaking of Thanksgiving," said Allen. "I told my mom about you, and she'd love to have you join us for Thanksgiving."

"Aw, that's really sweet of you, Allen. But I'm probably going to be too tired to have a big meal."

"Well, you're welcome to join us if you change your mind. Just shoot me a text."

Hannah smiled.

"I'll do that. But I really don't mind spending Thanksgiving evening alone, especially after working all day."

"Okay," said Allen. Though he was slightly disappointed she wouldn't be joining him.

They stood there for another minute.

"Well, goodnight," said Hannah.

"Goodnight," said Allen.

He leaned down and gave her a quick kiss on the cheek.

CHAPTER 34

On the subway ride home, Allen thought about Hannah. He'd had a good time, but it had felt more like hanging out with one of his friends than a date. Not that that was a bad thing. But he didn't get the same feelings around Hannah as he did when he was with Carly. He leaned his head back and closed his eyes.

He unlocked the door to his apartment and saw that the lights were on. Which meant that his parents were home. Sure enough, his mother appeared less than a minute after he walked in.

"How was the date?" she asked. "You have fun? Was Bradley Cooper good?"

"Bradley Cooper was very good. The date was okay."

"Just okay?" said his mother.

"It was fine. It's just…"

His mother waited.

Allen sighed.

"I really like Hannah, but…"

"No spark?"

If she only knew how ironic that statement was.

Allen shook his head.

"Give it time. Some of the best relationships begin as friendships."

"I know," said Allen. "It's just that you and dad met right after you got out of college, and you knew he was the one."

His mother smiled wistfully.

"I did, but we didn't get married right away. As a matter of fact, we broke up."

"You did?" said Allen.

This was news to him.

His mother nodded.

"I was at Teachers College, at Columbia, and I wasn't ready to get married. Your father said, 'Why delay when you know it's right?' And I said, 'Because if it's right, it'll still be right in another year.' And he got angry, and we broke up. Though we got back together a couple of months later. I'll never forget when he called me."

She smiled at the memory.

"What did he say?" Allen didn't remember hearing this story before.

"That he was sorry for pressuring me, and that he would wait."

Allen thought he saw tears forming in his mother's eyes. She sniffed and continued.

"We got married just over a year later."

"You have any regrets?"

"None. I was lucky. Your father was a good man. And so is Jonathan. We should all be so lucky to find true love twice."

Allen was hoping to find it once. He had thought what he had had with Sophie was love, but he realized it had just been infatuation.

"By the way, I don't think Hannah will be joining us for Thanksgiving."

"Did you tell her she was welcome?"

"I did, but she said she would probably be too tired to come over."

"Well, another time."

She looked at Allen and gently laid a hand on his cheek.

"I'm off to read in bed. Have a good night. And don't stay up too late."

He smiled at her. She still thought of him as her little boy, but tonight he didn't mind.

"Goodnight, Mom," he said. Then they headed off to their rooms.

Allen was taking a break from his article on Cyber Monday deals to check his messages when he saw he had an email from Blind Date. Edna had written to him.

"Hey, I saw *A Star Is Born* this weekend," Edna wrote. "Good film, though I didn't love it. It was kind of depressing. Did you wind up seeing it? If so, let me know what you thought.

"I have kind of a busy few days, Thanksgiving week and all. I'm probably not going to go home until early Thursday. (One advantage of living not too far away.)

"What are you doing for Turkey Day?"

She then closed with a joke.

Allen stared at Edna's message. Could she have gone to see the movie the same time he had at the same theater? Though the chances of that were slim. Still, it seemed as though their paths kept crossing.

As he was lost in thought, his phone began vibrating. It was a message from Eric, asking him and Molly if they were going to do their annual pre-Thanksgiving get-together.

Allen had completely forgotten about it. Every year, when they were in college, the three of them would get together for dinner before they went home for Thanksgiving. Not that any of them were going that far. But with their various family commitments over the four-day weekend, they wouldn't see each other. And the gathering was a good way to blow off a little steam before heading home.

"I'm in!" wrote Molly.

"I'm in, too," Allen replied. "When and where?"

"Tomorrow?" wrote Eric. "Though I could probably do Wednesday, too."

Allen waited for Molly to chime in.

"Wednesday's better for me," she wrote.

She had made plans to see Finn on Tuesday before he headed back to Massachusetts.

"I can do Wednesday," texted Allen.

"Great!" wrote Eric. "It's a date. What time and where?"

After a bit of back and forth, they had decided to meet up at one of their favorite student haunts in the Village at six that Wednesday.

Molly smiled as Allen and Eric walked into the restaurant. Something about her looked different, Allen thought.

She went over to them and gave them each a hug.

"I feel like I haven't seen you guys in ages, though I know it's only been a couple of weeks."

"You look different," said Eric, eyeing her. "Did you do something to your hair?"

Molly grinned. She was wearing it down, instead of in her usual ponytail.

"I'm surprised you even noticed."

"Something else looks different," said Allen, checking her out. Was she wearing makeup? And he could have sworn her breasts look bigger. Not that he had ever really looked at them. Though as he did he could feel himself blushing.

"Let's go sit," said Molly. "I could use a drink."

She ushered them over to the host stand and told him they were all there.

They ordered drinks once they were seated, then began talking all at once.

"Whoa!" said Molly. "Eric, why don't you go first, then Allen, then me."

Eric told them about school and what he'd be doing over Thanksgiving.

"It's going to be pretty quiet this year," he said. "Just my folks, me, and Emily. So you're welcome to come over if you need a place to detox."

"Thanks," said Molly. "I'd love to. But I'll be in Jersey, listening to my sisters go on about married life and the wedding."

She rolled her eyes.

"When is Fiona getting married again?" asked Allen.

"In May. So I've got another six months of listening to her drone on."

"I'm glad Emily didn't marry that idiot Bruce," said Eric.

"Was she engaged?" asked Molly.

"We're not sure. I'm just glad they broke up." He turned to Allen. "Be glad you don't have a sister."

Molly nodded.

"You say that, but I always wished I had a sibling growing up. Though you and Emily were the next best thing," he added, looking at Eric.

"Aw," said Molly. "Okay, your turn, Allen. Tell us what's going on in the exciting world of Hipster."

"If it's okay with you guys, I'd rather not discuss work. Unless you want to hear me recite my latest Top Ten list."

Molly and Eric shook their heads and Allen chuckled. Then he took a breath.

"I started working on my novel again."

"That's wonderful!" said Molly.

Eric nodded.

"It was painful to read through what I had written. But I'm glad I did. And I wrote a couple more chapters. This time, I'm not stopping until it's finished."

"That's the spirit!" said Molly, who was still hoping to write her own novel.

"You give yourself a deadline?" asked Eric.

Allen nodded.

"I want to have a first draft done by the end of the year."

"Whoa," said Molly. "That's not that far away. Give yourself some time."

"I did that the last time and look what happened. No, this time, it's full speed ahead. Even if it sucks, I just need to finish it. I can always go back and edit it."

"Well, I, for one, admire you," said Eric. "I know it's not easy. I don't how I'm going to write my thesis when it's time. It'll probably take me a year."

"If you like, I can show your manuscript to Constance. When you're ready, of course."

"I appreciate the offer," said Allen. "Though actually…" He looked down at the table, then back up at his friends. "I already found someone who said she'd take a look at it when I'm ready."

Molly raised her eyebrows.

"Is she in publishing?"

Allen nodded.

"I don't want to say anymore. Don't want to jinx it."

"Well, if your new connection falls through, hit me up," said Molly. "I know Constance is looking for books that appeal to Millennial guys and Gen Zers."

"Thanks," said Allen.

"So what are you doing for Turkey Day?" Molly asked him. "The usual? Having dinner with the fam?"

Allen nodded.

"Leighton and his fake fiancée, Tiffany, arrived last night. They're staying with us through Friday. Apparently Mommy Dearest doesn't approve of people sleeping together, at least in her house, before they're lawfully wed."

"How old-fashioned of her," said Eric.

"My folks won't let any of us sleep in the same room with a guy unless we're married," said Molly.

"That's because you're good Irish Catholics," said Eric.

Molly made a face.

"So is Leighton still an ass?" asked Eric.

Allen nodded.

"I'd love to meet him," said Molly.

"Why?" said Allen and Eric.

"Just curious to see if he's as bad as you both make him out to be."

"Trust me," said Eric. "He's worse. He and Liam used to bully all the younger kids at school. I still don't understand how Emily could have gone out with him."

He shook his head.

"Your sister went out with Allen's brother?"

"Stepbrother," said Allen.

Molly was still looking at Eric.

"Leighton was the captain of the football team, and Emily was the captain of the volleyball team. It was a match made in jock heaven."

"Huh," said Molly. "How long did they go out for?"

"Leighton broke it off at the end of senior year, right after the senior dance. Emily was devastated."

"He sounds like a real charmer," said Molly.

"Oh yeah. Of course, senior year she began dating someone else. I'll say this for my sis, she doesn't stay single for long."

"Nice for her," said Molly.

"So, tell us what's going on with you," said Eric.

"Well," said Molly, smiling. "I think I may have met someone!"

Both men stared at her.

"I don't want to jinx it," she said. "So I'm not going to say anymore, but…"

She was clearly excited. Maybe that's what was different about her thought Eric and Allen. Molly was in love.

"That's great, Molly," said Eric, though he didn't feel so great as he said it.

"Yeah," said Allen, who was trying to ignore an odd feeling in his stomach.

The server deposited their drinks on the table.

They raised their glasses.

"To friendship," said Eric.

"To friendship," said Allen and Molly.

"And to surviving Thanksgiving," added Molly.

"I'll drink to that!" said Allen.

They clinked glasses and drank.

By the time they had finished their meal (and a second round of drinks) nearly two hours later, they were all in a good mood. They paid the check, then made their way outside.

"We should do this again before Christmas," said Molly.

"I'm in," said Eric.

"Me, too," said Allen.

They remained standing outside the restaurant.

"Well, goodnight," said Molly.

"Goodnight," said Eric.

He headed west as Molly and Allen headed east.

"You headed back to your place?" asked Allen.

Molly nodded.

"Taking the subway?"

"I was planning on it."

"Shall we ride uptown together?"

"Sure, why not?"

They made their way over.

"You look happy," said Allen.

"That's because I am happy. I'm always happy to see you guys."

"That's not what I meant. You look different. There's a kind of glow about you."

He felt stupid as soon as he said it. But it was too late to take it back.

Molly turned and looked at him.

"Are you okay?"

"I'm fine. Why?"

"You never give me compliments."

"Sure, I do."

Molly shook her head.

"No, you don't."

Allen felt funny inside.

"Really, I never told you that you looked nice?"

"Maybe once or twice," said Molly. "But I always figured you just said it to be nice."

Allen stopped and looked at Molly. The moon was full, and he could swear Molly's face was aglow. Even her copper-red hair seemed to be shining. She looked up at him, her moss-green eyes searching his. And suddenly, he desperately wanted to kiss her. He started to lower his head, but Molly, sensing what he was about to do, turned and began walking.

"Come on," she said. "It's cold out. And I need to get up early tomorrow."

He nodded and followed her, his cheeks now pink.

They waited for the subway, neither saying anything, and silently boarded the train when it arrived.

It was only when she got off that Molly finally exhaled. She had sensed that Allen had been about to kiss her. And while a part of her had wanted him to, she remembered the other times he had kissed her, and the disappointment that had followed. Also, she was seeing Finn now, and it wouldn't be right.

But as she got undressed, she couldn't stop thinking about Allen and what might have been.

CHAPTER 35

Allen survived Thanksgiving dinner. Barely. He didn't understand how someone as self-effacing as his stepfather could raise two such self-absorbed human beings. Liam went on and on about his job working for one of the biggest sports management agencies and the various professional athletes he met and considered his friends. Allen worried he'd suffer eye strain from rolling his eyes so much.

And Leighton and his fiancée hadn't been much better, going on and on about their upcoming nuptials, to be held at one of New York's top hotels, with the best caterer, the hottest florist, the most in-demand DJ. Blah, blah, blah.

Allen made a vow that if he ever got engaged, he'd have a small wedding and wouldn't talk about it with anyone.

As Leighton and Tiffany continued to babble, now discussing their honeymoon on Maui, Allen wondered if this was how Molly felt when she got together with her sisters. He excused himself to go to the bathroom and surreptitiously texted her, apologizing for not being more sympathetic. He waited to see if she would reply, but his phone remained silent. No doubt she was being bombarded with wedding planning talk, too.

Allen returned to the table and asked to be excused from joining them for dessert, hoping to escape to Eric's. But his mother insisted he stay and eat pumpkin and apple pie with them. So he begrudgingly stayed, texting Eric that he was being held captive by a bunch of boring barbarians. Eric had replied with a laughing, tear-streaked emoji.

Fortunately, Leighton and his odious fiancée left the next day. Liam too. And Allen felt himself slowly begin to relax. Hannah had asked him if he wanted to come over to taste some more recipes and watch Netflix Saturday. And he would be getting together with Carly that Sunday.

He had also exchanged a couple of quick messages with Edna, whose Thanksgiving sounded similar to his own.

Soon it would be four weeks since they had begun corresponding, and they would be able to finally meet. Allen was surprised and pleased that they had made it this long. And they had both written that they looked forward to finally meeting.

Allen still had no idea what Edna looked like, but he felt as though he knew her. Which was the point of Blind Date, he realized, to get to know people without judging them just by their looks. Though he wondered how he'd feel about Edna once he met her. What if he didn't find her attractive, or she him? He swallowed as he thought about it, then put the thought out of his head.

Allen woke up Saturday morning in a good mood. He checked the forecast and decided to go for a run. When he got back, he found a text waiting for him from Hannah.

"Just checking to make sure we're still on," she had written. "Does 12 still work?"

Allen looked at his phone. It was nearly ten.

"Twelve is fine," he wrote. "Can I bring anything?"

"Just your appetite," she replied. "I think I went a little overboard. Though you'll be happy to know, no turkey. :-)"

"Phew!" wrote Allen. "If I ate any more turkey, I think I'd turn into one, or fall into a coma. I'll see you at noon."

Despite what Hannah had written, Allen felt weird about arriving empty-handed, so he picked up some flowers on his way over.

"Oh, thank you," Hannah said, upon being presented with the bouquet.

She invited him in. Allen sniffed. The place smelled of tomatoes, or rather tomato sauce, as though he had stepped into a trattoria, like the ones he had visited in Italy.

He sniffed again.

"Hope you like Italian food," said Hannah, smiling over at him. "Just before Thanksgiving, I got a panicked email from a cookbook editor I've worked with, asking if I could test a few dishes this weekend."

"It smells great," said Allen, following her to the kitchen.

"I made a Caprese salad, a vegetable lasagna, and pesto garlic bread."

She pulled the lasagna and pesto garlic bread out of the oven. The lasagna was bubbling, and Allen could practically taste the cheese and the tomato sauce, as well as the garlic from the bread. He hadn't eaten anything that morning, and the sight of all the food made his stomach growl.

"Just give me a sec, and we'll dig in."

Allen nodded, staring at all the food.

"Oh, and save some room for dessert. I made a ricotta cheesecake."

Allen looked at Hannah. She couldn't have weighed more than 110 pounds.

"How do you eat all this food and not get fat?"

Hannah laughed.

"I rarely eat what I make anymore. I learned that lesson the hard way. Now I just have a bite or two. Fortunately, I've found there's no shortage of people in New York happy to eat whatever I make. Here," she said, taking some of the Caprese salad and putting it on a plate. "Let's start with this. I found fresh mozzarella at a little stall at the Union Square farmers market, along with some fresh tomatoes. Thank goodness for greenhouses."

"This is amazing," said Allen, practically inhaling the Caprese salad. "You can really taste the cheese and the tomato and basil. And are these figs?" he asked, holding one up.

Hannah nodded.

"They are. They add just the right touch of sweetness, to balance the balsamic vinegar."

Allen polished off the rest of his salad.

"You're welcome to have some more," said Hannah. "Just save room for the lasagna and the garlic pesto bread—and the cheesecake!"

When they were done sampling all the food Hannah made, and Allen swore he couldn't eat another bite, Hannah made him a doggy bag.

"My mom is going to love this," said Allen. "You'll have to let me know when the cookbook is out."

Hannah smiled.

"I will. So, you want to watch something on Netflix? I've also got Hulu and Amazon Prime."

"You pick," said Allen.

Hannah looked at him, as though trying to figure out what he might enjoy watching.

"Have you seen *The Marvelous Mrs. Maisel?* Everyone says I should check it out."

"My mom's totally into *Mrs. Maisel*," said Allen. "Though I haven't watched it. But I'm fine checking it out."

"You sure?" asked Hannah.

"Positive," said Allen.

He smiled at Hannah, and she picked up the remote.

Two episodes later, Allen said he should shove off.

He had liked the show, but he was feeling restless. Rarely did he watch more than a couple of hours of TV at a time.

"Thanks for coming over," said Hannah.

She went into the kitchen and retrieved Allen's doggy bag.

"Don't worry about returning the containers. I've got plenty more."

"I should be thanking *you*," said Allen. "Everything was great."

Hannah smiled.

"Well, goodbye," said Allen, as he reached the front door.

Hannah was standing just in front of him. He looked down at her, then bent down and gave her a kiss on the cheek. Was it his imagination or did Hannah look disappointed?

"Attention everyone!"

Justin was standing in the middle of the floor, having called everyone together for an impromptu meeting.

"The Hipster New Year's Eve Bash is just over a month away, and I have very exciting news! I am happy to announce that Parquet Courts and King Princess, two of the hottest indie bands around, will be playing at our little affair."

There was lots of excited chatter.

"Did you hear that, dude?" said Dave, nudging Allen. "J.J.

got Parquet Courts! How cool is that?"

"Hmm?" said Allen. He had not been paying attention.

"The J-Man got Parquet Courts *and* King Princess for the New Year's Eve party!" said Dave.

"Really?" said Allen. "Wow."

Dave nodded.

"I wonder if I'll be able to get an autograph."

"And you know what happens right after the Bash," Justin continued. "The 'New Year, New You' edition of Hipster comes out. So I expect all of you to be working hard on your articles. I want to start 2019 with a bang!"

Everyone waited to see if Justin had more to say.

"That's it, everyone," he concluded. "Now get back to work!"

The staff slowly dispersed, with people chattering among themselves.

Allen went back to his desk and sat in front of his computer. He had been typing notes about his two dates that weekend before Justin had called everyone over. And he had been feeling guilty. It felt like he was exploiting Hannah and Carly to further his own career. Though he knew deep down that wasn't the case.

Carly.

He could feel his face growing warm and his pants getting tighter just thinking about her. They had gone back to her place on Sunday and had fooled around. He could still feel her tongue as it had slid from his ear to his neck to his mouth and then down his chest to his…

She had wanted him to spend the night, but he had left (hard as that was), explaining that he had to be at work the next morning. He also didn't want his mother asking him a lot of nosy questions, asking him where he had been. Though he didn't say that to Carly.

After their evening together, he had decided he would ask

Carly to the Hipster New Year's Eve Bash. Of the three women, he thought she would enjoy it the most and was the one most likely to impress Justin. Not that he cared about impressing Justin. But if Justin liked Carly, maybe he'd help her with her career. (He had mentioned Carly to Celine before Thanksgiving, but Celine hadn't seemed particularly interested.)

Allen had also decided that he and Hannah were destined to be just friends. He had no idea how Hannah felt and was nervous about saying anything. But he knew he should say something to her in case she had different expectations.

Then there was Edna. He had been feeling a mix of excitement and dread at the thought of meeting her. He had thought about waiting to see how their date went before inviting Carly to the New Year's Eve Bash. But after last night, he had decided not to.

He continued to type absentmindedly.

Towards the end of the day, he checked his phone for messages. There was a text from an L.A. area code. The only person he knew in L.A. was Sophie. But he hadn't heard from her in months. He thought about deleting the text, but his curiosity got the better of him, so he opened it and nearly fell off his chair.

"Hey, you," read the text. "It's Eric's annoying older sister Emily. Remember me? I was just scrolling through Hipster and saw your byline. How are you?"

Allen stared at his phone, then he continued to read.

"I had to bribe Eric for your number, btw," Emily continued. "Anyway, I'm back in NYC and was wondering if you wanted to have a drink & catch up."

Allen could feel his heart pounding against his chest. He didn't know how to respond. He checked the time stamp. Emily had texted him two hours ago.

"Hey," he finally typed. "Thanks for the text."

He paused, not knowing what to say. Had Eric mentioned

him over Thanksgiving? He looked at his phone again.

"Would be happy to meet," he continued. "What were you thinking?"

He hit "send" and waited, wondering if he should have just deleted the messages. Eric would probably kill him if he had a drink with his sister. Though they were both adults.

"Hey," Emily replied a minute later. "I was beginning to wonder if Eric gave me the right number. So by any chance are you free tonight? I know it's last minute, but…"

Allen suddenly felt hot. Did he have plans that evening? He couldn't remember. If he did, he'd cancel them.

He took a few deep breaths then responded.

"I think I can make it. Where do you want to meet?"

"How's 7 @ Balthazar? It's right by my office."

That was just a couple of hours from now. Again, Allen could feel his heart beating against his chest.

"That's fine," he wrote.

"Great!" Emily replied. "See you at 7."

Allen continued to stare at his phone. Then he looked down. His attire was definitely not date-ready. He stopped himself. Was this a date? He shook his head. He was just meeting an old friend. Granted, an old friend he used to lust after.

He looked at his computer. If he left now, he could get home and change before he had to be at Balthazar.

He saved the document he was working on and shut down his computer. Then he grabbed his bag and left.

CHAPTER 36

Allen arrived at Balthazar at a minute after seven. The place was packed, even though it was a Monday. He looked around, hoping to spy Emily. But while he saw lots of attractive blondes, he didn't see her. At least he didn't think so. It had been years since he had last seen her. Not that she would have changed that much between then and now. But you never knew. L.A. did things to people.

He stood over by the bar, positioning himself so he could see the door. A few minutes later, an attractive woman dressed in a blue wool coat, with flowing blonde hair and a slight tan, came through the door. He immediately recognized her. It was FlirtyFashionista, the woman who had blown him off. He continued to stare.

The woman turned and looked at him, then smiled.

"Allen?" she said.

And then Allen knew. FlirtyFashionista and Emily were one and the same.

Various emotions warred inside him. Was Emily just playing with him? Was this some game?

"Are you okay?" she asked, a frown forming on her pretty face.

"I'm fine," he said, coldly.

Emily tilted her head.

"You don't seem fine."

Allen decided to not beat around the bush. He had to know.

"You're FlirtyFashionista."

Emily studied him.

"So it was you," she said. "I wondered. I even asked Eric, but he said you hated online dating."

"So were you just messing with me?"

"No," said Emily. "I legitimately liked your profile."

"Then why did you blow me off?"

Allen was unable to hide the hurt in his voice.

"I didn't mean to. Come, let's get a table and have a drink, and I'll explain."

She reached for his arm, but Allen shrugged it off.

"Do you want me to go?" she asked him.

Allen looked at her, and all the old longing came rushing back.

"No," he said.

"Then come on."

She led him over to the hostess stand and asked for a table for two.

"You look good, by the way," said Emily, after they had ordered drinks. "I almost didn't recognize you."

Allen wasn't sure if that was meant to be a compliment.

"You look good, too. L.A. clearly agrees with you."

"Thanks," she replied. "Though I've had my fill of L.A." She studied Allen's face and what he was wearing. "So, you work for Hipster."

Allen nodded.

"You know, I would've never pegged you as the Hipster type."

"Oh?" said Allen, mildly irritated (though it hadn't bothered him before when people made the comment). "And what's that?"

Emily waved her hand.

"You know." A smile crept over her face. "Fun little fact, I once went on a date with your boss."

"You dated J.J.?"

Emily nodded.

"We only went out a couple of times. Though I'm surprised Eric didn't mention it. Then again, it may have slipped his mind. It was several years ago, when I was interning at Calvin Klein over the summer, just before my senior year at USC."

Allen wasn't sure if he wanted to hear about it, but he remained silent.

"He was over at Calvin, Justin, that is, trying to get them to buy ad space. Hipster had just started up. He saw me and asked Bo, he was my boss, to make an introduction. I had no idea who Justin was. But he invited me to some party Hipster was sponsoring. I barely saw him, but afterward he asked me out for dinner."

Emily's tale was interrupted by the server delivering their drinks.

They each took a sip.

"Now where was I? Oh, yes. Dinner. So Justin invites me out to dinner and takes me to this very fancy restaurant. I think it was Per Se? It was all so over-the-top. He was clearly trying to impress me, but I was totally not interested."

She took another sip of her drink.

"He asked me out again, and I stupidly agreed. I think I was hoping he might hire me after I graduated. But I finally had to tell him I wasn't interested in him that way."

"How did he take it?"

"Pretty well, actually."

"So why weren't you interested?"

This was the first time Allen heard of a woman not being interested in Justin.

"He just wasn't my type."

"And what is that?"

Emily leaned forward and smiled at him, and Allen could feel his heart pounding.

"The tall, dark, and handsome type."

Allen swallowed and took a large sip of his drink.

They had nearly finished their drinks when Emily announced she was hungry.

"Shall we get some food and another round?"

Allen nodded. It was like she was a spider, and he was trapped in her web. Not that he wanted to be free.

She signaled to their server, who immediately came over.

"Two menus, please."

While they ate and drank, Emily told Allen about her life in L.A. and her new job, working for a Milan-based fashion company. And Allen told her about his novel and what it was like working for Hipster. Then Allen got up the nerve to ask her why she had blown him off.

Emily sighed.

"I didn't lie to you," she said. "I really was out of town and then busy. Work has been nuts."

"But why reach out to me in the first place and then ask for a raincheck when you knew you were busy?"

He hated to sound whiny, but he needed to know.

"I had just broken up with Bruce and moved back to the city. I guess I was lonely. And a friend suggested I go on Spark. I saw your profile and thought you were cute. It didn't occur to me you were you until later. And then I saw you had deactivated your profile. So, did you find someone?"

Allen nodded.

"Is she nice?"

The question took him aback. Was Carly nice? She was certainly attractive. And talented. And a good kisser. But was she nice?

Emily was looking at him.

"Do yourself a favor, Allen. Before you get serious about someone, make sure they're nice, that they treat you well. That they listen to you. Take it from me, I learned from experience. Great sex and a pretty face alone don't make for a great relationship."

Emily signaled to their server and asked for a check.

"No coffee or dessert?" he asked them.

Emily shook her head.

"Just the check."

She turned to Allen.

"I have a busy day tomorrow. I'm flying to Milan later this week."

The server returned with the check and Allen immediately reached for his wallet. But Emily stopped him.

"My treat," she said.

Allen opened his mouth to protest, but Emily had already handed the server her credit card.

They stood outside the restaurant. There was a strong wind blowing, and Emily's hair was whipping around her.

"Thanks for meeting me," she said.

"No problem," said Allen, his hands in his pockets. He felt as though he was sixteen again.

She took a few steps closer, until she was standing right in front of him. Then she tilted her head slightly and kissed him, gently prying his lips apart.

Before Allen knew it, he was kissing her back.

The kiss seemed to go on forever. How many times had he dreamed of this moment? But now Emily was gently pushing him away, smiling as she did so.

"Had I known you were such a good kisser, I would have done that years ago."

Allen felt himself blushing.

"Well, as much as I'd like to continue our… conversation,

I really do need to be going," she said. "I'll give you a shout when I'm back from Milan."

"When do you get back?"

"In a couple of weeks."

There was a cab dropping off a passenger in front of the restaurant and she hailed it. Before she got in, she gave Allen a quick kiss on the lips.

"*Arrivederci!*" she said, before pulling the door closed.

That night, Allen found it impossible to sleep. He kept thinking about Emily, imagining getting into the cab with her and making out with her in the backseat. He felt himself getting hard and groaned.

When he got up the next morning, he checked his phone, but there was no message from her. He desperately wanted to see her again and thought about texting her. But he stopped himself. He didn't want to seem needy. Instead, he threw on his running clothes and headed to Central Park. When he got home, he took a cold shower.

There was still no message from her by the time he got to the office, so he finally decided to send her one.

"Thanks for dinner," he wrote. "Have fun in Milan. Let me know when you're back."

He felt a small twinge of guilt after he sent it. But it was too late now.

Wednesday evening he went to Pianos to hear Carly. Both of her roommates, as well as Ham and Gil, were already there when he arrived. He wished, not for the first time, that they weren't, but he knew he was being childish.

They greeted Allen politely and made room for him at the table. He ordered a drink, and a few minutes later, Carly went on.

The place was more crowded than last time, and there was lots of applauding and whooping when Carly was done.

Someone shouted "More!" which was joined by several other people calling for her to keep singing, and Carly obliged.

"So any of you from Chicagoland?" she asked the audience.

There was some more whooping.

Carly smiled.

"I was just back there over Thanksgiving, and I wrote this song about it. I hope you like it."

She strummed her guitar and began to sing.

Allen listened as Carly sang. It was the song she had sung to him in the video. He closed his eyes to better hear her. She had a beautiful voice, strong yet soft. He would have to talk to Celine again.

When she was done, he opened his eyes. She was glowing, her hair a blonde halo. Though he knew it was probably just the lighting.

She sang one more song, then wished everyone a good night. A few minutes later, she joined the group at their table.

Allen got up and offered her his seat, grabbing another from a nearby table.

"You were amazing tonight," said Ham. "Love the new song."

Gil nodded.

"What did you think, Allen?"

"You were incredible," he said, and he meant it.

Carly beamed.

And for the first time in days, he realized he wasn't thinking about Emily.

CHAPTER 37

Allen didn't stay for the second set. He was tired and wanted to go home.

Carly had been disappointed but said she understood.

She walked him to the exit, pulling him into a dark alcove before they got there.

"Did you really think I was good?"

"You were better than good," said Allen, breathing in her perfume, or maybe it was her shampoo? (Whatever it was, it smelled amazing.) "You were incredible, mesmerizing, breath—"

Before he could finish, Carly wrapped her arms around his neck and kissed him.

"Speaking of taking my breath away," he said when Carly finally released him.

"Sorry. I just get a bit weird when people give me too many compliments."

"No apology necessary. Remind me to give you compliments more often." He smiled down at her, but he could tell Carly was feeling self-conscious. "Didn't you hear how quiet it was when you sang and then how loudly everyone clapped after? They loved you."

"I did hear the applause, but I can't help thinking people were just being polite."

"They weren't. Believe me."

Carly shook her head.

"I don't know what's wrong with me. Ever since I came to New York, I've been doubting myself."

"New York has a way of doing that to people. But trust me, I wouldn't say you were good unless I meant it. And there were a lot of people in there who felt the same way."

Carly studied his face.

"You really are a prince, you know that?"

Allen didn't know what to say.

"You sure you can't stay for the second set?"

"I've got a big day tomorrow and need my beauty rest."

"You're good-looking enough. Come on, stay."

She took his hand and tried to pull him back into the club.

"I really do need to go," he said, resisting. "You free this weekend?"

"Unless someone asks me to play last minute."

"Hey, Carly!" someone called.

"Oops! Gotta get ready for my second set. Shall we say Saturday?"

Allen nodded and watched as Carly ran back into the club.

"So…?" said Felicity. She was leaning against Molly's desk. "Nick says Finn is totally smitten and missed you like crazy over Thanksgiving."

Molly smiled. She was pretty smitten, too.

"He says he's never seen Finn like this," Felicity continued. "So, is it serious?"

"We haven't even been dating a month," said Molly.

"So? I knew right after I met Nick that he could be the one."

"That's different," said Molly. "You guys had been messaging each other for weeks before you hooked up."

"Hey, speaking of messaging, you still communicating

with your Blind Date guy, Jay What's-his-name?"

"I am," said Molly. "And it's McInerney, like the writer."

"Yeah, yeah, yeah, whatever. So, you going to tell him about Finn?"

"No. Why?"

Felicity looked at her.

"Uh, hello?"

"Look, I have no idea where things are headed with Finn, and you were the one who insisted I try Blind Date and stick with it. It's only another week. Don't you think I should see it through?"

"I guess," said Felicity. "Though Finn might not be happy to hear you've been seeing someone else."

"First of all, I've never *seen* Jay. And secondly, it's not like we're having phone sex or sexting. Jay and I are just friends."

"Uh-huh."

Molly made a face.

"Well, the four weeks are almost up, and I want to meet him."

Felicity held up her hands.

"By all means."

"Just promise me you won't say anything to Nick or Finn about Jay, okay?" pleaded Molly.

Felicity crossed her heart.

"I swear."

"Good, thank you. I mean, it'll probably amount to nothing. Jay's probably some introvert who couldn't get a date the normal way. For all I know, he's really short, has acne, and wears a bowtie."

Though Molly never imagined him looking that way. In fact, she had always envisioned him looking like a young version of his namesake, who she found rather attractive. But she didn't say that to Felicity.

"Well," said Felicity, hopping off Molly's desk, "I need to

get back to work." She paused. "So you two want to double date this weekend? Nick wants to try out this new Vietnamese place."

"Sure," said Molly. "When were you thinking?"

"Saturday? And yes, I know Saturday is, like, the worst night to go out. But Nick's been so busy with work and travel and stuff…"

"I understand," said Molly. "Saturday's fine. I'll talk to Finn."

"Great. I'll let Nick know and then confirm."

"Sounds good."

Once Felicity had gone, Molly opened her email and reread Jay's latest message. He had mentioned that he had gone to hear Carly again at Pianos, and Molly wondered if Jay had a crush on her. Carly was quite attractive, in that blonde, girl-next-door way that guys seemed to go for.

She shook her head. They weren't even dating, and she was already jealous. Then another thought popped into her head: Would Jay find her as attractive as Carly?

Don't go comparing yourself to other people, a little voice in her head scolded. But Molly couldn't help it. She didn't consider herself a troll, but she didn't think of herself as the kind of woman men turned their heads for.

Well, she would find out soon enough if Jay found her attractive, assuming they actually met.

The thought of the two of them meeting, having dinner together, made her a bit nervous. Writing to each other practically daily was one thing. And she had come to treasure their back-and-forth. She felt as though she knew Jay, and that he knew her.

Did Finn know her, really know her? She quickly brushed the thought aside. Then she glanced back at Jay's email.

"Dear Jay," she wrote. "Can you believe that it's almost four weeks since we first 'met'? I know I can't. The time seems to have flown by, and I feel like I've really gotten to know you, or know you as much as Blind Date allows one to get to know someone. So, shall we meet? I know I'd like to see the man behind the mask, or emails."

Molly paused. What if Jay didn't want to meet her? She shook her head and continued typing.

"Hope you have something fun planned this weekend. I'm trying a new Vietnamese place with friends. Have you ever had Vietnamese food? I had it once and liked it. Will let you know how this place is.

"Okay, back to reading manuscripts. Hope to read yours one day. Ciao for now, Edna."

She reviewed what she had written and realized she had forgotten to include a joke. She opened a new tab and quickly searched for one, then added it in and pressed "send."

Eric had been exchanging messages with Doris daily, even though both were swamped with end-of-semester work. But writing to Doris had a therapeutic quality. Doris understood what Eric was going through, almost eerily. He wondered if she could be at Columbia. But surely if she had been, he would know, wouldn't he?

He had wanted to ask her at least a half-dozen times where she was studying. But the one time he had, his message had been flagged. So clearly someone at Blind Date was keeping tabs on them. Or it could have been their algorithm. Either way, he had been careful ever since not to ask or reveal anything too identifying.

He had just sent Doris another note, saying he was looking forward to finally meeting her—and being able to debate in person why British history was more interesting than American history. He smiled just thinking about it. They had already had several back-and-forths on the subject, each arguing that their course of study was the more interesting.

Some of the exchanges had been pretty heated, but it just made him want to meet Doris more. She was clearly smart and well-versed in American history. And she had told him she wanted to write her thesis on the roles women played in the War for Independence and the founding of the country, which Eric thought admirable. He frankly had never given much thought to the roles women played in the American Revolution and just afterward and said he would be happy to read a draft when she was ready.

But what if Doris decided she didn't want to meet him?

Eric frowned.

Stop it, he told himself. But as he waited for Doris to reply, he couldn't get the thought out of his head.

Allen looked down at his phone and saw that he had a new text message. It was from Eric.

"You wanna grab a beer later?"

Allen had promised his mother and Jonathan he'd have dinner with them that evening, but they didn't usually eat until seven-thirty or eight.

"I could grab a quick one," Allen replied, "if you don't mind meeting up near my place. I promised the 'rents I'd have dinner with them."

"No prob," wrote Eric. "You want to meet at Dorian's at 6?"

Allen looked at the time. It was a little after three.

"Make it 6:15."

"OK. See you then," Eric replied.

CHAPTER 38

Eric was seated at the bar, nursing a beer, when Allen arrived. He had saved the stool next to him and now removed his bag so that Allen could sit, which he did.

"So, what's up?"

He knew it must be something important for Eric to come to the Upper East Side.

"So, you remember Doris?"

"The woman you met on Blind Date."

Eric nodded.

"We've been corresponding for nearly four weeks now, and I really like her."

"That's great," said Allen.

The bartender placed a beer in front of Allen, and he took a sip.

"So what's the problem?"

"The problem is, we can now meet if we want to, and I'd like to meet her. But what if she doesn't want to meet me?"

"Did she indicate she didn't want to meet you?"

"No," said Eric slowly.

"Then what's the problem?"

Eric ran a hand through his short blond hair, causing some of it to stick up.

"You know I haven't had much luck with women."

"You dated Penelope," said Allen. "That seemed to have gone well."

"That was different."

"How?"

"She was British, and I was living in London."

"I don't see how that makes a difference."

"Things were different in London, and British females are more laid back."

Allen took another sip of his beer.

"Instead of getting yourself all worked up, why don't you just ask her?"

"I did."

"And?"

"I'm still waiting to hear back."

"When did you last write to her?"

"Earlier today."

"So maybe she's busy."

Eric sipped his beer, then turned to Allen.

"And another thing. Let's assume we do meet up. What if she takes one look at me and goes 'no way'?"

"Seriously?"

"I mean, I know I'm not the best looking guy, but I'm not hideous, right?"

"You are far from hideous," said Allen, suppressing a smile.

"Of course, I could take one look at her and want to run," Eric said, staring into his beer. He turned to face Allen. "So, what should I do?"

"What do you mean, what should you do?"

"Should I just call the whole thing off?"

"Don't be an idiot. You should meet her."

"But what if…?"

"No buts ifs," said Allen. "I'm sure she'll reply to your email. Then you guys should go on a date. And just keep an open mind. Remember what you liked about her. Talk to her like you did in your emails. She's probably nervous, too."

"Fine, I'll go on the date. But if she's a troll, or she thinks I'm a troll, I'm blaming you."

"Fine," said Allen. "Blame me. But just give it a shot. Now, can we please talk about something else?"

"Sure," said Eric. "What do you want to talk about?"

Allen was tempted to ask Eric if he had heard from his sister lately, but he didn't want to go there for fear Eric would ask him why. Instead he shrugged.

"I don't know." He took another sip of his beer. "You doing anything exciting this weekend?"

"Only if you call grading papers exciting. What about you?"

Allen thought about mentioning Carly but decided against it.

"Not much. Working on my novel, mostly."

There was a basketball game on the television, and they stared at it for several minutes, though neither was a big basketball fan. Finally, Allen said he needed to shove off and told Eric to keep him posted.

Molly enjoyed getting together with Felicity and Nick that Saturday. The Vietnamese restaurant had been great, and they had gone to shoot pool afterward, though neither Felicity nor Molly was very good. But the boys seemed to be enjoying themselves, and Molly enjoyed it when Finn wrapped his arms around her and pressed his body close when trying to show her how to properly hold a cue stick and shoot.

After a couple of games, Molly and Felicity begged off and told the boys to play on their own, neither of whom objected. As the men played, Molly glanced around the room. She wondered if Jay played pool. Then she stopped herself. Why was she thinking of Jay now? She shook her head.

"Molly?"

It was Finn.

"I've been calling your name, but you weren't responding."

"Oh, sorry," she said. "Must've been spacing out. What's up?"

"We wanted to know if you and Felicity wanted to play the next game?"

Molly yawned.

"Actually, I think I'm going to head out. I'm kind of tired."

"You sure?"

Molly nodded.

Finn made to go with her, but Molly stopped him.

"You stay. I'm fine."

But Finn insisted on accompanying her out of the pool hall and ordered a car to take her home. Molly started to object when he joined her but gave in.

"You okay, babe?" he asked her as they rode uptown. "You seemed a little preoccupied back at the pool hall."

"Sorry," said Molly. "Pool's not really my thing, and I guess I have a lot on my mind."

"Like?"

"Just work stuff. Constance keeps throwing manuscripts at me to read."

She was not going to tell him she had been thinking about another man.

"You're lucky," said Finn. "I'd love to sit around all day getting paid to read books."

Molly tried to hide her annoyance. That was one of the few things that irked her about Finn, his condescending attitude toward her job. She knew he wasn't much of a reader, but still. She didn't make snide comments about him being an accountant and adding numbers all day.

The car pulled up outside her building, and they got out.

Molly could tell Finn expected to go upstairs with her, but she wasn't in the mood and let out a fake yawn.

"Thanks for dropping me off," she said.

"You're not going to invite me upstairs?"

Molly let out another yawn. She knew she was probably overdoing it, but...

"I'm really tired, and Becca's home."

"We could just cuddle on the couch."

"Becca's probably watching *Saturday Night Live*."

Finn frowned.

"Are you trying to get rid of me?"

"I'm just tired. Why don't we get together this week?"

"I'm on the road this week. I've got to be in Chicago Monday, then I'm headed to the West Coast. I won't be back until late Thursday."

"Oh," said Molly. "Well, maybe Friday then?"

"Sure," said Finn, though he still seemed annoyed.

Molly took his hand and kissed him on the cheek.

"Thanks for dinner and pool."

He nodded and looked around. But the car had already driven off. He frowned, scanning the street for a cab. He turned back to see if Molly might let him upstairs, if only for a few minutes, but she had disappeared.

Molly leaned against the door.

"You okay?" asked Becca. She was sitting on the couch, the television on. "You look out of breath."

"I just ran up the stairs."

"Where's Finn?"

"Probably on his way home."

"You didn't invite him up?"

Molly shook her head.

"How come?"

"I don't know."

"You want to tell Aunt Becca all about it?"

She patted the cushion next to her, but Molly shook her head.

"Thanks, but I'm just going to brush my teeth and get into bed."

Becca shrugged.

"Suit yourself."

Allen had stayed over at Carly's Saturday, and she had convinced him to spend Sunday morning with her, too. He still felt awkward around her roommates, but she told him to get over it.

He had told his mother before he left that he might be out late and not to worry. But he was relieved they were out when he got home. Though he knew his mother would ask him where he'd been.

He took a shower and changed and got himself something to eat. Carly had asked him if he'd like to go out for brunch with her and Danielle and Brook, but he had politely declined, saying he needed to get home.

He had checked his messages after he left and realized he had never replied to Hannah's text, sent a couple days ago, asking him if he was free that Sunday, i.e., today. He immediately felt guilty. He had meant to get back to her but had kept putting it off.

After he had eaten, he wrote her back, apologizing for his tardiness in responding. Then he told her that although he thought she was great and an amazing cook, he didn't see the two of them as more than friends.

He read over what he had written, then hit "send" before he could change his mind. She would probably be pissed, unless she felt the same way. But he felt it was better to be honest than to lie or ghost her.

The email from Blind Date arrived in his inbox Monday morning, shortly after he arrived at work.

"Congratulations!" it read. "You did it! Now it's time to meet your match. Please hit 'Accept' to confirm you received this email and are interested in meeting Edna O'Brien."

Allen stared at the email. So this was it. He had made it. Four weeks, and now he could meet Edna. His finger hovered over the "Accept" button.

He thought about Carly. Would it be cheating if he went on a date with Edna? Though was it really a date? And he and Carly weren't officially a couple.

As he was debating with himself, a shadow fell over him. He looked up and saw Justin.

"Hey, Whit-man! What's up? Thinking those deep thoughts of yours?"

"No, just spacing," said Allen.

Justin glanced at Allen's computer screen, where the email from Blind Date was displayed. Allen silently cursed himself for being so careless.

"So, who's Edna?"

"She's the editor Blind Date matched me with."

"Edna, eh?" said Justin. "Not very sexy."

"Though isn't the whole point of Blind Date to not judge people by superficial things, like their looks or their name?" Allen retorted.

Justin patted Allen's shoulder.

"Right you are. So, will you be bringing Edna to the New Year's Eve Bash?"

"I haven't decided." Although he had, in fact, decided to

bring Carly. He just hadn't asked her yet.

"Tick-tock," said Justin, tapping his watch. "The Bash is just four weeks away. And I'll need a name to put on the guest list soon."

"I know," said Allen. "I'll let you know by the end of the week."

Justin stood there for a few more seconds. Then he looked at his watch, one of those big, expensive timepieces Hipster had said were the new fashion statements.

"Well, I need to go. Keep me posted."

Allen nodded and watched as Justin made his way across the floor. When the coast was clear, he turned back to his computer and clicked "Accept."

Molly sat at her desk, staring at her monitor. She had read the email from Blind Date but had yet to press "Accept." She wanted to meet Jay, but a part of her felt guilty.

Finn had texted her Sunday, asking if she was okay. And Molly had felt bad for blowing him off the night before.

Would it be cheating if she went out with Jay? She and Finn weren't exclusive. At least they hadn't said they were. Though she knew she'd be upset if she found out he was seeing someone else.

She bit her lip and reread the email from Blind Date one more time. Not that there was much to read. She either agreed to meet Jay or she didn't.

"Oh, what the hell," she said. "It'd be silly to have written to him for four weeks only to blow him off."

She hit "Accept" and let out a puff of air. Then she closed her email and went back to work.

Eric read the email from Blind Date and immediately clicked on the "Accept" button. He just hoped Doris had, too. He had been antsy all weekend, debating whether he should meet Doris or not, despite his talk with Allen. In a panicked moment, he had even texted Molly. She had called rather than text him back, telling him in no uncertain terms he should accept the invitation.

Now he waited to see if Doris had accepted, too.

While he was waiting, he checked the Blind Date FAQs (not for the first time), to see how the whole date thing worked. Per the website, once both parties accepted, Blind Date sent a list of potential meetup dates, asking users to pick three. Once that was done, each party would receive an invitation to meet at a restaurant run by one of their partners. They would check in using their Blind Date names. After that, it was up to each party how to proceed.

Eric sat back in his chair.

After staring at his screen for several more minutes, he minimized it and grabbed one of the history books from his pile. He cracked it open and began to read.

CHAPTER 39

After lunch, Allen received a new message from Blind Date, asking him to select three evenings out of a list of seven when he could meet Edna for dinner. So Edna must have accepted the meet-up invite, too.

He gazed at the list. The first possible date was that Wednesday, just two days away. Carly played at Pianos on Wednesdays, so that seemed safe. He clicked the circle to indicate Wednesday as one of his choices. Though would Carly expect him to go hear her? She couldn't really expect him to go every Wednesday, could she?

He leaned back, still staring at his screen. Then he leaned forward again and clicked on Thursday and the following Monday. Though what if Carly had lined up gigs for the weekend and wanted to see him Thursday? Maybe he should click on Friday or Saturday instead?

He pulled on his hair. Why was this so hard?

After staring at his screen another minute, he left things as they were, with Wednesday, Thursday, and the following Monday checked. Then he sent the email.

Molly was relieved when she received the follow-up email from Blind Date. She had been worried that Jay had changed his mind and didn't want to meet her after all.

As Finn would be away through Thursday, she checked off Wednesday and Thursday as possible days. Then she added Monday, figuring Finn would either be away or wouldn't want to get together then.

She hit "send," then resumed reading the latest manuscript Constance had given her.

Eric hesitated before opening the email from Blind Date. What if it was to tell him that Doris wasn't interested in meeting him? Then he heard Allen and Molly in his head and opened the email. He instantly relaxed.

Aside from having dinner with his parents on Sunday, he had no concrete plans that week. He looked at the list of possible days. The first was that Wednesday. Would he seem too eager if he checked off Wednesday? He thought about his schedule. He had a seminar Thursday evening, but he didn't have anything that Wednesday or Friday.

After going back and forth, he checked Wednesday, Friday, and Saturday. Though he wondered if he was a loser for checking off both Friday and Saturday. Then again, if he was seeing someone, he wouldn't have needed to go on Blind Date.

"Just be done with it," he said aloud and hit "send."

The next day, Allen received yet another email from Blind Date, informing him that he would be dining with Edna O'Brien at seven o'clock that Wednesday at Provence, a French bistro located near Gramercy Park. Allen hadn't heard of Provence and immediately Googled it.

The place had received good reviews and was known as a popular date spot. Figured. He checked out the menu. It reminded him of the places he and Molly had eaten in Nice junior year. He smiled. That had been a good weekend. Until he had fucked it up with that kiss. Though, if he was being honest, he had enjoyed the kiss. Really enjoyed it. But it had been wrong. He and Molly were just friends.

He reread the email and clicked to confirm that he would be there. Then he went back to work. But he was having difficulty focusing, as he wasn't particularly interested in the article he was working on, on how to rent a dog, the current hot trend.

"Provence," said Molly, reading the email.

She had never heard of the place. But it sounded nice.

She typed "Provence restaurant" into her search engine. The place had received hundreds of reviews and was listed as a top romantic spot to dine. She looked at photos, then went to the restaurant's website. The place reminded her of the cafés she and Allen had eaten at around Nice. She smiled. That had been a good trip. She had loved exploring Nice and the surrounding area with Allen. And that kiss.

She had forgotten about the kiss. Or told herself she had. But suddenly the memory came flooding back, of Allen kissing her, of her kissing him back, and then Allen freaking out and apologizing.

She made a face.

Well, hopefully, Jay wouldn't freak out if they kissed. Though what was she thinking? She had a boyfriend now. Sort of. She should not be thinking about kissing other men!

"No," she said aloud. "It's just dinner, not a real date. We probably won't even be into each other."

She convinced herself that it wouldn't be cheating, then confirmed that she would be at Provence at seven that Wednesday.

Eric didn't hesitate when he received the next email from Blind Date. He opened it right away. The email said to be at Le Bibliothèque at seven o'clock that Wednesday for his date with Doris Kearns Goodwin.

"Le Bibliothèque?" said Eric. He knew it meant library in French, but he had never heard of a restaurant with that name.

He did an online search and sure enough, there was a restaurant near the New York Public Library called Le Bibliothèque. He read a handful of reviews, then visited the restaurant's website. The place was lined with bookshelves and had a cozy reading room vibe to it. It was perfect for two people who spent most of their time in libraries. And maybe the dim lighting would prevent Doris from getting a good look at him.

He reread the email, then confirmed he would be at Le Bibliothèque at seven that Wednesday.

Wednesday arrived, and Allen didn't know why he felt so nervous. This was just another date. Though it wasn't. This date was different from the Spark dates. Although he had no idea what Edna looked like, he felt as though he knew her, even though he didn't know where she worked or had gone to school or the names of any of her friends or family members.

Again, he tried to picture her but was unable to. He had looked up the real Edna O'Brien online when he had first seen her name. But she was in her late eighties. Though she had been quite attractive when she was young, with wavy brown hair and hazel eyes. Maybe his Edna O'Brien did too.

But what if she had an annoying voice, or laughed too loud, or wore a ton of perfume? Or worse, what if she didn't like him?

He stood outside the restaurant, dressed in the suit Natalie had told him to wear. She had wanted to personally style him, offering to come over to his place with Paolo. But he had politely refused. He could dress himself, thank you. But she had insisted on picking out the outfit he would wear—and that Allen send her a picture before he left, which he did.

He took a deep breath and entered Provence. It was dimly lit, and he didn't see any women seated alone. He went up to the host and said he had a reservation for two under McInerney-O'Brien.

"Ah yes, Mr. McInerney, welcome," said the host. "You're the first to arrive. Would you like me to take your coat?"

"I'm good," Allen replied.

He glanced around again. The place was maybe half full.

"Shall I show you to your table?"

Allen nodded and followed the host to a table for two towards the back. He shrugged off his coat and placed it on the back of his chair, then glanced around a third time. It was a pretty place with little candles on each of the tables.

A busboy came by a minute later and filled Allen's water glass. Then a waiter stopped by to see if he wanted a drink.

As he waited for Edna and his vodka tonic, he checked out his social media feeds. He was scrolling through Instagram when he sensed someone coming towards him.

He looked up and saw the woman he had seen that first time at Pianos. She was even wearing the same slinky dress. Then he did a double-take and immediately stood up.

"Molly?"

Molly stopped and stared at him.

"Allen?" She seemed equally surprised. "What are you doing here?"

"This is Mr. McInerney," the host explained.

"No, it isn't," said Molly. "That's my friend, Allen."

"*You're* Edna O'Brien?" said Allen.

Molly slowly nodded her head.

"Where's the waiter with that drink?" said Allen, looking around.

The host pulled out a chair for Molly and she sat, still in a bit of a daze. Allen followed suit.

A few seconds later, the waiter appeared with Allen's drink and asked Molly if she'd like something. She nodded, and he returned with her white wine two minutes later.

They sat there, neither one speaking, for what seemed like several minutes. Then Molly began to laugh.

"What's so funny?" said Allen, not amused.

"Oh, come on, Allen! Surely you don't think it's funny that of all the people on the planet Blind Date matched the two of us—and that we didn't have a clue we were writing to each other?"

"I guess," said Allen, taking a sip of his drink.

"Though I'm surprised you were even on Blind Date. I thought you had sworn off online dating."

"About that," said Allen, his collar suddenly feeling a bit tight.

Molly raised her eyebrows.

Allen looked at her. She really did look beautiful with her fiery hair cascading over her shoulders, her thick brown lashes framing those inquisitive green eyes of her, and her lips looking so…

Get a grip, Whitford, he told himself. This was Molly. Though he was seeing her in a whole new way.

He breathed out, not realizing he had been holding his breath.

"I guess it's going to come out anyway."

Molly continued to wait and look at him.

"It was all Justin's idea. We have this whole 'New Year, New You' issue we do at the beginning of each year, and Justin wanted to do a piece on how to find your soulmate online."

"Your soulmate?"

Allen nodded, though he knew how corny it sounded.

"Justin had landed two new advertisers, both dating services: Blind Date and another one called Spark. And he thought a dating piece would appeal to them."

"I've heard of Spark," said Molly. "That's the one where women are supposedly in charge, right?"

Allen nodded.

"Anyway, Justin got the brilliant idea that someone from Hipster should be the guinea pig, check out both sites, and he picked me."

"Why you?"

Allen sighed.

"Because most of the other guys who work at Hipster are either in a relationship or not what Justin would consider good dating material."

"I see," said Molly. "Why not pick a woman instead then?"

It was a good question, and Allen wondered why he hadn't asked Justin that. Though for all he knew, Justin had asked one of his female coworkers to go on both sites, too, and hadn't told him.

"I don't know. All I know is that I had to find someone, either on Spark or Blind Date, to take to the annual Hipster New Year's Eve Bash."

"I see," said Molly. "Just any date or your *soulmate*?"

Allen winced.

"It was supposed to be my soulmate, but I told Justin it wasn't realistic to expect me to find my soulmate in two months, especially with my track record."

Molly was about to ask him another question when the waiter came over, asking if they'd like to order. They asked him to come back in a minute, then picked up their menus. Allen was relieved not to have to answer any more questions, even if it was only for a few minutes.

When the waiter returned, they ordered.

"I still can't believe you're Jay McInerney," said Molly, once the waiter left. "Though I should have known. I mean what are the chances of two guys writing about their parents dying in 9/11 and then growing up in a changed New York? That should have been a tip-off.

"By the way, I meant what I wrote, about taking a look at your manuscript," she continued. "I'd love to read it when you're ready. Or I can ask Constance if you feel weird about me taking a look."

"Thanks," said Allen. "It's still not ready for prime time, but…"

"You don't have to finish it before giving it to someone to read," Molly said, interrupting. "Just send an overview and some sample chapters."

"I'll think about it," said Allen.

By the time they had finished their appetizers and were on their second drink, both Molly and Allen were feeling more relaxed and had even begun to smile.

"So be honest," said Molly. "What did you think of the Blind Date questionnaire?"

"Oh my God!" said Allen. "Was that the worst or what?"

"Totally. I mean, some of those questions. Do people really answer all of them?"

"I know," said Allen. "Some of them were so weird, like the toilet paper question. I mean, who cares how you put the toilet paper on the holder, right?"

"Actually," said Molly.

"Oh no, don't tell me," said Allen, in mock horror.

Molly smiled.

"I could never date someone who placed the roll on the holder with the paper behind."

Allen smiled.

"Duly noted."

Their main courses came out and they paused to eat.

Allen had to admit, the evening had gone better than he had feared. Though he still couldn't believe Molly was Edna O'Brien. And that he had been writing to her for four weeks and hadn't a clue.

"Would you like dessert or coffee?" asked the waiter, after their plates had been cleared away.

Molly and Allen exchanged a look.

"What do you have?" asked Molly.

The waiter brought over two dessert menus, then went to check on another table.

"See anything you like?" Allen asked.

"Everything," Molly replied. "You want to share something?"

Molly knew Allen loved chocolate, so she suggested they share a piece of flourless chocolate cake.

"So, you never said," she said, after they had ordered dessert.

"About what?" asked Allen.

"You said that the point of the online dating exercise was to find some to take to the Hipster New Year's Eve Bash."

Allen suddenly felt very warm.

"So, who are you planning on taking?"

CHAPTER 40

Eric arrived at Le Bibliothèque nearly fifteen minutes late. It had taken him longer to get downtown than he had thought, and he was perspiring.

He went up to the hostess stand and said he was looking for the Bryson-Kearns Goodwin party.

She informed him that his date was already there and led him to a cozy-looking booth near the back. He gazed at the woman seated there. She was reading a book, her face pointed down, and seemed oblivious to his arrival.

Eric cleared his throat and the woman looked up.

He immediately recognized her, even though they had only spoken once before. But he remembered her pale, lightly freckled skin, the chocolate-brown eyes, and the shoulder-length brown hair.

"Caro?" he said.

Her eyes went wide.

"Eric? What are you doing here?"

"I'm here to meet my date," he said. "What are you doing here?"

"I, uh…" she said, her eyes looking downward. "I'm meeting someone too."

The hostess smiled at them.

"This is the table reserved for the Bryson-Kearns Goodwin party."

Both Eric and Caro looked at her. Then they looked at each other.

"*You're* Bill Bryson?" said Caro.

"Hey, I didn't pick the name," said Eric, defensively.

Caro grinned.

"What's so funny?"

"If you only knew," she said. "I kept picturing this paunchy pale guy with thinning hair…"

She continued to grin, and Eric found himself smiling too.

"Though I shouldn't talk. After all, Doris Kearns Goodwin isn't exactly romance novel cover material."

"No, but she's brilliant," said Eric. "And isn't the whole point of Blind Date to not judge people by superficial stuff?"

"True," said Caro, nodding. "So, you want to have a seat?"

Eric took the seat opposite her.

"So, have you read any of Doris Kearns Goodwin's books?"

She nodded.

"I have. Though not all of them. What about you?"

"I read *No Ordinary Time*, about Roosevelt and World War II. And my dad read *Wait Till Next Year*, her baseball book."

"My dad read that too!" said Caro. "He's a big-time Mets fan."

"You ever go to games?"

"Occasionally. You?"

"Occasionally. My dad's a Yankees fan."

"Of course," said Caro, rolling her eyes.

They smiled at each other.

Maybe this date would turn out okay after all, thought Eric.

The waiter arrived with Allen and Molly's flourless chocolate cake, along with two glasses of sparkling wine.

"We didn't order champagne," said Allen.

The waiter smiled.

"It's courtesy of Blind Date."

He placed the flutes on the table, along with the cake and two forks, and left.

Allen looked at Molly, who shrugged.

"Hey, may as well," she said, lifting her flute.

She was about to say "to us" but changed her mind.

"To friendship," she said instead.

"To friendship," Allen repeated.

They clinked glasses and drank, then dug into the cake.

"So, you still haven't answered the question," said Molly a couple of minutes later.

"The question?"

"Who are you planning on taking to the Hipster New Year's Eve party?"

Allen put down his fork.

"The truth is, I don't know."

Though up until that evening he had planned on inviting Carly. And had been planning on asking her but for some reason hadn't yet.

Molly took another bite of the cake.

"You don't know, or you don't want to tell me, because you don't want to hurt my feelings?"

Allen looked down at the table. Molly had always been able to read his mind. Or so it seemed.

"It's okay if you don't want to bring me," Molly continued. "I totally get it."

Allen felt conflicted.

"I'd like to bring you, but…"

He looked across the table. Molly's face was slightly flushed, and her hair seemed to be glowing in the candlelight. And the way she was looking at him. He wanted to reach across the table and stroke her face.

"The truth is, I met someone. On Spark. And I was planning on inviting her."

"I see," said Molly. "By any chance does she happen to sing at Pianos?"

Allen's eyes went wide.

"I thought so," said Molly.

"How?" said Allen.

"I'm not an idiot, Allen. You went on and on about her and to hear her play what, two, three times?"

Allen hadn't realized he had talked that much about Carly in his emails and felt embarrassed.

"It's fine," Molly continued. "I met someone, too."

"That guy you mentioned?"

Molly nodded.

"We've been seeing each other several times a week."

Molly could have sworn Allen growled.

"What's his name?" asked Allen, his hand unconsciously forming a fist in his lap.

"Finn."

"Finn? Is he part fish?"

"Very funny. No, he's an accountant."

"An accountant?"

"Hey, there's nothing wrong with being an accountant."

"I never said there was. So, is it serious?"

Molly paused before answering. Was it serious?

"Maybe," she said. "I don't know."

"So, you've been seeing this Finn while you were flirting to me?"

"Hey, you've been seeing Carly."

They glared at each other across the table. Suddenly what had been a fun evening had turned sour.

"Let's get the check," said Molly.

"Fine," said Allen. He signaled to the waiter.

"Dinner is on Blind Date," said the waiter when Allen tried

to hand him his credit card. "Though we would appreciate it if you would both leave us a review on social media."

"We'd be happy to," said Molly, forcing herself to smile.

They left a tip, Molly insisting they split it, then headed to the door. As they stood outside, with Molly shivering, Allen felt bad for the way things had ended in the restaurant.

"Come here," he said.

"Why?" Molly snapped.

"You look cold."

"I'm fine," she said, though she was freezing. Why had she worn her lightweight coat over that skimpy dress?

"You want to share a ride uptown?"

"I'm fine taking the subway."

She turned and started walking away. Allen thought about letting her go, then followed her.

CHAPTER 41

"What are you so happy about?" Emily asked her brother as they sat in the living room of their parents' apartment.

"Nothing," said Eric, but he couldn't help smiling.

Emily poked him.

"Come on, give."

Eric looked at her, as if deciding whether he could trust her.

"I met someone."

"Well, good for you. It's about time. So what's her name?"

"Caro."

"Caro?"

"It's short for Caroline."

"Ah," said Emily. "So, what does she do?"

"She's a History Ph.D. candidate at Columbia."

"Of course." She snorted, then picked up a carrot stick from the plate of crudité and bit off a piece. "So how'd you two meet, school?"

Eric nodded, not wanting to discuss Blind Date with his sister. And technically, he had met Caro at school.

"And...?"

"And what?" asked Eric.

"Is she attractive?"

"I think so."

Emily was looking at him, waiting for him to say more.

"Why do you care what she looks like?"

"Uh, hello, I'm in fashion. Besides, I'm curious to know what kind of woman my little brother finds attractive."

Eric debated how to respond.

"If you must know," he said a minute later, "she's a little shorter than me and has light-brown hair and brown eyes."

"Now there's a romantic description," said Emily, sarcastically. "If you can't properly describe her, just tell me her last name and I'll Google her."

"No way."

"Fine. I probably have enough information to go on. I'll just find her myself."

"Leave it alone, Em," Eric warned.

Emily looked at him.

"My, my. A bit touchy, aren't we? Fine. I don't really care that much anyway. I have my own love life to worry about."

"Please don't tell me you got back together with Bruce."

"God, no. I met someone in Italy. Actually, I've known him for a while, but we didn't really get to know each other until this trip."

She got a faraway look in her eyes.

"What's his name?"

"Giovanni. And he's totally dreamy."

She sighed.

"Are you even allowed to date people you work with?" asked Eric. "Don't most companies have rules about that?"

"The company's Italian."

"So?"

She gave him a look, the one that said, "You don't understand, and you never will."

Eric made a face.

"So, you and Giovanni, is it serious?"

"Well, he invited me to spend Christmas with him and his family."

"In Italy?"

"No, at Disney World. Of course, in Italy."

"Does Mom know?"

Christmas was a big deal for their mother, who was in the kitchen preparing dinner along with their father.

"I haven't mentioned it to them yet."

"Well, you'd better let her know soon."

"I will, but I'm a grown woman, and if I want to spend Christmas in Italy with my boyfriend…"

"What's this about being a grown woman and spending Christmas in Italy?" said their mother, emerging from the kitchen.

"Emily here has a new boyfriend who lives there and invited her to spend Christmas with him and his family," said Eric.

Emily looked daggers at him, but Eric just grinned.

"Is that correct, sweetheart?" asked their father, who was standing just behind their mother.

"I'm thinking about it," said Emily. "You don't know Giovanni, but he's amazing. So smart, and handsome, and…"

"Italian," said their father.

"Yes, very Italian," said Emily, smiling.

"I don't think I've ever heard you mention this Giovanni before," said their mother.

"I've known him for a while," said Emily. "But we just started dating. Frankly, I didn't want to leave. Milan is amazing."

"I see," said their father. "Well, you know how we feel about Christmas, especially your mother."

"I know," said Emily.

"But you're an adult now, and we can't force you to stay here," he said. "Though I hope you'll decide to spend Christmas with us. You know, you can always invite Giovanni to spend Christmas here."

Emily went over and kissed him on the cheek.

"That's very sweet of you, Daddy. But I'm pretty sure Giovanni wants to spend Christmas with his family, in Milan."

"Enough talk about Christmas and Italy," said their mother. "Let's go eat."

Eric and Emily dutifully followed their parents into the dining room.

Allen had been feeling miserable for days. He had texted Molly the day after their dinner, apologizing for the way it had ended, and she had texted him back that it was okay. No big deal. She understood. But he sensed that things weren't okay between them. That everything wasn't fine. And he wondered if he had made a mistake not inviting her to the Hipster New Year's Eve Bash.

He had finally invited Carly, and she had shrieked with pleasure when he'd asked her. That, at least, had made him feel good. At least temporarily. Lately, though, Carly had seemed more interested in her music than him. Not that she was ignoring him. It was just that every time he saw her, all she seemed to talk about was her career.

She had quickly developed a loyal following at Pianos, no doubt helped by the video Ham had posted of her playing there, which had received thousands of views. And now she was fielding calls from other venues.

However, her constant worrying about making it and her desire to be famous had begun to grate on Allen. He had no interest in celebrity or fame. Though he understood Carly's desire to have her music heard. But ever since his dinner with Molly, he had had second thoughts about Carly.

He had also thought about Hannah, who he hadn't heard from since he'd sent her that text. They had had such an easy rapport. Had he made a mistake writing her off so quickly?

And then there was Emily. He had sent her a couple of texts, but she hadn't replied.

Allen had been tempted to tell Eric about meeting up with her, lest it got out somehow. But he had stopped himself. He also wanted to tell him about Molly. But again that felt weird.

He sighed. Maybe he should see if Sara was around. After all, she was Hipster's advice columnist. But she didn't know him like Eric did. So after hemming and hawing, he finally texted him, asking if they could meet up later.

"So, what's up?" asked Eric, after they had been seated and ordered beers.

"I need to confess something to you," said Allen, looking a bit nervous. "And I could use some advice."

"Shoot."

Allen knew he wasn't supposed to tell anyone outside of Hipster about the whole dating experiment, but he knew Eric wouldn't say anything. And he owed it to him to tell him the truth. He'd find out anyway in a couple of weeks.

Allen took a deep breath.

"I lied to you."

"About?"

"The online dating thing."

The waiter deposited their beers and asked if they were ready to order.

"Can you give us a minute?" asked Allen.

The waiter nodded and went to check on another table.

"So what exactly did you lie about?"

"I knew all about Blind Date because I was on it too. And I was on Spark. It was part of an article I'm working on, on online dating."

"I see," said Eric.

"I wanted to tell you, but I wasn't allowed to discuss it outside the office. Justin made me swear."

"So whose brilliant idea was it for you to give online dating another try? I can't imagine it was yours."

Allen shook his head.

"It was Justin's. He got these two new advertisers, Blind Date and Spark, and thought it would be fun if someone from Hipster actually used them, tested them out."

"But why you?"

"I asked the same thing. But if you knew the other guys at Hipster, you'd understand."

"So, you gave online dating another shot. Why all the angst? You have a right to change your mind."

Allen ran a hand through his hair.

"There were some unforeseen problems."

"Unforeseen problems?"

"So, the article Justin wanted me to write was all about how to find your soulmate in two months or less."

"Kind of a tight deadline," said Eric.

"Tell me about it. But Justin wanted to make sure I found someone to take to the Hipster New Year's Eve Bash, which the advertisers would be attending."

"So…?"

"So I signed up with Spark and Blind Date, not thinking that I'd meet anyone who knew me, which, in retrospect, was probably naïve. And…"

Eric waited for him to go on, but Allen didn't know how to tell him he had gone out with his sister and Molly.

"Out with it already."

Allen took a deep breath.

"I went out with your sister."

Eric scowled. So Emily had lied to him. What a surprise. Not.

"She found me on Spark," Allen continued. "I didn't realize it was her. On Spark, everyone has a handle, kind of like Instagram. So I didn't know her real name. She reached out to me, then blew me off. Twice, actually. Then she texted me out of the blue and asked me out for a drink. And I, I went. And it was nice, but nothing happened. Swear."

Eric was looking at him.

"Please tell me you're not pissed at me."

Eric sighed.

"No, I'm not pissed at you. Though I am at Emily. She asked me a while back if you were on Spark. At the time, I thought she was crazy. Then later she asked me for your number. Said she wanted to ask you about Hipster. I thought it was work-related. But I should have known something was up."

"I should have said something."

"It's okay," said Eric. "I get it. Just tell me you didn't sleep with her."

"I swear," said Allen. "To tell you the truth, I haven't heard from her since we had dinner. Though I sent her a couple of texts."

"She was in Milan."

"Yeah, she said she was going. Did she say how her trip went?"

"Apparently, very well. Or should I say, *molto bene*? She even came back with an Italian boyfriend."

"She did?"

Eric nodded.

"Giovanni. He works in the Milan office of her company."

"Huh," said Allen. Well, that explained why he hadn't heard from her. She was seeing someone. He felt a slight twinge but nothing more.

"She's going back there over Christmas," Eric continued. "Giovanni supposedly can't live without her."

"Well, I hope she's happy. I'm just glad you're not pissed at me."

"Maybe a little bit," said Eric, grinning. He took a sip of his beer. "So was there something else you wanted to get off your chest?"

"Something else?" said Allen.

"You said you met a couple of people you knew.

"Right." He had momentarily forgotten.

"So, you come across someone from NYU?"

Allen nodded.

Eric looked thoughtful and named a couple of women they knew. Both times Allen shook his head.

"Okay, I give up then. Who'd you meet online?"

"Molly."

"*Molly*? Our Molly? She didn't tell me she was also on Spark."

"I met her on Blind Date," said Allen. "I had no idea it was her. Though in retrospect I should have."

Eric shook his head. How could Allen have not known he was corresponding with Molly?

"So…?"

Part of him didn't want to know. Then he realized, if Allen knew it was Molly, it must mean they had met and gone out.

"You two went out?"

Allen nodded.

"You should have seen the look on her face when she saw me. Mine, too. At first we laughed about it. I mean, you have to admit, Blind Date matching us, and neither knowing, is pretty funny."

Yeah, hysterical, thought Eric.

"Then what happened?"

Allen looked down.

"Uh-oh. I know that look."

"I told Molly about Carly."

"The woman from Pianos? Why? Are you seeing her?"

Allen nodded.

Eric shook his head.

"Wow, I've gotta hand it to you, Allen. Looks like the dating experiment was a big success."

Allen knew sarcasm when he heard it.

"So, did Molly get upset when you told her you were seeing someone?"

"Sort of. Turns out, she's seeing someone, too."

"That guy she mentioned."

Allen nodded.

"So how did you two leave it?"

"That's the thing. She was pretty pissed at me when we left the restaurant. She said she wasn't, but I could tell. And she's barely communicated with me since."

"And how does that make you feel?"

"What, are you my therapist now?"

"Hey, you asked me to meet with you."

Allen looked down at his beer, which was almost gone. He had asked Eric to meet with him. And what had he expected? Eric was just trying to be a friend.

"Do you have feelings for her, for Molly, I mean?"

Allen continued to stare at his glass. Did he have feelings for Molly? Of course he did. They were friends. Best friends. But he knew what Eric was asking. And if he was being honest with himself, he did have those kinds of feelings for Molly.

He nodded.

"But I can't date Molly! It's Molly!"

"Why not?" said Eric. "You know she's had a crush on you since freshman year."

"She has? Did she say something to you?"

"She didn't have to. It was kind of obvious." Though Eric had denied it to himself.

Allen didn't know what to say.

"So any advice?"

"About Molly?"

Allen nodded, and Eric looked thoughtful.

"Well, if you're seeing Carly and she's seeing What's-his-name, you should probably just let it be."

Allen frowned.

"Or you can tell her how you really feel."

The waiter came back over, and they ordered food and another round of beers. Then Allen asked Eric how his date with Doris had gone.

"Really good. It turns out we kind of knew each other."

"Oh?"

"She's also at Columbia, getting her Ph.D. in American History."

"Wow, small world. And you had no idea?"

"None."

"So you two must have had loads to talk about."

Eric nodded.

"We did."

"And does she have a name, other than Doris?"

"It's Caroline, though everyone calls her Caro."

"You two planning on seeing each other again?"

Again, Eric nodded.

"We're getting together this weekend."

"That's awesome! I'm happy for you."

"Thanks," said Eric, smiling. "I'm pretty happy, too."

Their food arrived and they made small talk while they ate.

"Well, good luck with everything," said Eric, as they parted ways.

"Thanks," said Allen.

He felt better for telling Eric everything, but he still didn't know what to do about Molly.

CHAPTER 42

Molly had been in a bad mood since her dinner with Allen. Things had been going so well, and then… She knew she should just move on, get over him already. But a little part of her—okay, maybe more than a little—had hoped that the two of them…

She had seen the way he had looked at her. Why was it so hard for him to admit he had feelings for her?

And really, another freaking blonde? Molly scowled. First that stupid Drama major, and now a singer? Well, if Allen preferred the pretty, superficial type…

"Argh!" she screamed, throwing her pillow against the wall.

"You okay in there?" called Becca.

"Sorry!" Molly shouted back.

A few seconds later there was a knock on her door.

"Okay if I come in?"

"Sure," said Molly, though she wasn't in the mood for one of Becca's pep talks.

"So what's up? I heard you scream."

Molly sighed.

"Why do men have to be such idiots?"

"You want the long answer or the short one?"

Molly smiled.

"Any particular man being especially idiotic?" asked Becca.

"They're all idiots, but I was referring to Allen."

"Ah," said Becca. "You want to talk about it?"

"Not really. I mean, what's there to say? He knows I like him. And I know he likes me. But he has this stupid idea that if we dated it would mess up our friendship."

Becca patiently waited for Molly to continue.

"And I know I have Finn. I mean, not *have* him. But, you know. And he's great. But Allen… It's like we have this special connection. If only he'd acknowledge it. But every time we get close, he shies away. And it's making me crazy."

She looked over at her roommate.

"What do I do, Becs?"

"Have you told Allen how you feel?"

"I would think it's obvious. And we'd just been corresponding for four weeks on that stupid dating app. So he had to know I was interested in him that way."

She squeezed the stuffed animal she was holding.

"But have you actually said to him, 'Allen, I really like you and would like to screw your brains out?'"

Molly scowled at her.

"I take it that's a no then." Now it was Becca's turn to sigh. "Look, Moll, if the guy means that much to you, you should say something. Make it crystal clear how you feel."

"Again, I would think it obvious."

"You'd be surprised."

"Well, it's too late anyway. He's seeing someone and taking her to the Hipster New Year's Eve Bash."

"You know the chick?"

"Sort of. She's a singer."

"A singer? Would I know her?"

"Maybe. Her name's Carly Carrera."

Becca looked thoughtful.

"Nope. Doesn't ring a bell. So have you stalked her online?"

Molly shook her head, and Becca gave her a look.

"Okay, maybe a little. She has a bunch of videos on YouTube and an Instagram and has thousands of followers. And now Allen. How can I compete?"

"You have Finn."

"I know. And Finn's great and all, but…"

"Look, Molly, I get it. But if you're not willing to fight for Allen, let him go and focus on Finn. It's just not worth making yourself crazy."

"I know. It's just hard."

Becca went over to the bed and gave Molly a hug.

"Allen's an idiot."

"Thanks," said Molly.

"I'm off to bed. You going to be okay?"

Molly nodded, even though she didn't believe it.

Christmas had arrived in New York, and the city had turned into a winter wonderland, with all the department stores along Fifth Avenue decked out, each one trying to outdo the other with their window displays.

Emily had gone off to Italy to be with Giovanni, much to Eric's relief. Though he knew their parents were disappointed.

He had asked Caro over for Christmas dinner, but she was having dinner on Long Island with her family. So they made a date to go ice skating at Rockefeller Center a couple of days after, and Eric was hoping the two of them could spend New Year's Eve together.

Allen had continued to see Carly, who had been peppering him with questions about the New Year's Eve Bash—who would be there, who'd be playing, what she should wear. A part of him regretted inviting her (she seemed to care more about the Bash than about him), but it was too late now. And he had been relieved when she had gone back to Chicago for Christmas.

As for Molly, she had taken Becca's advice and had done her best to block out Allen and be nicer to Finn.

Finn would be going back to Massachusetts for Christmas, but he told Molly he had a big surprise for her when he got back and to not make plans for New Year's Eve. Molly had tried to ferret out what the surprise was, but he had refused to answer her questions, only giving her a mischievous smile.

Just before Finn left, the four of them—she and Finn and Nick and Felicity—got together for dinner. They had shared a bottle of wine, and everyone was in a good mood. It was Christmastime, after all. And as Molly glanced around the table at her friends, she realized she hadn't thought about Allen in days and smiled.

Then it was New Year's Eve.

Finn had instructed Molly to be ready by nine.

"Where are we going?" she had asked him earlier that day for the umpteenth time. "I need to know what to wear."

But he had refused to divulge where they were going, only telling her to wear something sexy. As if that helped.

"Come on, at least give me a hint!" Molly begged as they rode to their destination. (Finn had picked her up at her place, looking stylish in a Tom Ford suit.)

Finn grinned.

"You'll find out soon enough."

"But why all the secrecy?"

"I just want it to be a surprise."

"I hate surprises," Molly grumbled.

"I bet you'll like this one," he said, still grinning.

A few minutes later they pulled up in front of Rockefeller Center.

"Are you taking me ice skating? If so, you should have told me. I'm not really dressed for it."

"Nope, we're not going ice skating."

He helped her out of the car and escorted her inside 30 Rockefeller Plaza. There was a large group of people waiting for the elevator. Molly read the sign posted there and paled.

"We're going to the Hipster New Year's Eve Bash?"

"Surprise! My boss got us tickets. It was a reward for all the extra time I've put in."

He looked over at her and saw that she wasn't excited and frowned.

"I thought you'd be excited. This is, like, *the* hottest ticket in town."

"Sorry," said Molly. "It's just…"

She was unable to finish her sentence as the elevator doors opened and everyone rushed to get in. Molly felt her ears pop as the elevator zoomed up to the 65th floor. Two minutes later, the doors opened to reveal one of the most beautiful and romantic spots in all of New York City, with killer panoramic views of Midtown and beyond.

"I've never been here," said Finn, glancing around the Rainbow Room. "And everyone's been telling me I should go."

The place was packed, and Molly grabbed Finn's arm.

He smiled down at her and led her over to the coat check, where she removed her coat and handed it to the young woman there.

"Wow!" said Finn, eyeing her appreciatively. "You look amazing!"

"Thanks," said Molly, secretly pleased.

She had gone shopping with her friend Tabitha, who had insisted she buy the sexy off-the-shoulder, form-fitting cocktail dress, even though it was more than she had wanted to pay. She had also had her hair trimmed, and Becca had insisted on doing her makeup, giving her a glam look that brought out her eyes.

"I mean it," said Finn. "You look like one of those supermodels."

Molly blushed.

"I wouldn't go that far, but thank you."

He took her arm and led her inside the restaurant. Waiters were circulating with trays of sparkling wine and Finn grabbed two glasses, handing one to Molly.

"To us," he said, raising his glass.

They clinked glasses, then drank.

As she sipped her sparkling wine, Molly nervously looked around, wondering if Allen was there.

"Come on," said Finn. "Let's check out the view."

CHAPTER 43

"Wow," said Allen, looking at Carly. "You look amazing."

She really did. It was like she was glowing. Her blonde hair fell in waves to her shoulder and looked like spun gold. And the makeup she was wearing seemed to have a sparkle to it. And that dress. It left little to the imagination. If he didn't know her, he'd swear she was a celebrity. Though, to her growing fanbase, she was.

Carly smiled.

"I'm glad you think so. It took me forever to decide what to wear and do my hair and makeup. Brook and Danielle helped. They said I needed to look more rock 'n' roll if I wanted to make a good impression on your boss."

Allen frowned. So this was about impressing Justin, not him. But he quickly hid his annoyance. After all, considering the people who would be at the party, this could be Carly's big break. And he knew how important her career was.

Carly talked nervously the whole ride over to Rockefeller Center, asking him again who would be there and if she really looked okay. Allen reassured her that she looked fine, better than fine, and said he wasn't sure who exactly would be there, not really caring about the guest list. In fact, he had been dreading the party, large noisy gatherings not being his thing. But he knew he had to make an appearance.

Natalie had insisted on dressing Allen herself and had even

commandeered Paolo to do his hair. Allen had protested, but
Natalie had overruled him, pointing out that representatives
from both Blind Date and Spark would be there, and Allen
needed to make a good impression.

They finally arrived at Rockefeller Center and headed to
the elevators that would woosh them to the 65th floor. Carly
peered at all the people standing in line and frowned.

"Do you think all the famous people ride in a separate
elevator?" she asked in a whisper.

Allen shrugged.

When they got upstairs, Allen offered to check Carly's
coat. Then they headed towards one of the large plate-glass
windows to take in the view. But Carly was more interested in
the view of the crowd.

"Wow," she said, glancing around. "Look at all the people.
And this place! It's amazing."

A waiter came by with a tray of sparkling wine.

"Thanks!" said Carly, taking a flute. Allen did the same.

They sipped from their glasses, both of them looking
around as they did so.

"How many people do you reckon are here?"

"Too many," mumbled Allen, who wished it was midnight
already, so he could escape.

"Finally!" said a female voice.

Allen turned and saw Natalie coming towards them.

"I thought you'd never get here."

"I was picking up Carly."

Natalie turned her attention to his date, immediately
assessing her.

"So this is the famous Carly," she said.

"That's me!" said Carly. "Though I'm not famous, at least
not yet. And you are?"

"This is Natalie, Hipster's fashion editor," said Allen,
before Natalie could reply.

Carly eyed her, taking in her dress, as well as her hair and makeup.

"I should have known. Nice dress, by the way."

"Thanks," said Natalie. She turned to Allen. "The CEO of Spark just got here. Give me a minute, then I'll bring you over and introduce you two."

"She seems nice," said Carly, after Natalie disappeared back into the crowd. "A bit intense, but nice."

"Intense is probably a good way to describe her," said Allen.

Carly glanced around.

"Is your music critic here?"

"Celine?"

"Unless you have more than one."

"No, just Celine," said Allen. "She's probably hanging out by the bandstand."

Amidst all the noise, you could barely hear the music.

"Let's go see," said Carly, taking Allen's hand.

"We should probably wait for Natalie," said Allen. But Carly pulled him across the floor.

"I'm sure she'll find us."

They made their way to the stage and Carly stopped.

"Oh my God! That's King Princess! You didn't tell me she would be playing!" Allen had thought he had mentioned it. "I love her."

Carly was clearly starstruck.

Allen glanced around and spied Celine a little ways away.

"There's Celine," he said, pointing.

"Would you introduce me?" asked Carly.

Allen nodded and led Carly to where Celine was chatting with a small group of people. He waited a minute, until there was a lull in the conversation, then cut in.

"Hey Celine, I'd like to introduce you to my friend, Carly Carrera. She's the singer I told you about."

"The singer," said Celine, eyeing Carly. "Ah, yes."

Celine was a good head taller than Carly, and Carly wasn't particularly short.

"Hi," said Carly, extending a hand. "Pleased to meet you."

Celine looked down at the proffered hand but didn't take it.

"I understand you play at Pianos."

Carly nodded.

"Every Wednesday, two sets."

"I know Pianos," said one of the men in the group. "Doesn't Maggie Rogers occasionally play there?"

Carly nodded.

"What kind of stuff do you sing?" asked one of the women.

"My own stuff plus covers. I love classic stuff, like Joan Baez and Joni Mitchell."

There was nodding among the group.

"You going to play tonight?" asked the other man.

"Oh no!" said Carly, blushing. "I'm just here as Allen's guest."

Everyone turned and looked at Allen.

"Allen is one of our writers," explained Celine.

"There you two are," said Natalie, making her way through the crowd. "I've been looking everywhere for you."

She grabbed Allen by the arm.

"Come with me." She turned and looked at Carly. "You, too."

"It was nice meeting all of you!" said Carly, as Natalie dragged them away.

Carly turned to Allen.

"Do you think Celine will come hear me sing?"

"What?" said Allen.

With all the noise, it was hard to hear.

"I said, do you think Celine will come hear me sing?" Carly repeated, practically shouting.

"Probably," shouted Allen.

"Ah, here we are," said Natalie, stopping in front of Justin and a handsome woman, probably in her late thirties or early forties. "Bettina Fredericks, I'd like to introduce you to Allen Whitford and Carly Carrera. Allen works at Hipster. Carly found him on Spark."

Bettina regarded Allen and Carly.

"I'm Justin Johnson, the publisher and editor of Hipster," said Justin, taking Carly's hand and gazing at her. "But you can call me J.J."

Natalie rolled her eyes.

"Nice to meet you, J.J.," said Carly, smiling up at him.

Natalie cleared her throat, and Justin let go of Carly's hand.

"As you can see," Natalie said to Bettina, "Spark works."

Bettina continued to eye Allen and Carly.

"So, Carly," said Bettina, "what attracted you to Allen?"

Carly looked up at Allen and smiled.

"That's easy," she replied. "He was super cute. But it wasn't just that. He seemed like a nice guy, you know? Really sensitive and caring. And I liked that he was a writer as I'm a writer, too. Though I write songs. Creativity is important to me."

"I see," said Bettina.

She turned her attention to Allen.

"And why did you accept Carly's invitation?"

"Well," said Allen, not sure how to answer. The first thing he thought of was that he had liked how she looked, but he didn't want to sound superficial. "I just really liked her profile."

He knew it was a lame answer, but he was feeling under pressure, and he never performed well under pressure.

"I see," said Bettina.

"They make a very handsome couple, don't you think?" said Justin. "Very happy, too, from what Allen's told me. And it's all thanks to Spark!"

"Mmm…" said Bettina.

"You should hear Carly sing," said Allen. "She's really good."

"Is that right?" said Justin, again eyeing Carly.

Carly continued to smile.

"Allen may be a bit biased, but I'd like to think I'm okay. My videos have gotten thousands of views and I have a regular gig at Pianos."

"Well, you must let us hear you sing," said Justin, continuing to look at her in a way that made Allen uncomfortable.

"Tonight?" said Carly, wide-eyed.

"Now that you mention it," he said, "why not?"

Natalie looked horrified.

"But I don't have my guitar."

"I'm sure you could borrow one," said Justin.

Natalie grabbed Justin.

"A word?"

"If you will excuse me," said Justin, smiling.

Allen watched as Natalie dragged him away.

"So," said Bettina, turning back to Allen and Carly. "What did you both think of Spark?"

"It's great!" said Carly. "I mean, what other dating app lets women be in charge? And you don't have to worry about the guy being a creep because you screen everyone."

Bettina smiled.

"What about you, Allen. Did you have a good experience?"

Allen nodded.

He saw Bettina looking at him and felt uncomfortable.

"Care to elaborate?" she said.

"Well, to tell you the truth," said Allen, "I'm not a huge fan of dating apps. But of the ones I've tried, Spark was the best."

"Thank you for your honesty, Allen," said Bettina. "And would you two recommend Spark to a friend?"

"Definitely," said Carly, nodding.

"What about you, Allen?"

"Me?" He had been watching Natalie and Justin argue about something in the distance.

"Yes, you," said Bettina. "Would you recommend Spark to your friends?"

"Um, sure," he said, seeing Justin and Natalie heading back over.

"We're back!" said Justin, smiling as though nothing had happened.

He signaled to one of the servers offering guests flutes of sparkling wine.

"A toast!" he said, picking up a fresh glass and indicating everyone else to do the same. "To Spark! May it spark many relationships!"

He raised his glass and the rest of them did likewise.

"To Spark!" they intoned, clinking glasses.

Allen, feeling nervous, downed his sparkling wine in a few gulps.

"Take it easy there, Whit-man," said Justin, patting Allen on the back. "The night's still young." He looked over at Carly. "So, Carly, tell me about yourself."

"If you'll excuse me," said Bettina.

She stepped away, leaving Justin, Allen, Carly, and Natalie standing there.

"I should go mingle," said Natalie, also excusing herself.

Allen suddenly felt like a third wheel.

"Allen, why don't you go get some food for yourself and your lovely date?" suggested Justin, still gazing at Carly, who seemed pleased by the attention.

"Sure," he said.

CHAPTER 44

Allen ran into several of his colleagues on the way to the buffet table, each of whom stopped him to chat for a few seconds. Then he had to wait in line to get food. By the time he returned to where he had left Carly chatting with Justin, they were nowhere to be found. And the place was even more packed.

He glanced around the immediate area but didn't see either one of them. Then he stared down at the plate of food he had brought for himself and Carly to share. He could feel his stomach grumbling, so he ate one of the chicken satays, a couple of shrimp, and a couple of cheese puffs. Then he went in search of his date.

As he passed by one of the bars, he stopped and got himself a vodka tonic. He knew it wasn't a great idea to mix drinks, but he didn't care. The noise and the crowd were getting to him, and he needed something strong if he was to make it until midnight.

Parquet Courts had just started playing, and he thought that might be a good place to find Carly. He had texted her, asking where she was, but she had yet to reply.

There was a large crowd gathered around the stage, and it was hard to see. He thought for a minute he spied her, but it was just another blonde who vaguely resembled her.

He stood to the side, listening to the band and wondering

what he should do. Then he felt a tap on his shoulder. He turned.

"Pretty cool, right?" said Dave, practically shouting.

"Yeah," said Allen, shouting back at him. He could barely hear himself.

"What happened to your date?" said Dave. "I heard she was a hottie."

"She's around," said Allen.

"Speaking of hotties," said Dave. "You see that blonde with Justin? *Muy caliente!*"

Allen looked down at Dave, who was several inches shorter than him.

"Did you say blonde?"

Dave nodded.

"Did she have wavy hair and was wearing a red dress?"

"Yeah, that's her. Is she a model or something? Though she didn't look tall enough to be a model."

"Do you happen to know where they went?"

"They were over there last I saw them," said Dave, pointing vaguely to the right.

"Thanks," said Allen.

"You going to check her out?"

Allen ignored him and headed off.

He scanned the area Dave had indicated, but there was no sign of Justin or Carly. He scowled and checked his phone again. He had sent her another text, but there was still no reply. Where were they? He started to make his way through the crowd, to the other side of the room, when he practically collided with Natalie.

"Hey, Nat, have you seen Carly?"

"Carly?" she said.

"My date. The blonde."

"Oh her. Did you lose her already?"

Natalie was clearly buzzed.

Allen made a face.

"Justin sent me to get food, but when I got back, I couldn't find them."

Natalie looked like she was trying hard not to laugh.

"What's so funny?" said Allen.

"You lost your date!" She giggled, then stopped herself and tried to look serious. "You should have never left her alone with Justin," she said, wagging her finger at him.

Allen frowned.

"How much have you had to drink?"

"None of your business," she replied, poking a finger into his chest.

Allen sighed.

"Well, have you seen Justin?"

"Nope!" She glanced around. "Not here!" Then she frowned. "I need another drink. Hope you find your date!"

Allen thought she had had enough, but he didn't say anything. Instead, he resumed his search for Carly.

Molly had had enough. She had had enough of Finn asking if that was so-and-so, every time he spotted someone famous or who looked famous, like some starstruck kid. (Celebrities didn't impress Molly.) She had had enough of the music, which was too loud. She had had enough of all the pushing and jostling, of people trying to move around in the crowded room. And she had probably had too much to drink, which only made her more anxious. What she needed was some air, or at least some space.

"Would you excuse me?" she said to Finn.

"Sure, babe, everything okay?"

"I just need to find a restroom. I'll be right back."

"I'll be here!" he said, not looking at her. He was too busy listening to the band and trying to spot celebrities.

Molly sighed and went in search of a bathroom. She finally found one a few minutes later. Of course, there was a line. But she didn't have to go that badly. She just needed to get away from the noise. And at least it was quiet there, or quieter.

Finally, it was her turn. When she was done, she washed her hands and stared at herself in the mirror. She had taken great pains to look good that evening. And Finn had said all the right things. But soon after they had entered the Rainbow Room, he had stopped paying attention to her, and she was annoyed.

Part of her understood. Even though Finn was no country bumpkin, he was still new to New York, and the combination of being in one of the famous restaurants in the world along with all the famous people gathered there, though most of the celebrities there were B- or C-listers, not the truly famous, would make most people a bit giddy. Just not Molly. She would have been happy to have watched the ball drop from her couch in her pajamas.

She finished staring at her reflection and sighed. Fortunately, it was almost midnight. And after the clock struck twelve, she would be leaving, with or without Finn.

Allen had nearly given up when he found them. They were huddled together in a dark corner. He had nearly walked right by them, but he had heard Justin's voice and had stopped.

He couldn't hear what Justin was saying, so he moved closer, hiding behind a nearby column. He caught a sliver of the woman. He was almost certain it was Carly. And she was giggling. Allen knew he should leave, but he couldn't tear himself away. He watched as Justin whispered something in her ear. At least he hoped he was just whispering. Then he heard the woman giggle again and saw Justin kissing her. They turned slightly, and Allen saw Justin snake his hand up Carly's dress and heard her moan. The next thing he knew, he was practically running.

Allen continued to run, not caring who he bumped into. He felt angry, though he wasn't sure who he was angrier at, Justin or Carly.

"Hey, watch where you're going!" yelled an annoyed guest, as Allen continued to push his way through the crowd.

"Sorry," said Allen, not really paying attention or caring.

He stopped a few seconds later, panting and running a hand through his hair. He thought about going back there and confronting them. But a bigger part just wanted to leave.

"Allen?" said a familiar-sounding female voice.

He turned and saw Molly looking up at him.

"Molly?"

He thought for a minute he was hallucinating. Then he took a closer look. Her hair was down, and she had on a lowcut, off-the-shoulder, form-fitting dress. And she looked worried. He grabbed her hand.

"Come on," he said.

"Where are we going?" she asked, as he pulled her through the crowd.

"Just follow me."

He spied an open bottle of sparkling wine in an ice bucket and grabbed it.

"Hey!" said an angry server.

"It's okay. I work for Hipster!" Allen called back.

Molly giggled.

He continued to lead her toward the elevators. When they got there, he pressed the button several times. An elevator arrived a minute later, disgorging around a dozen people. When it was empty, Allen pulled Molly inside, then pressed the button for the lobby.

"But it's not midnight," said Molly, as the doors began to close.

"Do you really care?" he asked her.

Molly shook her head.

The elevator quickly descended, and they could feel their ears popping.

When it stopped at the ground floor, Allen quickly got out, pulling Molly with him, the bottle of sparkling wine in his other hand.

"Where are we going?"

"Out," he replied. He was desperate to get some air and get as far away from the party as he could.

"But it's cold out, and my coat's still upstairs."

Allen looked at her. She was definitely not dressed for the outdoors. He felt bad, but there was no way he was going back up there.

"I'll keep you warm," he told her.

Molly looked up at him, and Allen saw the look in her eyes. Then he removed his jacket and placed it around her shoulders.

"Come on," he said. Then he took her hand and led her outside.

They made their way to the ice skating rink, which was all lit up.

Allen was cold, but he didn't care. The crisp night air felt good, and at least it wasn't freezing.

He put the bottle of sparkling wine to his mouth and drank. Then he handed the bottle to Molly.

They stood there, gazing at the ice skaters and the golden statue of Prometheus, taking turns sipping from the bottle.

"It must be almost midnight," said Molly, hearing people

blowing noisemakers and laughing nearby.

Allen took another sip. He was starting to feel numb.

"What were you doing at the Hipster New Year's Bash?" he asked her.

Molly sighed.

"Finn got us tickets."

"Finn the fish boy?"

He made a fish face, which made Molly laugh. She was pretty when she laughed. She should laugh more, Allen thought.

He stood there staring at her. Under the lights, she seemed to glow. And he wanted to take her in his arms and kiss her.

He made a move to do so, but Molly stopped him.

"What happened to your date? Isn't she going to be concerned that you skipped out on her?"

"Doubtful. Last I saw her she was making out with Justin."

"Oh," said Molly, taken aback. "Sorry."

They stared at the rink. Then people began shouting, "Happy New Year!" and blowing noisemakers.

"Happy New Year," Molly said, turning to Allen.

"Happy New Year," he replied, looking at her. Then he closed the distance between them and leaned down and kissed her.

This time Molly didn't stop him.

CHAPTER 45

Molly opened her eyes to see light coming through her window. She must have forgotten to close the shades. She groaned, then closed her eyes. Her head hurt something fierce and her mouth felt as though it had cotton in it. As she lay there, trying to ignore the pain, she registered the sound of snoring. Her eyes flew open and she rolled over.

Allen was lying next to her, his eyes closed and his mouth partially open, dead to the world.

She stared at him, trying to remember how he got there. She remembered Allen kissing her by the skating rink, a kiss that seemed to go on forever. Then she vaguely remembered him arranging a ride and escorting her back to her place, and him following her upstairs. The rest was kind of a blur. Though she knew there had been more kissing and then…

She lifted the covers. They were both wearing concert tees and underwear. Thank God for that. Though she didn't remember changing.

She glanced over at Allen again. Was that drool? She smiled. He even looked cute drooling. She made her way to the bathroom and swallowed two ibuprofen. Then she stared at herself in the mirror. She hadn't removed her makeup from the night before, and it was now smeared across her face. She grabbed the bag of makeup remover wipes and rubbed one all over her face. Then she took a second one. When she was done, she splashed herself with cold water, then headed to the kitchen.

She glanced up at the clock on the microwave. It was just past nine-thirty. She thought about going back to bed and snuggling next to Allen. How many times had she dreamed of the two of them together? Too many to count.

She scooped coffee into the coffee maker and hit start. Then she walked back to the bedroom. She climbed into bed and gave Allen a soft kiss on the cheek. He jerked awake, nearly butting heads with her.

"Where am I?" he said, looking alarmed.

"You don't remember?"

Allen's head felt as though someone had hit the back of it repeatedly with a baseball bat. He rubbed the spot where it hurt.

"You okay?"

"Were we attacked last night?" he asked her.

"Attacked?"

Allen continued to feel his head for bumps.

"I feel like I got hit with a baseball bat."

"More like a bottle of sparkling wine," said Molly. "You really don't remember?"

Allen shook his head, but that only made it hurt more.

"I'm making coffee. I'll get you a mug. Maybe that will help you remember."

Molly got off the bed and headed back to the kitchen, returning a minute later with a steaming mug of coffee.

"Here you go!" she said, handing Allen the mug

"Thanks," he said, sitting up and taking a sip as Molly watched.

"I have some ibuprofen, too, if you need it."

Allen continued to drink.

"So how did we wind up at your place? My memory's a bit hazy."

"As I recall, you insisted on escorting me home, then you followed me up the stairs."

"And then what happened?"

"I'm still trying to figure that part out. Though I'm pretty sure kissing was involved."

Allen brain suddenly formed an image of him kissing Molly against the back of her door, then carrying her into the bedroom.

"I see your memory's started to come back."

Allen took another sip of coffee and looked around the room.

"Any idea where my clothes are?"

"Hmm," said Molly, glancing around. "I'm sure they're around here somewhere."

"So, did we, you know?"

"I don't think so," said Molly. She had asked herself the same question. But she hadn't felt sore down there or noticed any wet spots on the bed. A part of her had been disappointed.

Allen rubbed his head again.

"I'm sorry."

"Sorry?" said Molly. "For what?"

"For making you leave the party early."

"First of all, you didn't *make* me leave. I had had more than enough by the time I bumped into you."

Allen looked relieved. Then he frowned again.

"What about your date?"

Molly had almost forgotten about Finn. She had yet to check her phone and didn't want to.

"He probably didn't even realize I had left."

"I doubt that," said Allen. He put down his coffee. "Come here," he said, patting the spot next to him.

Molly moved over. She could feel her heart speeding up.

Allen looked into her eyes and caressed the side of her face. Molly held her breath. If it was possible, he looked even sexier than he had the night before, with his hair tousled and his eyes slightly hooded. She looked down at his lips, which were parted, and wanted to kiss them.

As if reading her mind, Allen placed his hand behind her head and pulled her close. She could feel his breath on her face, and she wanted to pin him down and straddle him.

"Happy New Year," he said.

"Happy New Year," she replied.

Then he caressed her hair and kissed her.

This time when Molly got out of bed, she knew exactly what had happened. And she couldn't stop smiling as she stood under the shower.

Allen had showered first, and Molly had wanted to drag him back to bed when he emerged, a towel wrapped suggestively around his waist. She had tried to remove the towel, but Allen had playfully swatted her hand away and told her it was her turn.

When she emerged, Allen was dressed, having found his clothes.

"Do you have any food?" Allen asked her.

"Did you check in the kitchen? If not, we could grab a bite somewhere."

"I know where I'd like to grab a bite," he said, gently biting her neck.

Molly closed her eyes and sighed.

"If you keep doing that, we'll never get out of here."

He stopped, and Molly instantly felt disappointed.

"Get dressed," he commanded. "I'm taking you out for brunch."

"Oh you are, are you?" she said.

Allen nodded.

"I am."

Molly quickly pulled on a pair of jeans, a long-sleeved shirt, and a sweater.

"I'm ready. Where to?"

They had eaten brunch at a little place a couple of blocks away. It was a mild day, not that unusual for New York in January, a good thing as Allen only had his suit jacket.

Afterward, they went back to Molly's place and watched a movie on Netflix.

"I should go," he said, when the movie was over.

"Do you have to?"

She was curled up next to him on the couch.

"I told Eric I would stop by his folks' place. You're welcome to come with me. They're having their annual New Year's Day party."

"Thanks, but I think I'll pass."

"You sure?"

Molly nodded. She was nervous about how Allen would act around Eric. Would he act as though nothing had happened? She wasn't eager to find out.

"So is he still seeing Caro? Did they spend New Year's Eve together?"

"I think so. Come. You can ask him yourself."

Molly shook her head.

"You go. Tell him I say hi. Maybe we can double date."

Though as soon as the words left her mouth, she regretted them. Would Allen now freak out? But he was smiling.

"I think that's a great idea."

"You do?"

He nodded.

"I do. And now I should really get going, before Eric

wonders what happened to me."

He stood up and checked his phone, to see if Eric had messaged him. He had, as had Carly, Natalie, Justin, and his mother. He frowned. (This was why he hadn't checked his phone earlier.)

"Something wrong?"

"No."

But Molly wasn't so sure.

She followed him to the door.

"Have fun at Eric's."

He leaned down and gave her a kiss on her forehead.

"I'll text you later."

She watched as he headed down the stairs. Then she remembered.

"Hey, Allen!" she called.

He stopped and looked up at her.

"Do you think I could pick up my coat later? They wouldn't have thrown it out, would they?"

"Doubtful. Give the Rainbow Room a call. And if there's a problem, let me know."

"Okay," she said.

Allen then descended the rest of the stairs.

CHAPTER 46

When Allen got outside, he opened his messages. He read the ones from his mother first.

She was worried about him and wanted to know if he was okay and had asked him to please text her back, so she'd know he was alive.

He wrote her back, apologizing for not writing sooner. He was fine, he told her, and would be home later.

Next, he opened the messages from Natalie. There were several. She was pissed that he had disappeared, leaving her to explain to the head of Blind Date why he wasn't there. He felt guilty reading her messages. He should have told her he was leaving or at least messaged her.

He wrote her back, apologizing profusely, saying he hadn't been feeling well and had to leave. It wasn't a total lie, though it wasn't exactly the truth.

Then he opened the messages from Justin. If Natalie has been pissed, Justin had been furious, saying that Allen had made him look like a fool in front of the advertisers. Allen snorted. Talk about making someone look like a fool. Justin had said nothing about stealing Allen's date and making out with her.

Finally, he opened the texts from Carly. There were a half-dozen. He ran a hand through his hair. He knew it had been wrong to leave without saying anything, but she had been indisposed. And he had texted her, asking where she was, but she hadn't replied.

He began reading. At first, she had been apologetic, saying she hadn't seen his texts and was sorry for not replying sooner. She had claimed to have been chatting with people. Allen snorted.

Later, she texted asking where he was, saying she had looked all over but couldn't find him. Then she sent another text saying she had heard that he had left. Then still later she had asked if he was okay. Finally, she had texted him a short time ago, asking if he was ghosting her.

Allen sighed. Was he ghosting her? He hadn't meant to, but he knew it could seem that way. Frankly, he didn't really want to see her, the image of Justin with his hand up her dress seared into his brain. But he knew he should reply. But what to say? Finally, he began typing.

"Sorry I didn't reply sooner. I'm fine. You want to talk later?"

He didn't really want to talk to her, but he felt he owed her an explanation for his disappearance.

Molly had dreaded checking her phone. She knew Finn would be pissed at her. But once Allen left, she didn't have an excuse. She fished it out of her bag and check her messages. Finn was pissed all right.

"Where'd you go?" read the first text. Then the messages got progressively worse, ending with, "I can't believe you ran out on me on New Year's Eve. What kind of person does that? Fuck you, Molly Malloy."

Molly cringed, but she knew she deserved his wrath. She should have at least texted him and told him she wasn't feeling well and had gone home. But she had been so caught up in the moment, and Allen, that she had blown it off. (And frankly, she had been pissed that Finn had been ignoring her.) Now, however, she felt bad.

She sighed and stared down at her phone. Then she began to type.

"I understand if you don't ever want to see me again or talk to me. What I did was totally wrong. I was feeling overwhelmed and had a panic attack and just needed to get out of there. I should have texted you, but, like I said, I wasn't thinking.

"Let me know if you want to talk."

She read over what she had written, then deleted the last sentence. She didn't really feel like talking to Finn, but she would pick up the phone if he called her. Then she hit "send."

Next, she opened a series of texts from Felicity. Of course, Finn had written to Nick, who had told Felicity what had happened.

"Hey, Moll, I hope you're okay," read the first message. "Finn is really worried about you. Please text him back and let him know you're all right. Me too."

The next two messages were more of the same, with Felicity becoming increasingly panicky, wondering if she needed to start calling hospitals. There were also voicemails.

Molly immediately called her friend, who picked right up.

"Oh my God, you have no idea how worried we were! Are you okay? What happened?"

"I'm fine," said Molly. She paused, not sure what or how much she wanted to tell her friend.

"What happened?" Felicity asked again. "Finn was worried sick about you."

"I'm sorry. I had a panic attack and needed to get out of there. I wasn't thinking."

"I'm sorry about the panic attack, but you should have at least texted him. He was ready to call the cops."

Molly blanched.

"I know. I screwed up. I already wrote to him. And I understand if he doesn't want to talk to me."

"So where have you been? Why didn't you answer your phone?"

"I've been home. I guess I didn't hear my phone."

"Well, I'm relieved you're okay, but you're going to have to make it up to Finn, big time. He was worried sick about you."

"I know."

There was silence for several seconds.

"Well, I need to go," said Felicity. "Nick's dragging me to some New Year's Day party. You sure you're okay?"

"I'm fine," said Molly. "See you at work."

"There he is!" said Eric, as Allen entered.

"Caro, I'd like you to meet my best friend Allen Whitford. Allen, this is Caro, aka Doris."

Allen smiled. He hadn't seen Eric look so happy in ages.

"Nice to finally meet you, Caro. Eric has been telling me about you for weeks."

Caro smiled back at him.

"And Eric's told me a lot about you."

She glanced around.

"Where's your friend?"

"My friend?"

"Eric told me you were dating a singer. Carly, right?" she said, looking at Eric.

Eric nodded.

"About that," said Allen.

Eric could tell from Allen's expression that something was up.

"Is everything okay?"

"We can discuss it later."

Eric turned to Caro.

"Would you excuse us for a minute?"

"Sure," she replied. "Is everything okay?"

"I just need to ask Allen something. I'll be right back."

Caro shrugged. Then Eric then led Allen to his bedroom.

"So, what's up?"

"Who says anything's up?"

"Well, for starters," said Eric, "you look like you slept in your clothes."

Allen looked down. He had forgotten he was still wearing his suit, the one he had worn to the party the night before.

"Secondly, I know that expression."

"What expression?"

"That one. The one you get when you're uncomfortable talking about something."

"Remind me not to play poker with you," said Allen.

"Are you kidding? You're probably the only person I could win money from."

Allen smiled.

"So, seriously, what's wrong? Why isn't Carly with you?"

"About that," said Allen, his expression turning sober.

Eric waited.

"I caught her making out with Justin at the party."

"No way!"

Allen nodded.

"The two of them were going at it in some dark corner, and I kind of lost it."

"You didn't punch anyone, did you?"

"No, I just drank too much and left."

"Totally understandable," said Eric. "Though, did Carly say anything when you confronted her later?"

"Actually," said Allen. "I haven't spoken to her."

"But you texted her, right?"

"Sort of."

Again, Eric waited. Allen ran a hand through his hair.

"When I couldn't find her, I sent her a text. Actually I sent her a couple of texts. But she didn't respond. Then I found her with Justin, and I just wanted to get out there. Then I bumped into Molly and—"

"Wait," said Eric, interrupting him. "You bumped into Molly at the Hipster party?"

Allen nodded.

"What was she doing there?"

"She was there with her date, who was ignoring her. Anyway, one thing led to another and we wound up leaving."

"Together?"

Allen nodded again.

"Do I want to know the rest of this story?"

"I don't know. Do you?"

Eric looked up at his friend, then back down at his clothes and sighed.

"It was probably inevitable."

"What was?" said Allen.

"That you and Molly would get together."

"How did—"

But Eric stopped him from finishing his sentence, holding up a hand.

"Please, give me a little credit."

Allen looked uncomfortable.

"So?"

"So?" repeated Allen.

"Are you and Molly…?"

"Maybe. I don't know."

"Well, let me know when you've figured it out. Now I should get back to Caro. And you should say hello to my parents. They were asking about you."

"Sure," said Allen, following him out of the bedroom. "Lead the way."

CHAPTER 47

Molly had yet to hear back from Finn. She had returned to work after New Year's, but Finn had neither texted nor called her. Though Allen had. Repeatedly. In fact, the two had been texting or calling each other daily and had made plans to get together that weekend.

Then Friday, Felicity delivered the news. Finn was seeing someone. Molly was shocked. It had only been a few days since the party, and he was already seeing someone else? WTF? She immediately texted her friend back.

"Already? We haven't even officially broken up."

"Sorry," wrote Felicity. "I was pretty shocked when Nick told me. Apparently, she's on his team at work."

Molly didn't know whether to be angry or relieved. She was a bit of both. Not that she still wanted to see Finn, but. He could have at least waited.

"How long have they been seeing each other?" Molly asked.

"I don't know," wrote Felicity. "I'm really sorry."

"It's okay," Molly typed.

She thought about telling Felicity about Allen.

"You sure you're okay?" Felicity texted.

"I'm sure," Molly replied.

"Okay, but if you need to talk, just message me."

Molly sent her a thumbs-up emoji, then put her phone away.

Allen thought about not going into work. But he had to finish his article, which was already late. And he had no vacation days. Though he thought about calling in sick.

Fortunately, both Natalie and Justin were no-shows. In fact the office was surprisingly quiet. Though it wasn't a huge surprise. No doubt many people had taken the week off, what with New Year's falling on a Tuesday.

Allen enjoyed the peace and quiet and was able to finish his article, which would come out first thing Monday.

He had thought about texting Carly again, having not heard back from her. But he decided not to. She knew how to find him if she wanted to talk.

That Saturday he met Molly at a movie theater close to her house. The plan was to see a film, then Molly would make him dinner at her place. Allen had said that wasn't necessary, but Molly had insisted. Ever since he had told her about the tasting party, she had wanted to prove that she could cook, too.

She had made an Irish stew with lamb and vegetables, which Allen had declared delicious. For dessert she made ginger molasses cookies.

Becca was away, so Allen had stayed over.

Molly watched Allen as he slept. She still couldn't believe they had finally gotten together, that he hadn't freaked out and run away. But the next morning it seemed as though something was bothering him.

"Is something wrong?" she asked him over breakfast. "Did I do something?"

He looked at her, confused.

"You? No, why?"

"You seem… I don't know. Like something's bothering you."

Allen looked at her.

"It's my article. It's coming out at midnight. And I'm worried."

"Why are you worried?" Then she remembered. "Is this the dating piece?" She had forgotten about that.

He nodded.

"Promise you won't hate me?"

"Why would I hate you?"

Allen got his phone.

"Here," he said, handing it to her.

Molly read through the Google doc.

Allen watched her nervously. When she was done, she handed him back his phone.

"Let me guess, you hated it."

She tilted her head.

"Why would you think that?"

"Well, I doubt you loved it, judging by your expression."

"On the contrary, I thought it was very thoughtful. It wasn't in the least bit gossipy or mean."

"So you don't mind that I dated all these women? You're not angry?"

Molly looked up at him and smiled.

"How could I be angry with the man who called me his soulmate?"

The article, titled "Tinder Fella: A Shy Guy's Guide to Online Dating," was an immediate hit, blowing up on social media. It wasn't the kiss-and-tell that Justin had wanted, but he had begrudgingly agreed that it was a good piece, which had surprised Allen. Though it was probably because Allen had said nice things about Spark and Blind Date, which he knew would make Justin happy. He had also taken pains not to say anything negative about any of the women.

Just as popular as the main article, if not more so, was a shorter, ancillary piece Allen had written titled "Ten Tips for Getting a Date Online," along with Natalie's before-and-after piece on Allen's transformation from shy guy to stud, which had modeling agencies calling her asking who the guy was and if he had representation, which had sent Natalie into fits of laughter.

As for Allen's family and friends, their reactions to the articles were varied. Most of his male friends thought the article was cool, while his mother and stepfather's responses had been muted. His stepfather told Allen he didn't understand today's young people, while his mother said she was just glad that the experiment was over. Though she wanted to know who this soulmate of his was, Allen having disguised Molly.

As for Eric, he had teased Allen mercilessly about the before-and-after piece, as had some of his friends. But he knew most of them were probably just jealous.

The biggest surprise had been the women. He hadn't used their real names, but clearly some of them had figured out who he was talking about. Hannah had texted him a day after the article appeared, saying she had read it and had no hard feelings, which Allen had been relieved to hear. He had even heard from Hillary and Grace Kelly, whose real name was Deborah. He had no idea how "Grace" had figured it out, but she had written him that if things didn't work out with "Holly," he should hit her up.

It took over a week for things to die down, but they finally did, and Allen had been happy to move on.

As for his social life, he was still seeing Molly, and the two of them had finally gone out with Eric and Caro, who were still hot and heavy, or as hot and heavy as two introverted History Ph.D.s could be, and the four of them had plans to get together again.

In his spare time, Allen had continued to work on his novel. He had extended his self-imposed deadline after deciding to rewrite it. It had been a painful decision but the right one. He was not the same angst-ridden teenager he was when he had begun, and he wanted the novel to reflect that.

He was a long way from finishing it, but at Molly's insistence, he had given her a few sample chapters. She had loved them and had insisted on him allowing her to share them with her boss.

Allen had been hesitant. He thought the chapters needed more work. But Molly told him he was overthinking it, and that if he had seen some of the crap that crossed her desk, he would think differently. So he had given in at the end of January, and Molly told him the next day she had sent the chapters to Constance.

Two weeks later, they attended the launch party for Yasmin Farhi's new book, *Love Among the Ruins*. Molly had been talking about it all week, and had made sure Allen dressed appropriately, as she wanted him to make a good impression on Constance.

Allen felt nervous as they entered the venue, a former bank that had been transformed into a party space.

Felicity was checking in people and was too busy to talk to them, though she told Molly that Constance hadn't arrived yet.

The place was crowded, and they had to wait at the bar for a drink, but neither minded.

"This is so exciting!" Molly told Allen, squeezing his arm.

She led him over to the line to meet the author, who was busy signing books.

"It shouldn't take too long," she said. "I just can't leave without getting a book and having you meet Constance."

Molly gushed to the author when it was her turn, telling her she loved her first book and looked forward to reading the new one. Ms. Farhi smiled as she signed the book to Molly, who blurted out that she and her boyfriend were both aspiring authors.

When she was done signing, Molly thanked her, then looked around for Constance. Finally, she spied her, speaking with some woman Molly didn't know. Molly waited patiently, then cut in.

"Constance, I want to introduce you to my friend Allen Whitford, the one whose sample chapters I gave you."

Constance took him in.

"Molly speaks very highly of you, Mr. Whitford."

"Molly is a good friend," Allen replied, feeling awkward.

"She also has a good eye," Constance continued. "I read those sample chapters Molly gave me, and I think you have a lot of promise."

Allen thought his heart would leap out of his chest.

"You should find yourself a literary agent. When you do, have her talk to me. I'd like to have a crack at publishing your book."

Allen stood there, speechless, as Molly squeezed his arm.

"Thank you," said Allen, not knowing what to say. "I'll do that."

"Now, if you two will excuse me."

Molly and Allen nodded, then watched as Constance went to talk with someone else.

"Oh my God!" said Molly, practically squealing. "Did you hear that?"

Allen nodded. He was in shock.

The next several months were a total blur. When Allen wasn't at Hipster, he was hard at work on his novel.

Molly had helped him find a literary agent, who had, in turn, shopped the novel to several publishing houses, including Molly's. There had been a bidding war, and Molly's company had won. Allen would receive a $50,000 advance. While it was far from the biggest advance ever paid to a first-time author, Allen had been stunned and had thought about quitting Hipster. But Molly had advised him to stick it out, at least until his book came out.

Now it was the big day, almost exactly a year since he had met Constance at the book launch party for Yasmin Farhi's last book. His own book launch party would be much smaller, but that was fine by him.

Molly would, of course, be there. She had just been promoted, and they had recently celebrated their one-year anniversary.

"I still can't believe it," he said, as he glanced around the room. He had just been introduced to the editor of the *New York Times Book Review*, which would be publishing a piece on his novel that weekend. Already people were talking about it, and about Allen being the next big thing. A couple of the older people in the room had even compared him to a young Jay McInerney, which Molly had found hysterical.

"Believe it," said Molly, squeezing his arm.

But Allen was finding it hard to. He had dreamed of one day becoming a famous author, but in his wildest imaginings, he never thought it would happen so soon.

"Just promise you won't forget me after Reese and Jenna tell everyone about your book and women start throwing themselves at you," said Molly, only half teasingly.

Allen looked down at her. How could this beautiful, caring, intelligent woman think he could ever forget about her? If it weren't for Molly, he wouldn't even be here.

"I could never forget about you, Molly," he said. Then he took her face is in hands and kissed her.

Acknowledgments

First, I'd like to thank *you* for reading this book. If you enjoyed it, please leave a review or rate it on Amazon and/or Goodreads.

Next, I'd like to thank my first readers, Stephanie Cabot, Robin Muth, Bellamy Printz, and Abby Schiff, for their invaluable advice—and my mother, Sue Lonoff de Cuevas, for proofreading the manuscript and suggesting changes.

I would also like to thank Molly Burton of Cozy Cover Designs for the terrific cover and Polgarus Studio for the great job on the interior. It really does take a village, at least to publish a book.

Finally, thank you, Kenny. I met Kenny (aka my husband) many years ago, before there were dating apps, when I was working at HarperCollins Publishers and he was working for a natural living publication (put out by a hip alternative press). While I fretted that I would never be able to write a novel, Kenny never wavered. He knew I could do it. Thank you, Kenny, for believing in me.

About the Author

Jennifer L. Schiff is a native New Yorker who met her husband on a blind date. After a successful career as a journalist and editor, she began a second career as an author, penning the bestselling Sanibel Island Mystery series. *Tinder Fella* is her first novel.

Made in the USA
Monee, IL
28 October 2020